Persephone:
Goddess of the Not So Undead

Regan Wolfrom

Cover Art by Christa Holland of Paper & Sage Design

ISBN: 1927903025
ISBN-13: 978-1927903025

1

THE BLURSTEST DAY EVER

October 14th, 2023 was both the best and worst day of my life. You know, so far.

That was the day my step sister and I finally started getting along; it was also the day I accidentally shot an arrow through her lung.

I'm sure Dad would have rather just had his new and improved daughter along for the hunt, but his new wife had invited me to come out for the weekend, so when Dad had loaded up his gear and Fender the less-than-stellar hunting dog, he had two fifteen-year-old girls climbing into the truck, both of us awkwardly pretending that we knew something about killing things.

The last thing I wanted to do was kill an animal. I was way more interested in what the turkeys were thinking than what they might taste like. Iris was still a meat-eater back then, but I doubt she wanted to do any hunting, either.

But we both had an easily-distracted father to impress.

Daddy Schmidt traded up when Mom got sick, right after she'd lost her job at the hospital, when she'd started telling us that the parasites in the cat's litter box were rewiring her brain. His new wife was pretty, and god was she young; she'd had Iris when she was eighteen, the babydaddy apparently long forgotten, and that made her a good ten years younger than my parents.

Not robbing the cradle... more like scoping out the middle school.

Iris and I are the same age, always have been. But Iris has always looked older than me, in a good way. Longer legs, less plump, bigger boobs... I used to console myself that one day she'd have some serious back problems. She has long blond hair with just a touch of curls, while my poop-colored hair — matches my poop-colored eyes — always swings violently between straight-and-sickly and a giant frizzy mess.

You know it's a bad hair day when you look like there's a giant squid nesting on your scalp.

My nose is a little bigger, too. You can see right up it if you're a couple inches shorter than me. But don't worry. Iris doesn't have to see my snot since she's always been taller... perfectly long legs, remember?

Iris was like the daughter Dad had always wanted, the two of them hitting it off like his time with me had been a terrible, terrible mistake. She even took his name, so he'd have a Schmidt girl that he could be proud of.

A Schmidt girl he'd actually tell his friends about...

Anyway... Dad had taken us down to Fort Ransom, right across the road from the empty field that, if you believe the sign, was once a military fort. There's a bank of trees that Dad had named Turkey Shoot Forest, since... I guess there's no need to really explain that.

Dad had slathered paint all over his face and was dressed head-to-pac-boot in camo. He always brought the orange vest just in case the game warden came around, but I'd never seen him put it on. Of course, he made both of his daughters wear theirs, to match the dog's. I guess the hypocrisy is how you know he still loves you. As much as the mutt, at least.

Dad had two bows, his fancy overweighted one, and the slightly patronizing "lady bow" that he'd bought for me, but passed on to Iris when they'd all moved in together. I clearly didn't need a bow any-more, since I was stuck living with mom in that two-room apartment on South University, watching that kitty-poop brain rewiring in real-time.

So with one bow and two teenage girls, Iris and I would have to share, while Dad and Fender attended to the real hunt.

But it ended up being a lot of fun. Iris had snuck some malt cool-ers into the cart at Happy Harry's without Dad noticing, against his solemn diktat that hunters should only drink beer. We didn't get drunk, not because we're way underage, but because we're not idiots; we did have enough to drink that we'd started to feel a little more at ease with our *clusterfuddle* of a family life.

Iris told me some ridiculous stuff about her boyfriend-of-the-month, Sargent, like how he recounts lines from action movies in his sleep. I told her about Errol, even though we weren't really together anymore by then, and how he insisted on holding the car door open for me and would lose his mind if I dared try and do it myself. Ah, passive sexism. So romantic.

And we talked about Dad and his ridiculous face paint, and the blind he'd set up that was the size of a minivan. He shushed us at least a dozen times as we chuckled like a couple of losers, reeking of cherry-flavoured sludge.

About two hours and no turkeys in, we decided to humor Dad a little. We shut up and knelt down in the blind, or at least I did, since despite the sheer size of the thing, there somehow still wasn't enough room in there for all three of us.

Iris giggled as she picked up one of the decoys and kissed it on the beak, then took it with her to a stand of boxelder behind our blind, while I held the bow and waited.

I tried my best to stay quiet. That's not easy for me.

"Gobble, gobble, *motherlover*," Iris called out from her place in the trees.

"Please, Iris," Dad said. "Just give me ten minutes of peace."

"Ask the turkey, Dad. No... beg the turkey..."

"Dang it, Iris."

"It's the turkey's fault."

"Maybe you should take the turkey on a hike," I said. "Show him the historic nothing of Fort Ransom."

"Heh," she said. "Good idea. Fake turkeys love military history."

"Make sure you're wearing your vest," Dad said.

Iris and her plastic tom set off for the road, gobbling most of the way.

"Thanks, Seffy," Dad said. He gave my shoulder a squeeze.

I was going to say something back... I just didn't know what...

But Dad pulled out his gobble call and got down to it.

It didn't take long before I sighted a jake heading toward our remaining two decoys. Fender had spotted it, too.

"Too small?" I asked in a whisper.

"I'll take anything at this point. Well... you will."

"You first, Dad."

"*Ladies* first, Seffy. You know the rules."

"Yeah. Rule number one: don't call me Seffy. My name is Persephone. You know, Iris and Persephone... remember how cute that was for a while? Greek mythology... so hot right now..."

"Pick up the bow, Seffy."

I took the bow. I loaded the arrow and I aimed. I drew back.

I heard a shriek.

I jerked to the right.

"This fake turkey's getting fresh with me!" Iris yelled.

I hadn't realized what I'd just done. When I saw the arrow hit her, I didn't realize where it had come from.

I'd forgotten I was even holding the bow.

I heard Dad scream "oh my god" and I saw him run over to her.

And I... I just couldn't move. If anything, I wanted to disappear into that blind. I wanted to slap on some of Dad's face paint and stay perfectly quiet and still.

I didn't want Iris to see me. I didn't want her to know what I'd done.

I heard her gasping.

I didn't want to hear it.

"You shot me," she said. Slowly and quietly. "Seffy... you shot me."

"I know," I said. "I'm sorry."

"Down one daughter," she said. She closed her eyes.

I started to cry.

❧

Iris wasn't the first person in the greater Fargo-Moorhead area to get the botshot. I remember watching the story about the anonymous seventy-year-old woman who'd paid over a million dollars to try and reverse her aging. The thing is, they did the story right after the injection, so no one knew if she was getting any younger. I don't think they ever followed up on that.

But Iris didn't need to look any younger. She needed a new lung and half a new trachea. Well, I guess the lung was optional, assuming she didn't mind cutting back on her running, but the windpipe was pretty important. So when they transferred her to Sanford Federal, it wasn't really a question of whether or not Dad and Beth *wanted* to get her the shot, or whether or not the government would approve the use of the experimental treatment on a non-vetted patient. She'd get it or she'd never be able to breathe on her own. That was considered enough of an emergency to bypass the FDA panel.

So my step sister Iris had thousands of little robots injected into her arm. And within a couple of days they'd multiplied to several million.

And Iris' bots built her new lung and patched up the lower half of her trachea, and the bronchi thing and whatever. And I realized that my perfect step sister had gotten even *more* perfect.

Botshots don't allow the existence of silly things like acne or dark circles under the eyes, and I doubt they'll ever let you have boob and back problems. In fact, from what the doctor said, there was a strong chance that Iris wouldn't even have problems with things like gaining weight or looking older, that the bots would actually work to keep her body in near-perfect shape. So already-perfect Iris would somehow be more perfect, or perfect forever, I guess.

I'd always thought she'd get everything she ever wanted in life, but with those bots it seems like she's get it all and keep it all, until long after I'm dead and forgotten.

I'd felt like a piece of grot for shooting her with that arrow, and then I felt even worse that I was jealous of her for it.

The "experimental surcharge" Dad and Beth had to pay ended up cancelling university for both of us daughters, and forced Dad to put off his retirement for at least another ten years. And it became clear not long after Iris got out of the hospital that he wasn't planning on spending much of those ten years with the likes of me.

So I went back to the apartment on South University, to my lumpy sofa bed and my crazy-eyes mother, while Iris reached new heights of being *perfection*.

It's like cutting the head off a cute blond hydra. With perfect teeth.

Sometimes I think the worst part of what happened is that she still wants me in her life. She wants us to be sisters, and has no idea that half the time we're together I get so jealous and so sick of myself that I just want to find my way back to that hunting blind and disappear for frickin ever.

2

THE PARKING TICKET THAT EFFED AND/OR SAVED MY LIFE

It's been three years since I mistook my stepsister for an overly loud turkey. And in true dramatic style, her life's gotten better as mine's gotten grottier. She makes enough tips at the Radisson lounge to start NDSU next year in mechanical engineering, while my education plan is that I have no plan. I read articles and I've memorized everything written by the biggest experts in ethology, but that's where it all comes to a screeching halt.

You can't get a PhD based on blind hope.

Iris tried to support me, coming up with stupid "experiments" we could do together, reanimating a rat, messing with Iris' bots, but she couldn't change where my life was headed. I guess I deserve my plodding descent into forgotten dreams, having been the girl holding the compound bow.

If you'd told me when I was fifteen that winning the 9th grade science fair with cloned cockroaches would be the high point of my biology career...

Mom had her rTMS appointment this morning, and since she lost her license with that whole overriding the autonav and trying to run over her neighbour incident, it was my job to take her in; her car won't budge now without a valid card to read.

The perfect day already. And in the bathroom mirror I found a nice chin zit to add to my enjoyment.

I called Errol and let him know that I'd be late. I don't like putting him in that position, but he's the barely legal toolbag who decided to hire me. And it's not like you really need a full time dispatcher for a plumbing company with two trucks.

Sometimes minimum wage is just too damn high.

They don't do rTMS at Sanford Federal itself, at least, not for out-patient stuff. I think that's better for Mom, since she doesn't have to go back to where she used to work, where people she knows still work and say hello with that tinge of pity in their voice.

Instead of Sanford they opened up a little office on 3rd Avenue North, with mood lighting and abstract art and no indication from the street that they're strapping people to gurneys and zapping them. Well, okay… it's not really like that, but when Mom had first told me about the treatment, I couldn't help but think of that shock therapy bunk they used to do, where they'd stick a rubber ball or something in your mouth and go to town.

It just seems like a strange thing to do in the age of over-the-counter gene therapy, and 3D-printed antivirals, and of botshots moving from experimental to everyday. And rTMS and bots definite-ly don't mix. I read the pamphlet at the outpatient clinic… those electrical shocks or whatever can murder millions of those little guys. Although I do wonder what that would really do; it's not like pulses in your head is going to reach down and get bots swimming in your intestines.

But still, if Iris somehow lost those bots… it'd suck, probably worse than having never had them. Her whole lifestyle's changed now, not just because she's *bothot* now, but because she's gotten a little bit reckless.

I remember watching her climb a quarter of the way up a radio tower. Sometimes I wish I could be that fearless.

If they'd issue them for acne maybe I'd already have gotten my shot. And I'd be more than just me, even if they have started putting restrictions on just what those bots are allowed to do.

You see, you can't just have what Iris has been having. They spend more time in the lab now designing what those bots aren't al-lowed to do. They've basically closed the door on her kind of *bothot* perfection. But anything's better than nothing.

To be honest, I think that old-fashioned rTMS treatment is working, even if it's just placebo. Mom gets out of bed most morn-ings now, and I didn't have to do anything to get her into the car today.

She'd still been a little jittery about a news story from yesterday, about a couple of civil engineering students disappearing just west of town, leaving their truck and equipment behind. Mom had told me with complete conviction that the rapture had begun. I don't know why she thinks it will come in stages, like it'd start off with a dress rehearsal or something.

The nurse practitioner had said that soon they'd start reducing the visits to one every two months, and that the eventual goal was to eliminate them completely, that in a year or two they'll have rewired whatever part of her brain it was that made my mother think that Satan lives in our toilet bowl.

So I guess it's working, which is good, obviously, even if it is about six or seven years too late.

It's not like Mom getting better can undo everything else that's happened to our family.

And even though she is getting better, I wasn't about to just drop her off in front. I had to get the car to park somewhere and then I'd have to walk her in, and I'd have to sit with her in the tastefully-appointed waiting room until they called her name. After the session she'd be Aunt Callie's problem to pick up, but until she went in she was mine. And naturally, we waited there for forever.

And that's how I got another grotty parking ticket.

They give you three days now to pay it, or else they double the fine. I don't know why they ever put the meters on third anyway, since they've been broken for over a month and no one's bothered to come and fix it. And why the hurr do they still use parking meters? Even frickin Grand Forks has it automatic.

There was no way I was paying sixty five dollars for a broken parking meter. I mean, I'm practically a starving college student... well, you know, without the college part.

So I called Errol yet again and told him I'd be a little later than late, since I had some justice to pursue.

He laughed. I think he knows the whole job is a joke. Sometimes I wonder if it's pity that brings that paycheck, or if it's something distinctly creepier, like hidden cameras, or stray hairs and skin flakes collected and stored in some locked toolbox in the back of the shop.

It's possible Errol takes after his Uncle Pat...

Errol used to be that edgy kid with the dark clothes and the purple nail polish, the one you could date not just to rebel but because he was kinda hot.

Now he's just getting kinda weird. Buzzcut hair, perpetually wearing those stupid aviator sunglasses, even when it's cloudy and miserable, like it's been since Halloween and will probably remain until long past Thanksgiving… I guess he thinks that's the look women want. Maybe he thinks that's the look I want.

First rule of women: we don't know what the heck we want. Not until we see it, and even then…

I told the car to drive to our gray and charmless city hall, with my photographic evidence and best look of righteous anger to contest the ticket. The woman at the desk took care of it pretty quickly; I wonder sometimes if other girls see my chin zit and diarrhea-brown tentacle hair and take pity on me. I wonder if Iris gets treated worse by other women, because she's just so… Iris.

I know that doesn't happen. Women don't think like that. I don't think like that. Sometimes Iris makes me want to set up camp in a bottle of ill-gotten Jack, but it's not like I ever want to smash that bottle over her perfectly-shaped head.

I love my sister.

A fat stack more than I love myself.

❧

I decided that since it was already 11:15, I might as well call it a half day. I called Errol yet again, and he agreed, asking me if I had plans for lunch.

That was the last thing I wanted to do today. Or any day. Quit living in the past, Errol.

But… if you don't play nice, people tend to realize that you're not providing any real value. And then you have to go back to folding shirts at Herberger's. Which doesn't get you as many hours, and puts you in close proximity to people a buttload harder to deal with than Errol and his weird Uncle Pat.

He asked me to meet him at Cafe Manon, at 11:30. I think I mentioned once in middle school, like well over five years ago now, that I like French food, and since then Errol always wants to take me out for beef bourguignon and escargots, conveniently forgetting that I've been a vegetarian since before we ever knew each other.

But I do love the cheese...

I was a few minutes early, so I waited in my car. I tried some concealer on the pimple on my chin, but it didn't really help. It was less the redness and more the terrain change that was making that stupid thing stand out.

I checked my feeds; there were a few photos Iris posted of our last ride down to visit her new boyfriend. I only get to see her once or twice a month, so getting out on horseback with her happens even less.

I made a few stupid comments about the horses and that way Iris puts her heels up when she rides, then I closed the gallery once it got to pics of Iris and David... *canoodling*. I'm not jealous... I'm just... uh... uninterested?

Errol never showed up.

And didn't answer when I called him.

Prick.

It seemed like a strange way to tell someone they'd been fired. At least buy me a frickin cheese plate.

After around fifteen minutes I grabbed a takeout veggie wrap from a much cheaper restaurant and headed toward the shop, eating as the nav drove me.

That's when things got weird.

I ran into a backed up fudgefest of bad driving coming up on University Drive, right before the tracks, a white tanker truck turned near ninety degrees, blocking both lanes of traffic and hugging the side of a school bus.

The bus looked empty aside from a very angry driver.

I didn't see anyone in the tanker truck.

Fargo Septic & Sewer.

I was pretty sure I could smell it. Lunch ended pretty quickly for me.

Naturally, before mom's car could turn around, I had cars come up behind me, and I couldn't do much of anything but sit back and enjoy the stench.

I monkeyed with the console. I found no word on why someone would decide to park in the middle of North Seventh, no word on much of anything. This is Fargo, right? So I checked my social feeds and waited for something to happen.

I read Iris' latest screed about her boyfriend, trouble already, and Luis G's most recent rant about the mileage tax. Nothing from Mom or Aunt Callie.

I saw someone moving up the road in my direction, a man in an orange jumpsuit and an NDSU cap. He was dirty, but it looked like grease or some other byproduct of a day job, something like septic and sewer instead of the delicate dirt tracings of a hobo.

I was pretty sure he was the toolbag who'd ditched the poop truck smack in the middle of frickin everything.

He wasn't moving like he was drunk or high or brain damaged. He just looked... unaffected. Like he was just going for a walk in the middle of the road, spreading his own brand of traffic congestion and liquid human waste.

The one thing I noticed about him were his eyes. Bloodshot... not like a wispy pink, but like shark week. Heavy flow.

That didn't look healthy.

He was walking between the waiting cars, knocking his elbow against the mirror of the blue car to his right as he passed. He stopped at the driver's side door of the red SUV that was idling in front of me. He pulled on the handle.

I don't think the driver had been expecting that.

The door opened slightly, but the thirty-something man in the SUV quickly yanked the door shut. And he looked big enough to make sure that door stayed shut.

But the man in the jumpsuit tried a second pull anyway... and soon gave up. He turned to the small blue car on the other side.

I could see a middle-aged woman in the driver's seat; she was staring at his orange and black plumage and not really doing anything else.

I can't say I'd have been doing things any differently.

The man in the jumpsuit pulled open the passenger door.

That's North Dakota. The poor woman hadn't even thought to lock it.

The man climbed into the passenger side.

For a split second I thought about intervening, but I wasn't really sure what I was even looking at. Maybe he was just trying to bum a breath mint, or asking for a ride to Hardee's.

And let's not forget, there were other people around, like a guy in an SUV who was closer and significantly bigger than I was, and he didn't seem to be doing anything. If anyone's allowed to hide behind the bystander effect, I'd say it's someone short and wimpy like me. I got suspended from the Davies Track Team once — two whole weeks — for being too skinny. That was before the day I discovered the nachos at the Kum & Go... things have changed a little since then.

But it's not like I'm any stronger. Just less spindly.

Less like Iris.

So I didn't intervene. I just waited and watched.

After remembering to lock my own doors.

The woman in the blue car seemed calm at first, gesturing a little at the man in the jumpsuit but not giving off too much heat.

Then I saw him grab her by the elbow.

She started yelling at him. Really indignant.

I got out of my car, hoping that just seeing someone paying attention would be enough to get him to back down. Or would at least get the barrel-chested man in the red SUV off his fat ass.

Nothing changed.

So against my better judgment, I rushed to the passenger side of the blue car and knocked on the window.

The man in the jumpsuit let go of the woman's arm. He turned to look at me.

He didn't look like he was all there.

I suddenly regretted getting out of my mom's car.

He turned back to the woman in the driver's seat.

I knocked again. Or pounded, really. I figured you'd just distract him like you would a small rodent.

This time he didn't bother to look back to me.

He yanked the woman's arm for a second time.

She needed help.

I'd left my phone back in the car, snapped into the console. I glanced at the red SUV. I had no way of knowing if that do-nothing toolbag had even bothered to call the cops.

I made a little phone to my ear gesture at him.

I knew he saw me. I saw him shrug.

I heard the woman shriek. It sounded a little like the squeal you'd expect from a terrified poodle. Then there was a low whine.

I almost didn't turn back to look.

But I did. I looked.

The man in the jumpsuit had bitten her in the arm, right above her elbow. He'd bitten her, and I didn't think he had actually spit anything out.

There was less blood than I would have expected.

Less blood, and that haunting whine of hers that kept on going. Like when you know you're dying, but you can't do anything about it... so you do the only thing you can... you make a sad little noise.

I grabbed the door handle.

But I stopped myself from opening the door.

I knew there was nothing I could do to save her.

I watched him take another bite on her arm.

And another. Above the shoulder.

I was sure of it by that point.

He hadn't spit anything out.

And the whining had stopped.

I let go of the door handle.

I saw another man walking on the road, this time between us and the oncoming traffic. He had an orange jumpsuit as well. But he had red-brown stains to go with the black grease. And his bloodshot eyes were matched by fresh blood on his chin.

He'd had someone to eat as well.

And he was looking at me. I was new on the menu. Local fare.

I heard the engine rev from the red SUV. Like he'd taken it off the autonav.

Was I about to get run over? That's basically all people tend to do once they take over for the car-driving robot. Which is why most of the newer cars won't even let you do that in the middle of a city.

Like my mother's.

I grabbed the handle of the SUV's rear sliding door. It wasn't locked.

I climbed in.

Then I heard the click of the door locks.

The man in the SUV didn't say a word. It seemed like he might have wanted me to get in. Who doesn't love a damsel in distress who looks like she's got a filthy mop head glued to her scalp?

He rammed the back of his SUV into my mother's car. He pushed it back, right into the minivan behind it.

He kept trying to push it, flooring the pedal.

But he couldn't get it any farther back.

"Why aren't they moving?" he said. "Goddammit."

"You can get through," I said. "Onto the sidewalk."

"There's a goddamn pole in the way."

"There's room."

He swung his steering wheel and shifted gears.

He pulled the SUV over the curb and onto the sidewalk, running over a "stop here on red" sign and nearly side-swiping a building.

He brought us up to the crossroad, University, where traffic was slowly moving around the septic truck. He turned right, heading north.

He kept glancing over at me. Not at my chin… lower, actually. Like he was evaluating my refugee claim.

He looked like your average ND farm boy, or what they look like when they're a good ten years past being a boy anymore. He was heavyset, but not unhealthy-looking, with a Vikings cap covering his greasy hair.

He had a bit of a baby face, to be honest. I know it's not cool for me to admit, but I have trouble taking guys like that seriously.

"What the hell was that?" he asked.

"I don't know…"

"He was eating her."

"Yeah…"

"Look… I suppose I can drop you off somewhere, or…"

"I was trying to get to work."

"Yeah. Me, too. But I feel like we should get the heck out of town."

"Did you call the police?"

He shook his head.

Idiot.

"Well, I don't have my phone," I said.

"Console," he said, speaking at his dashboard, "call 911."

His phone started making those little dialing noises.

But it didn't connect.

The phone was beeping, long, loud beeps.

"What's going on?" I asked.

"Line's busy."

I didn't know what that meant. But it seemed like he expected me to understand, so I didn't ask for an explanation.

"How many people could possibly be calling this in?" he said.

"Should we go to the police?"

"Like, drive there?"

"Maybe…"

"I can hear the sirens," he said. "They don't need our help."

"I can't hear any…"

"Well, I can. They know what's going on…"

"Yeah, okay," I said. "But we're witnesses."

"They don't need witnesses. There's a guy with half a woman's arm in his stomach. You know what? I think what we really need is a goddamn drink."

"I'm only eighteen, hey?"

"Does that matter?"

"Depends on the drink."

He reached over to my side. "I'm Lucas, by the way."

He pulled open the glove compartment, shoving his right hand in and starting to rifle through. He wasn't spending near enough time looking out his front windshield.

I was worried he'd forgotten that he was the one driving.

"I can find whatever it is you're looking for," I said. "You know… self-preservation…"

He pulled back and returned to driving. "My sister works for Allegiant Air… every once in a while a bottle of artisan whiskey goes missing… got a nice collection back at the farm."

I saw a minibottle, sporting an off-white label with an angel on it. And another matching bottle, just as little.

"Why do you need two?" I asked.

"In case I rescue an attractive young lady from a horde of zombies."

"That's not funny."

"What? Zombies?"

"Any of it. I don't know what was wrong with those guys. That second guy… he's bitten someone, too. I saw the blood."

"I saw it, too. Pass me one of those bottles, alright?"

I didn't argue. I handed one over.

He unscrewed the cap and took a gulp. A big one.

A zombie-apocalypse-sized gulp. The kind you shouldn't take when you've taken your car off the auto-nav.

"I want to know what that was," he said, as we drove on past the university. "It's pretty crazy, I mean… two psychopaths chomping on human flesh…"

"That sums it up."

"That's not something you see in real life."

"Maybe it's a publicity stunt," I said. "Like that giant squid attack in Japan. We'll see it go viral..."

"Check my console."

I looked.

Someone had posted a video on Lucas' feed. Titled "Fargo Zombie Attack". I didn't want to watch. I didn't want to find out my stupid face and hair — and my stupid pimple — were all over it.

"Fargo Zombie Attack," I said. "This is ridiculous. And embarrassing. And stupid. They didn't even have any good, like, zombie makeup on..."

"So viral marketing," Lucas said. "You were right. They're bringing zombies back. Maybe a reboot. That'd be pretty awesome. Romero or *Walking Dead*... either/or is fine with me..."

"Viral marketing. Ugh. Now I just feel like an idiot. But it looked so real with that woman's arm..."

Lucas chuckled. "I know. They got us good, huh?" He nodded toward the glove compartment. "But don't worry... you can still have that drink. Even if we don't need to head for the hills."

"We don't have hills around here."

"Ha! Hey, have a drink, there. That other bottle."

"No, thanks..."

"I'm not trying to get you drunk or anything. But that way we know we each get as much as we want..."

"Yeah... um..." It didn't make sense to be hanging around in his grotty SUV anymore. "Can you take me to my work?"

"What?"

"My work. 29th Street North. Right near the tractor plant."

"Yeah... okay... gotta turn right back around, though..."

He was disappointed. I wasn't sure if it was because his wild-caught eighteen year old girl was moving on, or because he'd just found out that he'd been scared half to death by some ad company that had lowballed the special effects.

"Well, thanks for rescuing me," I said. "Even if it wasn't real. It's the thought that counts."

"You sure you don't want to have a drink with me?"

"I'm sure. Sorry, Lucas."

"Yeah, okay. Whatever."

He restored the autonav and directed the car to 29th Street North.

"And 3rd," I said.

"And 3rd," he repeated. "You know, you still haven't told me your name."

"Oh, sorry… it's Luna." Not the first time I'd done that. I'd learned from Iris that you can't just hand out your first name to people anymore. It's bad enough they might take a pic of you when you're not looking.

"Good to meet you, Luna."

"Yeah, okay."

He took another gulp from his minibottle. A little smaller.

"I guess you got a boyfriend."

"I guess I'm only eighteen."

"I get it."

"Okay."

"It's just been a weird day, you know? Almost the end of the world."

"Yeah. I know."

He handed me his bottle. "Can you put that away for me?"

"Sure."

Zombie apocalypse averted.

❧

Errol's red pickup truck was in the parking lot.

I parked right beside it.

I walked in through the front.

No one was at my desk.

I walked back to the shop area.

I didn't see anyone, just an empty shop and the three ridiculous welding helmets hanging on the wall, like witch doctor masks.

"Hello?" I called out.

There was still music playing, Coldplay or Mumford or some other kind of old man grot. Probably Dan's, since the only reassuring thing about Errol these days was that he had better taste in music than his father.

And a better concept of boundaries than his uncle. But I won't bother getting into that.

No one was there.

The building was empty, and unlocked.

Maybe Mom was right. Victims of the slowest rapture ever.

I called the trucks, to see if they were on schedule and to pretend like I was working.

Dan was down in West Acres, doing a commercial estimate, while Pat had just finished up a residential in Davies, with what he gleefully described to me as a 'hungry, hungry housewife'.

I'm not sure why he thinks I want to hear that.

Neither had heard from Errol.

I imagined that some beautiful woman had shown up right after he'd gotten off the phone with me. Some leggy blonde... they're always leggy blondes, right? Like Iris. Some woman had swept Errol away, and he'd just left everything behind to help his own damsel in distress with her blocked-up sink drain. Leaving his truck behind, as well...

That wasn't Errol.

It sounded more like Uncle Pat.

I was surprised that I was starting to get a little worried. Like if you get so used to a massive cockroach infestation and then they suddenly stop showing up dead on your kitchen counter. It makes you ill-at-ease, like... like what happened to my vermin? And on that note, why doesn't he paint his fingernails purple anymore?

I started to feel bad for comparing him to a cockroach. He was worth more than that.

There was a time when he seemed interesting, or at least his interest in me was interesting. Then I grew up and stopped rebelling, or maybe found different ways to rebel.

I still feel *something* for him, like a cousin or a frenemy or a neighbor who brings you lemonade on a moderately hot day. I'm not even angry anymore, for all the things he did when he was young and stupid, which were likely brought on by equally stupid things I'd done.

Wow. Am I ever wise now that I'm eighteen. So much wisdom. It's overflowing like a broken toilet.

I tried calling him again.

His phone rang. Still no answer.

Maybe he'd left it in his truck.

But again. That wasn't Errol.

I decided to play a round of *Sewer Saga* on my phone. Killing subterranean zombies usually makes a girl feel better. But the sewers and the flesh-eating weren't sitting well with me anymore. I kept thinking of that woman in the little blue car.

It didn't matter if it was staged or not.

It still bothered me.

Errol came back just after 1. He walked in through the front door, buzzcut and aviators, wearing the same blue dress shirt he always wore, with the same pipewrench logo. And the same khaki pants. And same brown workboots.

I wonder sometimes if his closet is just filled up with fifteen sets of the same outfit.

He didn't smile, or nod, or do that strange lip curl he does, for me and only me.

He just walked up to the desk and stared at me.

"Can I help you?" I asked.

He didn't answer.

He just kept staring.

"You said 11:30, Errol. I waited for like a half hour and couldn't get a hold of you."

No answer.

I picked my phone up off the desk and dialed his number, trying to make a point.

I heard his ringtone, a turkey call. Coming from his pant pocket.

He didn't take it out.

"Are you serious?" I said.

Still no smile. No response to the rise he was getting from me.

So I switched gears.

"Did you take one of the work trucks out? Because your pickup was still out front."

All I was getting out of him was a series of blinks, perfectly spaced. Leave it to Errol to find some weird new kind of silent treatment.

"I've got work to do," I said.

He didn't move from in front of the desk.

"What the *hurr*, man? What are you trying to do here?"

I stood up from the desk.

I turned around and took a couple of steps back, toward the shop.

He took a couple of steps, too.

And stopped.

"This isn't funny," I told him. "You know what? You're making me uncomfortable… I'm serious, Errol."

He was still staring at me. Not at my eyes, and not at my chest. Somewhere in between.

"It's just a stupid zit, you jerk."

He puffed out his cheeks. Just for a second.

"What is wrong with you?"

It sounded like he was about to burp… some kind of rumble in this throat.

"I'm going to have to tell your father about this," I said. "This is really over the line, Errol."

"Ssssss…"

"What?"

"Ssss-eh…" He exhaled, hard. I noticed he was sweating. But his eyes were still staring, blankly, and directly at the blackhead on my chin.

"You're a complete toolbag."

I turned around to head to the shop.

I felt him grab my right arm.

"Don't touch me!" I yelled.

"Sss-ehh…."

I turned and gave him a shove.

He didn't move. He'd held steady, like I hadn't even made contact. He still had my arm. He was holding it. And staring.

"Ssss-eh-eff…"

I pulled at his hand, trying to pry his fingers off of my bicep. I started to scratch, digging my nails into his thumb. I'd sliced into his skin, but he hadn't flinched.

I was thinking quite hard about whether or not I should make an attempt at gouging out his eyes.

But he wasn't doing *anything* else. He had my arm and I couldn't get away, but he wasn't trying to pin me against the wall, or grope me… he was just holding me. And muttering… *something*.

"Ss-ss-e-e-eff…"

Seffy. God, I hate that. So much.

"Yes," I said. "Seffy. You're calling me Seffy. What else?"

"Sss-eff…"

"Yeah… I got that part."

"I-I…"

"What happened to you?"

"B-b-b…"

"What?"

"B-b-bitt… b-b-b-bitten-n-n…"

"What the fuck, Errol? Bitten? Yeah, great. You saw the video. I'm probably in it, too. This is some kind of zombie roleplay now?"

"B-bitten… b-b-bit-t-t…"

"Then where's the blood, asshole? If you got bit, show me the bite marks."

His head moved. A little. Up and to the left.

I looked at his neck. Nothing there.

A stupid prank.

And he still was wearing those damned sunglasses so I couldn't see his unzombified eyes.

"B-b-b…"

"Shut up."

Then I saw it. It wasn't a bite. But his shirt was stained. Brown on the blue collar, right at the back of his neck.

Dried blood. Running down the back of his shirt.

"But you're not bleeding," I said. "There's still no mark there."

"B-b-b…"

"Bitten, yes. And blood. I got it, okay? I get the joke. Okay. Can you just let me go?"

"N-no…"

"You win, alright? I'll believe whatever the hell you want me to believe. Just let go of my arm."

"I… I… I can-n-n't…"

"Then I guess I'd better bite off your fucking arm, then. Since that's the gag, right?"

I felt his grip open.

I pulled my arm away.

His hand was still there, as if he was still latched on to me.

And he still had that stare.

Something inside told me to run, to get the hell out of there. To not care that all that was happening was just an idiot being an idiot.

I listened to that voice inside me.

I ran through the shop, out the back fire exit.

I heard the alarm sound.

I didn't look back. If that idiot was chasing me, he'd still be chasing me if I saw him. Looking back would just slow me down, or get me to do that horror movie victim thing where you trip on a rock or a branch…

I ran past the garage door company, toward the railroad tracks.

Past a tanker truck from Fargo Septic & Sewer.

That seemed less a coincidence and more an extension of the same stupid viral campaign. Was Fargo Septic & Sewer even a real company? Or a front for some zombie show about to come out? Set in frickin Fargo?

I didn't stop running. Not until I'd reached a gas station across the tracks, on Main Avenue.

I turned back to look.

I couldn't see Errol.

I wasn't about to go back.

3

THE EMPTY SOAP DISPENSER OF DOOM

The first thing I needed to do at that gas station was sit down and pee. I nodded to the man at the counter as I walked by. He gave me a wink.

That was... uh, not that pleasant, really.

I passed by an old lady perusing the Fantas. She didn't notice me, and saved me having to say hello. Old people like to talk; I guess they don't know how to text with those gnarled little fingers...

Wow, I felt like a douche.

I went into the bathroom and found both stalls occupied. So I had to wait.

And check out the ten-years-out-of-date wall map of the greater Fargo-Moorhead area. And listen to two girls talking to each other through the stall doors.

"Happy Harry's," one of them said. "We need to go there next. I remember my brother always telling some pretty great stories, and they always started with buying party supplies at Happy Harry's."

"Why do they call it Happy Harry's, anyway?" the other asked. I couldn't tell if there was a punchline coming.

"Drunks are happy, I guess. You know, until they're not. Wait... I totally forgot..."

"What?"

"North Dakota, bitch."

"Yeah. Happy Harry's Bottle Shop."

"Drinking age is twenty one."

"Oh."

"Yeah. Oh."

It wasn't that I was trying to listen, or that I have some kind of problem with being patient, but I had to say something.

"Look, ladies," I said, "it's great that you're having such a fun convo, but I haven't heard a splash since I came in here. Do you think maybe you're ready to start with the wiping?"

"Are you joking?" one of the girls said.

"I don't know… are you pooping?"

She giggled. "You're like a toilet detective."

I heard two flushes, almost perfectly timed.

And two stalls opening.

And two young women coming out, slim brunettes that could almost be sisters, with matching studs in their noses. They were decked out in standard Canadian prairie plumage, gray hoodies with Winnipeg Jets logos. Slap on a team name, and suddenly no one cares that they're wearing the same outfit as everyone else.

And probably haven't washed the thing in two months.

The only thing that differentiated the two of them were their gawdy belt buckles. One was a silver beaver, the other two crossed handguns with the words "Pistol Packin' Mama".

How delightfully ironic. And preachy.

So very Canadian.

They both smiled at me.

It didn't seem bathroom-appropriate, but for whatever reason I smiled back.

And then I took the first girl's stall, the giggly one with the beaver buckle. Those were seriously the only two differentiating factors.

"Dangit," she said from in front of the sinks. "No soap."

"Great, Jetta," the other girl said. "Now that you've announced it, the whole place knows."

"So?"

"So now we can't just sprinkle some water on our hands and leave. Now we have to find soap or be branded a couple of dirtballs."

"No one cares," I said from my place in the stall. "Just rinse and move on."

"Oh, but I'll care," the second girl said. "And Jetta will care, right?"

"I don't care," Jetta said. "So hey… Curlicue…" She started knocking on the door of my stall. "Hey…"

"Are you talking to me?" I asked.

"Yeah… Curlicue, you know? The curly hair… we've known each other long enough to require pet names."

"What do you need? No hand soap in here…"

"You twenty one yet?"

"No."

"You sure?"

"Pretty sure, yeah."

"Know anyone who's twenty one?"

"Well, my father… his wife… the state governor…"

"So no one who can go cooler shopping with us…"

"No. Sorry."

"Ask to see her ID," the second girl said.

"I'm not showing you my ID," I said.

"I'm joking. Maybe."

"Oh… okay."

"I'm Jetta," Jetta said, talking to my stall door. "This is my friend Leona."

"Can't shake hands A-T-M," I said.

"We're Canadian."

"I gathered…"

"Well, aren't you going to introduce yourself? Isn't that how this works?"

"I don't do many intros from the throne room."

"Well, we might not still be here once you flush and all."

"Yeah, okay…"

"So? What's your name, Curlicue?"

"Funnily enough," I said, "you got it right. And on your first try, too."

I heard her chuckle. She seemed to think I was enjoying the light banter from my seat on the crapper.

"I'll go out and ask about the soap," Leona said. "Thanks to you, Jetta."

"But they'll know you haven't washed," Jetta said.

"Not if you shut up for once."

Leona left, while Jetta didn't. She was standing right in front of the stall door, staring at it, I guess.

"I don't usually do this in front of an audience," I said.

She laughed. "So hey… do you know what there is to do around here on a Tuesday night?"

"Hopefully not more of this."

"There must be some clubs or something, right?"

"Not for people under twenty one, no. There's a reason eighteen year olds from North Dakota keep going to Canada."

"Oh… have you come up yet?"

"No," I said. "I guess I didn't realize how many cross-stall conversations I was missing out on."

"You seem tense, Curlicue."

"I'm uncomfortable, yes. And I've had a… a weird day."

"And this isn't making it less weird, right?"

"You got it."

"Sorry about that. I've just got some kind of broken faucet disease."

"What?"

"I just keep talking. Just keep letting it pour on out. I can even hear myself, and wonder why I won't shut up… but I… I just… I won't shut up."

"Oh."

"You're good at it, though… not talking."

"Thanks."

The door to the bathroom opened again.

"Oh my god," Leona said. "Oh my god."

"Norwegians?" Jetta asked. "I heard they have Norwegians here. Tall, blonde…"

"Some guy just attacked the cashier."

"What?"

"Some guy… he grabbed the cashier by the shoulder and yanked him onto the counter. And *bit* him."

"Hold on," I said. "Did you say he bit him?"

"Yeah," Leona said. "With his teeth. On the neck."

"Like a vampire?" Jetta asked.

"No, like a cashier-eating serial killer guy."

"Holy schmo… did he see you?"

"Yeah."

"And so you came back here so he could eat all of us?"

"We have to keep him out of here," I said.

"Well, obviously," Jetta said.

"No, listen… I saw the same thing an hour ago. I thought it was a prank."

"I don't think it's a prank," Leona said.

"The door pushes to the outside," Jetta said. "I don't see how we can keep it closed."

"We can't," Leona said.

"Well... you need to," I said.

"Then come out here and help us," Leona said.

I wiped as fast as I'd ever wiped. It felt like a front-end wedgie.

I came out and quickly rinsed my hands, since Leona hadn't brought any emergency soap back with her. Which bothered me more than it should have, all things considered.

I scanned the bathroom. Everything was bolted to the wall. If I aimed to improvise, I had a pretty empty toolkit to work from.

"We wait," I said.

"What?" Leona said.

"He hasn't come in yet, right? Maybe he's already left. Can you hear anything?"

"No," Jetta said.

"We should go out there," Leona said.

"I think we should wait," I said. "Just wait. Quietly."

"With no soap," Jetta said, in a whisper.

"No soap."

"Okay."

The three of us stood at the back wall of the bathroom, close enough that I could feel Jetta's breath on my right cheek. We were all pressed up against the tile, as though an extra hair's width or two of space from the door would somehow keep us safe from whatever was on the other side.

Whatever it was. Or he was.

Probably not a viral marketing campaign about particularly not-dead-looking zombies, but it sure as heck couldn't be real zombies. Because real zombies aren't real, because it's impossible to die and come back as a flesh-eating monster.

Because *Science*.

No one talked for a good thirty seconds.

"Was there only the one?" Jetta asked.

"The one what?" Leona said.

"The one biting guy."

"Only saw the one, yeah. Why would there be more?"

"Did you see that same guy, Curlicue?" Jetta asked me.

"I don't know," I said. "I didn't happen to see this guy. Was he wearing an orange jumpsuit? And could you please stop calling me Curlicue?"

"Jumpsuit? Like a tall, blond fighter jock?"

"He's about six foot, short brown hair," Leona said. "Dressed like a lumberjack, almost."

"Lumberjack? Like flannel?"

"Yeah. Flannel."

"Don't think it was one of the guys I saw."

"Wait," Jetta said, "so there are more guys? You say more than one?"

"I saw two," I said. And Errol. "Or three."

He hadn't been playing a joke on me.

"So that makes four," Jetta said.

"And that makes for a very bad weekend in the States," Leona said.

"Zombie apocalypse," Jetta said.

"What did you say?" I asked her. Not that I hadn't heard.

"I said 'zombie'. Uh, yeah."

"It's not crazy," Leona said. "They have zombie ants, don't they?"

"It's a fungus," I said. "Infects the ants and changes their behavior. Gets them to just sit still while the fungus eats away."

"You know about this stuff?"

"I'm a hobbyist. And two-time science fair champion."

And someone who should be doing more with her life...

"Maybe this is a fungus," Jetta said. "Could be the same one."

"A fungus that traveled all the way up here from the rainforest?"

"They heard about the Norwegians."

I turned to Leona. "What's wrong with her?"

"I babble when I'm nervous," Jetta said.

"And when you're not," Leona said.

"Fargo Septic & Sewer," I said. "Saw two trucks, each one near one of these outbreaks."

"So funky sewer water?" Leona asked.

"Maybe. And that guy out there was unlucky enough to run into one of those red-eyed guys in the jumpsuits."

"Oh," Jetta said, "you mean like a coverall. Like the Domo guys wear."

"It's not Japanese. Listen, we need to just shut up and listen."

"Okay."

So we waited. And listened.

No screaming. No mad dashing that we could hear.

You don't hear footsteps too well on concrete pads. No squeaks on the tiles, because there's no air gap to make them. I'd say gas stations are made for ninjas, with or without orange jumpsuits.

"Someone should take a look," Leona said.

"You sure you want to do that?" I asked.

"Not me... I already looked. Your turn."

"Not a chance."

"Well, I can't go," Jetta said. "The babbling..."

"That's ridiculous," I said.

"No," Leona said, "it's kind of a big problem."

"I hate you both."

I slowly moved toward the bathroom door.

I tried to think rationally. If it was some kind of infection, something from bad sewage... whatever was eating away at its victims — and eating away at Errol — it was making them sluggish, right?

I can outrun a slug.

I pushed open the door, just a little.

I looked out.

An empty convenience store.

The cashier was gone, no customers around. Some blood at the counter. Some blood on the floor near the pop cooler, less than ten feet from where I was standing. The old lady by the Fantas.

They'd been bitten. And then they'd gotten up and walked out. All within maybe five minutes.

They were infected.

Because there'd be no other way for them to have walked out after all that blood.

I let the bathroom door close.

"It's clear," I said. "From what I can tell."

"You didn't actually check," Leona said. "You couldn't possibly know for sure."

"I didn't say I knew for sure."

"Don't be a jerk, Leona," Jetta said. She looked over to me with a polite smile. "Did you see any soap?"

"It's an infection," I said. "People are bitten, and that's how it's transmitted."

"You know all that from an empty store?" Leona asked.

"We need to get away from here."

Leona nodded. "We need to get back to the car."

"If we keep our eyes open, we should be able to see them before they see us. Whatever this is should have slowed their response time."

"Like with zombies," Jetta said. "Amirite?"

I led the way, pushing open the bathroom door.

We moved straight toward the exit.

There was a flicker of movement. To my right.

I looked over.

The old lady.

She was walking toward the checkout.

Holding a bottle of Fanta Orange.

"Are you okay, ma'am?" Jetta asked her.

No response.

I hadn't expected one.

Just a blank stare. From bloodshot eyes.

"She's infected," I said. I'd said it quietly, as if I was worried it'd offend that poor old lady.

"Are you sure?" Leona asked.

"She was bitten. The blood on the floor. Her eyes…"

"We should make sure."

"Don't be an idiot."

"*Yee-ouch*," Jetta said.

"Let's keep moving," I said.

I reached the door. Outside looked just as quiet as inside the store. Traffic was still moving on the streets, but I guess an infection wouldn't take every car off its predetermined route.

I walked outside.

Leona and Jetta followed.

The old lady seemed to be following, too, but she wasn't moving quickly enough to worry me.

"Which car is yours?" I asked.

"The green one," Jetta said.

At the EV pump. The farthest one from the door, naturally.

"Is it unlocked?" I asked.

Jetta took out her tablet. "Okay. Done."

"We should make a run for it," Leona said.

"Just walk," I said. "We're okay as it is."

"Come on," she said, as she took off in a jog.

Jetta looked over to me and shrugged.

She followed after her friend.

Leona screamed.

I saw the cashier just as he grabbed her, wrapping his arm around her neck. He'd been behind a column, by the pumps. Not hiding, just out of our sightline.

Jetta froze.

We both watched as the cashier ripped into Leona's neck, taking his first bite.

I ran over to Jetta, pulling her by her hoodie.

"We need to get to the car," I said.

"We need to help her."

"We can't."

Leona was lying on the ground, bleeding.

Her eyes were open, but she wasn't moving.

The cashier was moving on to us, less than a half-dozen strides away.

I pulled harder on Jetta's hoodie.

She took a step back, away from Leona.

Not fast enough.

The cashier would reach us.

She still had her tablet in her hand. It could start the car, too... not just unlock it.

I didn't need to bring her with me.

Not if she didn't want to come.

Not if she was just going to stand around and let him take a bite.

Yeah... I could just steal her only means of escape...

I yanked even harder. "Let's go, Jetta," I said.

She finally started moving. With less than six feet between her and the biting cashier.

He lunged. Pulling at her sleeve.

He had it.

"No," Jetta said. "No..."

I kicked my leg out, aiming for the biter's stomach.

I almost fell over as it hit.

He fell back, onto the ground. Losing his grip on Jetta's hoodie.

I yanked on Jetta's hoodie again.

We reached the car. I took the driver's seat. And her tablet, docking it.

The console asked for our destination.

"145th Avenue SE," I said.

"And watch out for zombies," Jetta said, tears in her eyes.

We watched the city pass by as Jetta's little car drove us out. From the street you couldn't just tell who was infected, not if you couldn't see the whites or reds or pinks of their eyes. And they didn't stumble around like drunks or Minnesotans. The only way you'd know is when one guy would approach another guy and then he'd lunge. People don't lunge in everyday interactions.

I counted four attacks by the time we passed Bonanzaville and hit I-94.

That was what I'd seen on the way out. The lunges, the blood. That wasn't any indication of how much the infection had already spread.

Well, it was some indication. That things were worse than I could have expected. If the problem really had come from some bad sewage somewhere, and started with the workmen in a couple of sewer trucks... that meant I'd seen one of the first attacks at lunchtime, and — I looked at the console — it wasn't even 2:30 in the afternoon.

No disease moves that quickly. Not influenza, not dengue fever...

And I'd left my mother in the middle of it. And Aunt Callie.

"Is Leona dead?" Jetta asked.

"I don't know."

"But those zombie ants... they're dead..."

"This isn't the same thing. This is new."

"New? Like bioterrorism?"

"Yes. In Fargo."

"Seriously?"

"No, Jetta. Terrorists go to places like New York and LA. No one comes to Fargo to make a statement."

"Except for Chuck Klosterman."

"What?"

"I don't know. Just babbling."

"I don't know what's happening. But when an epidemic happens, the best place to be is far away from the infected."

"So where are we going?"

"My father's place. A farm. Hopefully we can stay clear of whatever this is."

"The console's blank," she said. "No feeds."

"No service, maybe? Network might be down." I took a closer look.

The network doesn't really go down anymore. Hasn't for years, anyway. The only time I remembered seeing a blank console on a car was our trip to visit crazy Uncle Dane in Green Bank, West Virginia; that's that area people move out to when they want to get away from the invisible death rays of technology, or something equally redonk-ulous.

But it looked the same way. Like with Uncle Dane.

And then the car stopped.

Not pulling onto the shoulder for some nav issue. Just stopped in the middle of the interstate. Gentle braking followed by not moving at all.

"We just charged it," Jetta said.

I looked out the window.

Every other car had stopped.

"Kill switch," I said.

"What?"

"Department of Homeland Security. Making us all a little bit less secure. I'll bet they know about the infection now..."

"This is a Canadian car."

"Doesn't work like that. Any autonav car within a given area can be shutdown on order of the government."

"Damn nazis."

Network shutdown. Autonav shutdown.

"Isolation," I said. "They don't want us to spread it."

"But it's not us," Jetta said. "We're not zombies."

"They're not going to take any chances. They're probably treating it just like they did the avian flu outbreak. They kept half of Idaho locked up for three weeks. No one in or out."

"But I'm only off work through Sunday..."

"We're just past Mapleton," I said. "Too far to walk."

"What's in Mapleton?"

"I mean to get to my father's farm. It'd take hours."

"Well, we don't need his farm, do we? Can't we just go some-where else? Or just wait in the car?"

"We can't just sit here," I said. "We don't have any food or water..."

"We do, actually."

"We do?"

She leaned over and checked the back seat. "We went to Target already. Picked up a few things we can't get at home. Let's see... refried beans, a box of chocolate-covered blueberries..."

I took a look, too.

"That's it," she said. "All I've got."

"What about those truffles?"

"Oh. Those are Leona's."

"Uh, okay..."

"Yeah, I guess they're ours, now."

"Any water?"

"Oh, wait... we didn't buy any water. I was going to pick up a Pepsi Tru at the gas station. This isn't enough food, is it..."

"We'd have to find a way to get that can of refried beans open... but you'd be surprised how far we could stretch this out..."

Jetta reached over and squeezed my hand. My mind flashed back to that empty soap dispenser. She kept holding it.

"Someone will come for us," she said.

"I'm not sure about that." I looked out the window, at the cars and trucks stuck on the interstate.

There was one vehicle moving. A red SUV.

It drove up beside us and slowed down.

The driver peered into our car. A heavyset man with a Minnesota Vikings cap. I thought I'd never have to see him again.

"Zombies can't drive," Jetta said, "right?"

"That's Lucas," I said. "I doubt he's infected..."

"Wait, you know him? How small is this town?"

If I was lucky he wouldn't realize it was me.

It wasn't that I was scared of him. On a normal day I wouldn't have a problem playing nice with a guy like Lucas. But it wasn't a normal day. It wasn't a good time to have someone like him around.

Jetta let my hand go. She reached over and honked the horn.

The SUV pulled in front of us and stopped.

Jetta opened the door.

Lucas got out of his car and started toward us.

"Hey, Lucas," Jetta said. "That's you, right?"

He smiled. "Do we know each other?" he asked, with extra enthusiasm.

"I'm Jetta. You know my new friend here?" She nodded to me.

I crouched down a little in my seat.

"Hey," he said. "Luna. Pretty sweet coincidence, huh? I've still got half a bottle..."

"Hey, Lucas," I said.

"So it's not a viral marketing thing. Saw another lady bite it. Or get bitten... you know..."

He almost sounded excited.

"I know," I said. "We saw more of it, too."

"And now the cars have been shut down... well, most of them... some of us know enough to make a few modifications so we can strip out the autonav when we need to..."

"I still don't get that part," Jetta said.

"You didn't tell me you're from Canada," Lucas said, staring at me.

"I'm not."

"I'm from Canada," Jetta said.

He looked over at her. Not at her chin, either.

He grinned.

"I'm Lucas," he said.

"I heard. And already knew."

"I like the nose ring... and your little beaver."

"Oh, uh... thanks," Jetta said.

"The belt buckle."

"Yeah."

"So I live just up the road a ways," he said.

"Really? How far up the road?"

"Maybe five minutes. Unless you're walking. Which we don't have to be. Because of my ride..."

"We've got a place to go," I said.

"You said it was too far, Luna," Jetta said, now also using what could probably be my stripper name.

"We'll get there."

"Oh. Okay."

"You can see I have a running vehicle," Lucas said. "Don't be stupid, Luna."

I shook my head. "Poor choice of words, Lucas."

"You know what I mean. I can keep you safe. Like before."

"Like before?" Jetta said. "What do you mean?"

"He got me out of a pretty unpleasant situation," I said.

"Those other zombies you ran into."

"Yeah."

"I'm a hunter," Lucas said. "I've got a Remington 12 Gauge back at my place that would do well versus whatever this is. Pretty sure they're zombies…"

"We're okay," I said. "Thanks, though."

Jetta was trying her best to shoot a message to me. Something along the lines of asking why I didn't want to join up with him.

I didn't know how to send the right response back to her. That the last thing I wanted to do was put my faith in some random guy and his shotgun.

"This is ridiculous," Lucas said. "Just come with me. I'm not trying to get in your pants or anything."

"No… thanks…"

"It's the end of the world, Luna. Do you get that?"

"It's not the end of the world —"

"Things are going to get worse, not better. It won't just be zombies soon… people are going to panic. People are going to start getting dangerous."

"More dangerous than zombies?" Jetta asked.

He nodded. "The most dangerous animal of all."

"I think I've made it clear," I said. "And I'm trying to make this clear to you. We're not interested in your help."

"Hey… don't get all bitchy about it."

"Just go away, Lucas."

"How about you, Jetta?" he asked. "You want to come with me? And survive?"

She looked over to me.

I shook my head.

"What else are we supposed to do?" she asked me. "You want to just lock the car doors and start rationing the refried beans?"

"You need to come with me," Lucas said. "Don't expect this one to keep you safe."

"We should go with him," Jetta said. "We shouldn't be out here alone."

"She's right, Luna. The next guy who comes along might not be your friend."

"I don't need friends who call me a stupid bitch, thanks," I said.

"We'll go with you," Jetta said.

"Jetta…"

"I'm going, Luna. Come with me, okay?"

"I don't want to."

She climbed out of the car. "Should I bring my refried beans?" she asked him.

"Please do… I'm sure I have tortillas or something at home. Just gotta scrape off the mold…"

Jetta laughed. "You seem nice, Lucas. Like not rapey at all."

I groaned a little.

Then I got out of the car.

Being left there alone sounded like the worse of two really bad decisions.

4

THE ZOMBIE NUT

Lucas drove us off the interstate, northwest toward Casselton, then a wide circle around it and farther to the west.

His farm wasn't anything more than a small house on a neglected yard site, with both a garage and a shed that had long ago collapsed.

"Not a family farm or anything," he said. "Bought it cheap a few years back. My sister stays with me when she's in town."

"Is she in town?" I asked.

"Nope. She's far away from this mess. I hope that ends up being a good thing."

"I'm sure she'll be okay," Jetta said.

"There's no way to know that," Lucas said. "So don't say it again."

"Take it easy, Lucas," I said.

"Sorry... I'm just trying to channel my inner badass. Build up the old courage."

"I get that," Jetta said.

"No," I said. "He's being a jerk."

"A jerk who's saved you how many times now?" Lucas said. "Twice?"

"I didn't want to go with you."

"Then you can walk back to your dead car, sweetheart. Jetta and I can handle things here."

"So where's the gun?" Jetta asked.

"In the basement. I'll get it. You girls come inside and see if you can find something to eat."

"Oh, I'm not that hungry."

"I could eat," Lucas said. He got out of the truck. "Make sure you girls bring in those supplies."

I turned to Jetta after he walked away.

"I don't trust him," I said. "And I don't like him."

"There's two of us, Luna," Jetta said. "And just one of him. We just need to stick together."

"Don't you wonder why his car didn't shut down?"

"Yeah…"

"There's something not right about him."

"Yeah. Maybe… but it's safer inside that house than not."

"I don't know about that."

We went inside. Jetta found her way to the kitchen.

I took a seat on the couch. I wasn't going to start making food for that farmboy idiot.

But I didn't feel like I could just sit still.

I saw a bookcase, overflowing with paper books.

I walked over.

The Walking Dead comics, episodes one through one million. So… zombies.

And then… more zombies. *Night of the Living Dead, Victorian Undead, Zombies vs. Cheerleaders*… and then it got worse.

"What the frick," I said.

But not loud enough for Jetta to hear.

So I went to the kitchen. I decided not to bring any samples from the bookcase. You know what guys do with those kinds of pictures…

"Zombie porn," I told her. "He has reams of it. On his bookcase, out in the open…"

"Let me see…"

She came out and checked out the collection.

"It's no big deal," she said.

"You're joking."

"It's like cult classic, exploitation-type stuff. Like so over-the-top that it's funny."

"This isn't funny. *Zombie Slavegirls #13*. Like, they made at least twelve more of these."

"It's patently ridiculous," she said. "It's not like you can do it with a zombie…"

I saw a strange leather strap hanging from the side of the bookcase. Hanging from what looked like a randomly-placed screw.

Two straps, actually, with a rubber or plastic ring in the middle. Like the world's strangest belt and an even stranger belt buckle; that's saying a lot considering what Jetta was using to keep her pants up.

"What is that?" I said.

"Looks like a conversation starter," Jetta said. "And probably not something you'd be into." She was giggling.

"This isn't funny, Jetta. This guy is a total creep."

"I think you're overreacting."

"Overreacting? About the strange man with the zombie porn and what... some sex toy or whatever... and who's downstairs looking for his shotgun?"

"Okay... I can see your point of view on this. But it's not like we can just leave now, right?"

"I don't know... I'd like to..."

I heard the sound of Lucas climbing back up the basement stairs.

"Oh," he said, seeing us by the bookcase. "I'm a bit of a zombie nut." He had a bag over his shoulder. It was long, and looked pretty heavy.

Seemed like he'd found the shotgun.

"Some of this is pornography," I said.

"Wow," Jetta said. "Right to the point, eh?"

"Don't get all judgy, alright?" he said. "I think it's kinda cool. I'm sure you two have plenty of weird little secrets."

"I like eating sugar," Jetta said. "Like, by the spoonful."

"I think you should drive us back to the interstate," I said.

He shook his head. "It's not safe, Luna." He put the gun bag down, leaning it against the bookcase. Like he was trying to emphasize the point.

"We're not staying here."

"I'm not going to chain you to the floor. But I'm not about to drive you around the entire county after you just insulted me."

"I didn't insult you. It's because of your bookcase, Lucas."

"So what?"

"So you're a pervert. And a creep. A creep who plies eighteen year old girls with alcohol."

"I was being polite."

"You were being skeevy."

"Let's just leave it there," Jetta said. "There's no reason to argue. It's not safe outside, so we'll stay here for now. Until being here somehow seems worse than out there."

"It's getting worse," I said.

"You suck, Luna." Lucas said. "Like truly."

"Whatever, Lucas."

"So," Jetta said, "how about some food? We've got hot dogs, beef burgers..."

"I'm a vegetarian," I said.

"Figures," Lucas said.

"I can work with that," Jetta said. "As long as you aren't vegan."

I nodded.

"Sweet," Lucas said. "You know, you kinda rock, Jetta."

"Wow, thanks. That's what my grandpa used to say to me."

I laughed.

❧

We had lunch, with Lucas eating three burgers and Jetta and I sharing a can of tomato soup. Apparently for Lucas, the rationing hadn't started yet.

I begrudgingly started to clear the table. Because Jetta had fed me, too. And she would have just picked up the dirty dishes herself.

"We'll need to go out on a run," Lucas said.

"A run?" Jetta said.

"To get supplies. I've got a barebones 3D printer for widgets and stuff, but it's pretty basic. And it can't print us anything to eat."

"I don't think we should go back into any populated areas," I said. "We should check to see how much food you have right now."

"It doesn't matter what I have. We need to gather as much as we can, as quickly as we can. By the time everyone else realizes what this is, we'll be sitting on top of five years' worth of stuff."

"I don't have any money, really," Jetta said.

"I don't think he's talking about a shopping spree," I said.

"Tell me what I'm talking about, Luna," he said.

"Looting."

"Yes, Luna. Looting. Or keeping us alive. Whatever you'd like to call it."

"It's been like three hours," I said. "Do we really need to start pillaging?"

"I'm the expert on this, alright? I've been reading about this for years."

"In your porno comics?"

"I've forgotten more about survival than you'll ever know."

"I know that the first rule of survival is to cut the douches out of your life. So really, Jetta and I should get going now..."

"Luna," Jetta said, "please... be nice, okay?"

"That's what he's counting on. That we'll just 'be nice' and let him push us around."

"My house," he said. "So my rules, alright?"

"No, it's not alright."

"Then there's the door, sweetheart."

"Enough, guys," Jetta said. "Seriously."

"We're not going on looting runs," I said.

Jetta sighed. "We shouldn't dismiss it."

"Are you serious?"

"If you're right, Luna... about this quarantine..."

"Quarantine?" Lucas asked. "What quarantine?"

"She thinks that's why they shut the cars down," Jetta said. "To keep us from getting out."

"Getting out of what? We got out of Fargo."

"Maybe it was already outside of Fargo when they drew the isolation line," I said.

"That's a fat pile of supposition."

"Yeah... like three-burgers-for-lunch fat." I wasn't proud of that.

"The network's down, too," Jetta said. "At least it was for us in my car. And I saw it was in your SUV, too."

"It's down here, too," Lucas said. "I already checked."

"No transportation," I said. "No communication..."

"But zombies can't drive," Jetta said, "can they?"

"Not according to what I've read," Lucas said.

"Also from your porno magazines," I said.

"That's cute, sweetheart."

"Maybe the network isn't down on purpose," I said. "Maybe that's just a byproduct of things going bad."

"Maybe it's more than just Fargo," Lucas said. "Maybe this outbreak is all over the country. All over the world..."

"That's what you're hoping for, isn't it?"

"That's not funny," Jetta said.

"It's not meant to be funny," I said. "Lucas wants there to be zombies. He's spent so much time pretending to fight zombies that now he thinks *he actually knows how to fight zombies.*"

"I know how to kill," he said. "That's what the shotgun is for."

"They're people," I said. "You know that, right?"

"They're dead people. Killed by some kind of infection."

Jetta gave out a little sob. She tried to hide it.

"I don't think they're dead," I said. "They don't look dead. And one of them tried to talk to me."

"Yeah, sure," Lucas said. "What did he say? 'Yum'?"

"A guy I work with," I said, more to Jetta than to the idiot in the room. "He was infected, but he... I think he was trying to warn me... even as he was coming after me."

"What do you mean?" Jetta asked.

"I think the part of Errol... that's his name, Errol —"

"That *was* his name," Lucas said. "Now he's just another zombie."

"He's not dead," I said. "And I don't think Leona's dead, either."

"Who the heck is Leona?" Lucas asked.

"Shut up," Jetta said. "Please."

He seemed surprised by that.

I wasn't.

"I don't know what I'm talking about," I said. "But I think there's still hope. For a cure, for some way of fixing this. Of saving the people who've been infected. We just need to hold on."

"There's no hope," Lucas said. "Anyone who's bitten is long past dead."

"I told you to shut up," Jetta said.

"My house, Jetta. Remember that."

"You know what would make things fair?" I said. "If we took a vote."

"A vote? Come on."

"I agree," Jetta said. "We should each get a vote."

"Of course you agree," Lucas said. "You two will agree on anything... just to spite me. So I'll automatically lose every time. There's no way I'm agreeing to that. I'm in charge. I'm older, I'm wiser, I'm stronger..."

"Fine," I said. "You win, Lucas."

"What?"

"Your house. Your rules." I turned to Jetta. "We'll start walking. Find someone who can help us, or else we'll just keep on until we reach my father's place."

"What are you trying to do?" he asked me.

"She's calling your bluff, snowflake," Jetta said.

"What bluff? You girls can leave anytime. It doesn't matter to me."

"You'll have to go find some new girls to play house with," I said. "Because we're not in the mood."

"Whatever."

"Let's go," I told her.

We started walking toward the door.

"I could make you stay," he said. "Don't make me make you."

"You'll have to kill us," I said. "That's what it'll take."

"Don't push me, Luna."

"Yeah... my name isn't Luna."

"It isn't?" Jetta said.

"I'll get into that later."

"Alright," Lucas said.

"Alright, what?"

"You win."

"We win what?"

"Take a vote."

"What exactly are we voting on?" Jetta asked.

"It doesn't matter," Lucas said.

"I vote we take the SUV to my father's farm," I said. "We'll pack up the supplies and we'll bring the shotgun."

"Sounds good," Jetta said. "Or, uh... I vote yes on proposition get-the-heck-outta-here."

"What's your vote, Lucas?" I asked.

"It doesn't matter," he said.

At least he was starting to understand how the world works.

∽

We got back into the SUV, supplies and shotgun included. Jetta took the back seat, while I sat up front beside Lucas. Someone had to take the hit.

And I think Lucas still thought he had a shot with Jetta.

He drove us east on 31st Street until we hit 145th.

He turned left.

"I hope your father's place hasn't been hit," he said.

"Hit by what?" Jetta asked.

"A horde or something."

"Have you seen any hordes out here?" I asked. "Or anywhere?"

"Zombies travel in packs."

"Says no reputable source on anything."

He didn't respond to that, other than an unintelligible mumble.

"Is it just your father living there?" Jetta asked.

"My stepmother's there, too," I said. "And Iris, my stepsister."

"Stepsister, huh," Lucas said. "I bet I'll like her better than you. Bet she even has a real name and everything."

"That doesn't upset me, Lucas. Sorry."

"So what is your name?" Jetta asked. "It's not Curlicue."

"It's Persephone."

"Persephone?" Lucas said. "That's like the worst name ever."

"Stop being a dick, Lucas," Jetta said.

"I remember high school," I said. "I doubt you can come up with something worse to say on it."

"So what do people call you?" Jetta asked. "Can't just be 'Persephone this' and 'Persephone that'..."

"That's all they call me."

"Bullcrap," Lucas said. "I know you're lying."

"Not much you can do about it."

"Persy."

"No."

"Fifi."

"No."

"Seffy."

"Shut up."

"That's it, isn't it?"

"Seffy?" Jetta said. "I like it."

"Don't," I said. "I hate it."

"Then come up with an alternative," Lucas said. "Otherwise..."

"What's that?" Jetta asked.

"What?" I said.

"In front of us," Lucas said. "I see it."

"I can't see it..."

"You need your eyes fixed, then."

"It's a horde," Jetta said.

"No way," I said.

"She's right," Lucas said. "There's a crowd up there, at the overpass. Dozens of them."

"Dozens of people, maybe. But I doubt it's zombies. Probably just people who got stranded when their cars got zapped."

"How will we know?" Jetta asked. "It's so hard to tell if they're infected."

"We assume they're infected," Lucas said. "We assume the worst. At all times."

"You must be real fun at parties," I said.

"You're like a walking cliché. The third member of the team, the third wheel. The cold bitch who thinks she's hotter than she is."

What it is with guys pretending you're no longer any good when you make it clear they're below your pay grade?

"Stay focused, guys," Jetta said. "Okay?"

Lucas slowed down as we neared the mass.

"If they're people, they'll clear the road," Lucas said. "Only dead people don't mind getting run over."

But as we got closer, the crowd seemed to congregate more in our direction.

"They aren't infected," I said. "They're just panicked."

"That's just a blind guess," Lucas said. "Check their eyes."

"Just don't hit anyone."

"I can't promise that. I'm not slowing down under thirty. I'm not going to risk it."

"Doors are locked?" Jetta asked.

"They're locked."

There were two men at the front of the group, waving their arms like air traffic controllers. They didn't look like zombies.

"They want us to stop," Jetta said.

"I don't care," Lucas said.

He pushed on, moving into the crowd. People started banging on the hood of the car, tapping on the windows, trying their best to pull open the doors.

"Help us," one of the men said. "For the love of god."

"What does he expect from us?" Jetta asked. "It's not like we can shove fifty people in the back."

"Just try not to make eye contact," Lucas said. "Don't let them think we're wavering for a second. Don't show weakness."

"What about the guy with the axe?" Jetta said. "What do we show him?"

I hadn't seen that. He was standing near the back of the crowd. He was waiting, calmly. He looked like a man who knew exactly what he intended to do.

"Where's the shotgun?" Lucas asked.

"Down here," Jetta said. "At my feet…"

"Take it out and show them."

"I don't know how to use a shotgun."

"Do you know how, Persephone?"

"Yeah," I said.

Jetta passed the bag up to me. I unzipped it and pulled out the shotgun.

"Point it at him," Lucas said.

"Is it loaded?" I asked.

"Does it matter? You're not actually going to shoot him, are you?"

"Is it loaded?"

"Yes. It's loaded. So don't shoot me by mistake."

"Yeah," I said. "By mistake…"

I pointed the barrel of the shotgun at the man with the axe.

The crowd started rocking the vehicle.

"Bad idea," Jetta said. "I think we've pissed them off."

"Then we speed up," Lucas said. "We're the ones in the two ton SUV."

I lowered the shotgun.

"No," Lucas said. "Keep it aimed. Don't show weakness."

"It wasn't working," I said.

He slammed on the gas pedal.

At first the vehicle barely moved. Then it happened. We pushed through the crowd, shoving people aside. People were being pushed clear, and for a moment I thought we'd get through without anyone being killed. Then I heard the thump, as the right side of the car lifted up and over something.

Lucas kept going.

The man with the axe took his swing, missing the windshield and coming down on the frame beside it. Another few inches would have launched that axe right into my face.

I'm too pretty to have my head chopped open.

"Stop the car," Jetta said. "I think you killed someone."

"You're insane," Lucas said. "They'll rip us to shreds."

"Do you care that you might have killed someone?" I asked.

"Just shut up, alright?"

We passed over the interstate and down the other side of the overpass. A second, smaller crowd was gathered on beside the road. They didn't try to block our way.

"I don't want to be a part of this," Jetta said. "This isn't okay."

"It's done," Lucas said. "We're past it."

"They weren't infected," I said. "Those were just normal people you ran over with your car."

"They would have done the same to us."

"There's no way that's true."

"I'll pull over in another mile or so, then. And you two can get out and head on back. Maybe all you need to do is hike up your skirts, bat your eyelashes and apologize. That should fix it."

"We're not wearing skirts," Jetta said.

"I understand why you did it," I said. "But we're allowed to feel bad about it. We're allowed to think this sucks." He didn't really deserve the understanding. But it felt like the right thing to hand over, the best way to keep Jetta and I safe.

He turned and looked at me. "If you're going to waste time on feeling bad about the things we need to do, you're not going to have much time for anything else."

"What's that supposed to mean?" Jetta asked.

"It means that we're just getting started. It's the beginning of the end. There's a lot more end coming up."

"You're not actually any more prepared than the rest of us," I said.

"What are you talking about?" he said.

"This tough-guy act... the chomping at your bit to start looting and running people over... it doesn't help things."

"I'm keeping us alive. Those people would have torn us apart."

"We don't know what's happening... we don't know how this will end."

"No, Luna... or Seffy... or whatever. You're wrong. I know exactly how this will end. With a ninety-nine percent fatality rate. With a handful of survivors. And I intend to be one of that one percent."

"You sound a little insane," Jetta said. "Is that what you want people to think?"

"Creeping normality… you all look around and think things are like they always were… not seeing the little changes here and there."

"Everything changes," I said. "All the time. What's your point?"

"This has been coming for a long time."

"Then I guess you should have told someone."

"We all should have known. I mean, what's the carrying capacity of the Earth anyhow?"

"I feel like this car is already a little too filled up," Jetta said.

"Climb out, then," Lucas said. He slowed the SUV down.

Then stopped it completely.

"Look out there," he said, pointing right across me and out my window, his arm almost swiping my nose.

I took a look.

There was browning grass, more browning grass… and what looked like a pile of old clothes. People think you can just dump your garbage anywhere…

Then I saw what it was. A body.

"What do you think?" Lucas asked. "Zombie or not? Either way, that girl's dead."

"Girl?" I said.

I looked again.

She had brown hair, not much straighter than mine. Her eyes were open, staring up at the sky.

"Let's take a closer look," Lucas said. "See if she's a zombie."

"I'm not going out there," Jetta said.

"But this car… it's so full…"

"I'm sorry…" Jetta was starting to cry.

"Don't treat her like that," I said.

"Like what?" Lucas asked. "The way you two have been treating me from the very start?"

"I'm sorry," Jetta said.

I climbed out of the SUV.

Anything to get him to leave her alone for a minute.

He got out, too.

We walked toward the body, me in front.

I didn't need anyone to hold my hand.

I reached the body and knelt down.

"She's not a zombie," I said.

"How can you tell?"

"I'm guessing that zombies keep going unless you kill the brain. That's almost how bots work, at the best of times."

"Can you tell how she died?"

"I don't know, Lucas. But my guess is that if she was a zombie, she wouldn't be dead."

She was younger than me.

Back in high school, she'd have been a freshman, probably… maybe a junior… maybe…

That made her just a kid. The kind of kid who wore too much eyeliner and thought more foundation was a miracle concealer. The kind of kid who still thought boys were worth impressing.

And she was lying in the browning grass. No sign of what had happened to her.

"Her neck," Lucas said. He traced his finger just over the bruising.

Someone had strangled her.

Someone had taken the chaos as what, an opportunity? A chance to do whatever sick thing they'd wanted to do all along?

Had she known the person who'd killed her?

"This is what we're up against," Lucas said. "Not just zombies. But people who know this is it, and who have a different endgame in mind."

"What are you even talking about?"

"There are three ways to respond to the end of your world, Persephone. You can run around like a chicken with its head cut off, or you can be like me, and start coming up with a plan to survive. Or you can do this."

"Get murdered and dumped in a field?"

"Some people don't panic and they don't try to survive. They cash in their chips, and they walk out of the casino."

"What?"

"What would you do if you knew today was your last day on Earth?"

"Apparently waste my time out here with you."

"Well, someone decided that this is what he wanted to do. Someone who probably isn't very far away from here."

I looked back to the SUV.

Jetta stared back at me, her face tired and red from crying.

5

THE SCHMIDT FAMILY REUNION

We got back into the SUV. I didn't have anything else to say about the dead girl in the field.

Lucas started driving again.

No one spoke for at least a minute.

"My father's place is just up there," I said. "At the top of that hill."

"Hill?" Lucas said. "This is North Dakota. Your father lives at the top of a freaking mountain. But that's good... good for sightlines..."

"It's only a hill on the one side... it's actually called a valley..."

"Still, though..."

Lucas pulled into the gravel drive. He didn't make it far before I sighted my father and his hunting rifle.

My father had already lowered the barrel.

"Seffy," he said, jogging toward the car door. I didn't recognize this kind of behavior from him. "You're okay?"

I climbed out of the SUV. "I'm fine," I said. "Do you know what's happening?"

"I know enough, yeah."

"You're supposed to be at work, Dad."

"This deserved a sick day."

I noticed that Fender was on the porch, too, but on a leash tied to the railing.

Fender doesn't really do leashes.

He was wagging his tail at me, but he seemed subdued... like he was a little embarrassed to be seen like that.

Lucas and Jetta got out of the vehicle.

Fender started his low-pitched intruder growl. His tail had stopped wagging.

"Easy, Fender," Dad said. "Who are they?"

"Name's Lucas Berg," Lucas said. "I live up near Casselton. I picked your daughter and her Canadian friend up on I-94."

Fender was still growling. I don't think he was big on Lucas. A dog with reasonably good taste, aside from the occasional hankering for his own poo.

"The cars have all been disabled," I said.

"I know," Dad said. "Mine are both out, too."

"Where's Iris?" I asked. "And Beth?"

"They're inside."

I started walking toward the front porch.

"You stay out here," Dad said. "I could use the help."

"I can help," Lucas said. "I've got a Remington 12 Gauge in my vehicle."

"Just everyone stay together, okay?"

"Yeah, okay," I said. "You okay, Dad?"

"As good as can be expected, right? They're talking pandemic. Pretty loaded word."

"It's bad… really bad."

"Have you heard from your mother or your Aunt Callie?"

"No. Network's down." *And I left them to get bitten.*

"Yeah. I know."

"Mr. Seffy's Dad?" Jetta said.

He looked over to her. "You didn't introduce yourself," he said.

"You didn't, either. I'm Jetta. Uh… I need to use your bathroom… is that okay?"

"Not really, no. But there's an outhouse by the machine shed. Composting toilet, actually."

She looked over to me.

I looked over to my father. "Are you joking?" I asked him.

"I'd rather keep the house secure," he said.

"You're starting to sound like Lucas, here."

"Outhouse is fine," Jetta said. "I've started a habit of not washing my hands after I'm through."

"I should go with you," I said.

"You should stay with me," Dad said.

"I'll go with her," Lucas said.

Dad nodded. "Yeah. Good idea."

Lucas went to the SUV to retrieve his shotgun.

Jetta gave me a second plaintive look, like she expected me to pull rank on my father. She didn't seem to understand that even the barn cats outranked me at my father's house.

"I'm a little thirsty, too," Jetta said. "Haven't had much to drink today."

"I can't help you with that right yet," Dad said.

I glared at him.

He saw, but didn't seem to care.

"What about that pump in the garden?" Lucas asked. "Can she drink from there?"

"I wouldn't," Dad said. "The well water around here tends to give people some pretty bad runs. We don't drink the stuff anymore."

"But you water the plants with it?" Jetta asked.

"Just the flowers… nothing we eat. We're not that kind of thrill-seeking."

Jetta looked at me one more time.

I gave her a little shrug, and she walked off toward the machine shed, Lucas following behind with his 12 gauge, playing hero.

The bad water. It made me think of the men in the sewer jump-suits. But there were no sewers here. Just wells and septic fields. A different world.

"You shouldn't have brought them here," Dad said to me. "Do you even know anything about them?"

"Yeah… Jetta's Canadian, and Lucas is nuts."

"You're putting my family in danger, Seffy."

"*Your* family?"

"And you, too."

"God, Dad."

"Mind your mouth, Seffy."

"I wouldn't be here if it wasn't for both of them," I said. "Lucas got me away from a couple of infected guys, and Jetta gave me a ride out of town in her car. And then, when it shut down, Lucas found us."

"When her car shut down?"

"Yeah."

"But she's Canadian, right?"

"What difference does that make?"

"Was it a Canadian car?"

"Manitoba plates, yeah."

He shook his head. "Canadian cars don't shut down the same way."

"No, Dad, they do... I was there when it happened."

"Canadian cars have an override. They only allow five minutes of shutdown before you can restart. Same as the Europeans."

"You're serious?"

"Of course."

"God... I'll bet he knew that."

"Who? That, uh... Lucas?"

"He wanted us to come stay at his place. There's no way we would have gone with him if we'd known about Jetta's car."

"Are we going to have a problem with him?"

"I don't think so. Other than having to put up with him in general. But that doesn't make me feel any better about how my day's going. You know... Errol's infected."

"I'm sorry, Seffy."

"I'm still hopeful..."

"For what?"

"I'm hoping that this thing can be cured. That people can be brought back... I think he's still in there... I think he's still alive."

He looked back at the house. "I hope so, too," he said. "Lord... I hope so."

"Listen, Dad... I'd really like to go inside..."

"In a bit, okay? Let's wait for your friends to come back."

"Yeah, okay. It's just —"

He shushed me.

He pointed toward the road.

Two figures walking up from the south.

"I'll bet they're infected," he said in a whisper.

"Why?"

"Just wait..."

The figures came closer. I could see that they were a man and woman, both around their early forties.

I couldn't tell if they were infected. Their eyes looked... okay. I couldn't see any red flush... but that might have been because of the distance.

And they were walking at a normal pace, like nothing was wrong.

Or was that a sign they *were* infected?

Fender was watching them, too, obviously. He wasn't barking, or growling… not yet.

"This won't end well," Dad said.

"What do you mean?"

"I'm going to have to shoot them, Seffy."

"Just wait… you don't know they're infected… and maybe they'll just keep on going."

"They aren't the first ones I've seen."

"What?"

I glanced around.

I didn't see anyone else. No one… lying in the dirt…

"You shot someone?" I asked him.

"I didn't have to," he said. "But these two…"

"Wait, Dad…"

"You there!" he called out. "Don't come any closer."

The two walkers seemed to slow down, but they didn't stop.

Dad pointed his rifle toward them. "Tell me your names," he said.

"Help… us…" the woman said. Her voice was disjointed, panicked maybe.

"Your names."

"Help us," she said again.

"They're not infected," I said. "She's talking to you, isn't she?"

"Tell me your names," Dad said again.

"Jack," the man said.

He didn't lower the rifle.

"What are you doing, Dad?" I asked.

"Full names," Dad said. "Both of you."

"Jack Rood," the man said. He sounded like he wasn't quite sure.

"Sam Rood," the woman said.

"They're infected," Dad said quietly to me.

"Are you nuts?" I said.

"Do you hear how they're talking? The words don't sound right to me."

"They've been through a lot."

"Now I need you to stop where you are," he said to them. "Just stand still."

They both stopped walking.

"Now," Dad said, "I need you both, one at a time, to say 'lollapalooza'."

"Dad…"

He shushed me again.

"Say 'lollapalooza'."

Neither responded at first.

"I'm not joking. Either you can say the word back to me or I'll have to shoot you."

"Help us," the woman said.

"Please," the man said.

Dad fired the rifle.

The man doubled over.

"Don't... don't shoot," the woman said.

"Don't move," Dad said.

"This isn't okay," I said. "You can't just shoot people."

"I shot him in the thigh, Seffy... that's not fatal."

"It can be fatal, Dad. Since there's no way to get him to the hospital."

"Trust me, Seffy. It won't be fatal to him."

The woman stood silently.

My father kept his rifle aimed.

The man he shot was sitting on the pavement.

The man hadn't cursed my father, he hadn't tried to crawl toward the ditch. He was just sitting there, on the road.

And the woman was still standing there beside him.

She hadn't tried to help him up.

"There's something not right about them," I said. "I know that."

"They're infected," Dad said. "I told you that already. Now wait... and watch him..."

After another thirty seconds or so I saw the man start to get up off the pavement. He stood up beside the woman.

"Help us," the woman said.

"They can talk," Dad said. "They can walk and they can talk. After a couple of hours after they've been infected, you'd almost think there was nothing wrong with them. Except that they can't seem to say some of the bigger words."

"Like 'lollapalooza'? Isn't that a music festival?"

"Well, they couldn't say it, could they?"

"How do you know all this?"

He fired the rifle again.

The man dropped.

Another round.

The woman fell, too.

He'd shot them both in the head.

"Come and see," he said.

"What the hell is wrong with you, Dad?"

"Just shut up and come with me."

He untied Fender's leash and gave him a pat.

We walked over to where they'd landed. I felt my whole body shaking.

Fender was guarded, but he seemed to know that the threat had passed.

Half of the man's right cheek was gone.

The woman's head was more whole, but I could see the blood from a wound near her temple.

And I could see that her eyes didn't seem bloodshot at all.

"Look at his leg," Dad said.

"What?"

"His leg."

I looked down to the man's thigh. One and then the other.

"The blood's there on his pants," Dad said, "but the wound's gone."

"It's been repaired," I said. "He must have had a botshot like Iris."

"Bots don't work that fast, Seffy. By design. You know that. Heck, you and Iris got in trouble for tampering with some of hers."

"But it wouldn't be impossible to reprogram them somehow…"

"This infection… I think it's connected to the bots."

"Bots wouldn't take a person over like that," I said. "It's not remotely possible."

"Well, how would you explain it? When people get bit, the wound gets repaired. They don't even look like anything happened. People who have never had a botshot…"

"You think the bites are spreading the bots to another person, but I told you, that's not possible. Bots are coded to their carrier's DNA. They don't spread."

"Well, something went wrong, Seffy."

"I don't know, Dad… there's still too much we don't know about this."

Dad had stopped listening somewhere along the way. He'd started walking back toward the house. "Your friends… they're not back yet.

You need to find them."

"You don't think something's happened to them…"

"I think they have a listening problem."

"Well, it's a little weird, isn't it, Dad? Not letting Jetta use the bathroom?"

"Find them, Seffy, okay?"

"Okay."

"And it you see anything off, you make some noise. Make sure I can hear you."

I walked over to the machine shed.

The outhouse was empty.

I'm not enough of a bloodhound to tell if Jetta had used it.

I called back to my father. "Is the house locked?"

"Yeah."

"Could Iris or Beth have let them in while we weren't watching?"

"No… if they're inside, they broke in."

"Come on, Dad… take it down a notch."

"We need to find them."

"Just… wait on the porch, okay? I'll find them." The last thing I needed was my father assuming that somehow Jetta and Lucas had gotten infected and kill-worthy in the last couple of minutes.

I walked over toward the machine shed. The door to the outhouse was open; compost toilets are great, but you still want to make sure you close the door afterward.

They weren't there.

I heard noise from the back of the house.

The aluminum window frame had been ripped down. I watched the backside of Lucas making his way through the new hole in my father's house.

I couldn't see Jetta.

I almost called out to him with a few choice expletives, but I remembered my father and his frame of mind.

And I thought of what Fender might do to that farmboy backside if my Dad were to drop the leash.

I ran over.

I climbed in behind him. Into the dining room.

"Lucas," I said. "What the heck are you doing? Where's Jetta?"

"I'm thirsty, alright?" I heard Jetta say. She was already out in the hallway, heading toward the kitchen.

"My father's not going to like this, Jetta."

"Your father's kinda weird."

I walked to the kitchen, Lucas following behind.

Jetta was standing at the kitchen sink, holding a glass.

"This filter," she said, pointing at the nub on the faucet. "This filters out the bad stuff?"

"That's the core concept," I said.

She filled the glass and drank the water in one gulp.

She filled the glass again.

"What was your plan, exactly?" I asked. "Were you going to just walk out the front door and apologize for the break-in?"

"Nope... back out the window..."

"Why wouldn't he let us in?" Lucas asked. "This is really weird."

"I don't know," I said.

"Where's your sister?" Jetta asked.

"I don't know."

"They're not here," Lucas said. "No one came at us when we climbed in."

"Yeah... how did you know you wouldn't get shot?"

"Jetta was in front. She's like a hot little canary."

"That doesn't feel like a compliment," Jetta said.

"No, it is." He was leering at her.

I was equal parts angry and grossed out. But that wasn't important.

"I need to find them," I said.

I checked the living room, then I made my way down to the bedrooms. Iris' was empty. The bathroom was empty.

I opened the door to the master bedroom.

And I found Iris and her mother.

Each one duct taped to a dining room chair, both chairs having been dragged into the bedroom for the occasion. Wrists bound, ankles bound, even the elbows and shoulders had been wrapped up in silver tape.

And both had duct tape covering their mouths, wrapped all the way around their heads. I could see a bit of purple sock protruding from Iris' mouth.

"Oh my god," I said.

They were both looking at me.

Iris started moaning, or muttering... trying to say something through her sock. Beth — her mother, not mine — didn't do much of anything.

"What the unholy frig is wrong with your father?" Lucas asked. He'd come up behind me. He walked into the room. "Get some scissors."

"Don't touch them," I said.

"We need to get them away from him."

I heard Jetta gasp. "What did he do to them?" she asked. "Is he going to hurt us? What do we need to do here, Seffy?"

"I think they're infected," I said.

Iris shook her head. And kept trying to talk.

"She doesn't agree with that assessment," Lucas said.

"She's not infected," Jetta said. "Look at her. For one thing, she's got less red in her eyes than you do."

"No," I said. "You guys don't get it."

"Does she look like a freaking zombie?" Lucas asked.

"I need to talk to my father," I said. "Don't do anything yet, okay?"

"They could choke," Jetta said. "I saw that in a movie once. Guy vomited and the stuff in his mouth blocked it, pushed it up and blocked his nose, too."

"They're not vomiting, are they?"

"It's just not safe. At least let us take the socks out."

"If your father didn't have something to hide," Lucas said, "he wouldn't have gagged them in the first place."

"Okay," I said. "Just the socks. But don't cut them free. Not until I talk to my father."

Iris made another sound. I was starting to understand her enough to know that she owed at least a couple of bucks to the swear jar.

Jetta closed the bedroom door.

Lucas pulled a pocket knife out from his pants.

"Don't cut them free," I said again. Not that he was listening.

I stepped toward him.

Jetta started wrapping her arms around me, kind of like a bear hug. And I learned that Jetta is surprisingly strong.

She had my arms pinned against my sides. I was close to lifting a leg and hoofing her in the crotch... but I held back. I haven't kicked a girl in the crotch since grade two. Aside from one blurry incident from a senior-year house party in Anna Kellum's basement... there's a reason Anna doesn't invite me to any of her parties anymore.

I wasn't going to kick Jetta. Lucas was the one in harm's way.

He cut the tape at Iris' wrists.

He stepped back.

"You heard what Persephone said about you," he told her. "She thinks you're infected."

Iris nodded.

"But you're not infected, right?"

Iris shook her head.

She wriggled her arms and shoulders against the tape.

She mumbled something through the sock.

Lucas cut more of the tape, freeing her arms.

"I'll let you handle taking the tape off your mouth," he said. "Might not feel so great."

She slowly started peeling the tape.

"No," Jetta said, "go quick. One fast pull..."

Iris yanked on the tape.

And shrieked.

And glared at me like it was somehow my fault.

"That hurts so very much," Iris said. "Now I'll have tape herpes or something."

I wanted to believe her. Not about the tape or the STI, but that she wasn't infected. I wanted to, but I just couldn't be sure.

Iris started tearing off the tape from her legs. She'd been unlucky enough to have been wearing capri pajama pants; we'd all hear her once she got down to the tape around her ankles.

I struggled against Jetta's arms. "You can let go now," I said.

"Oh," Jetta said. "Sorry about that." She dropped her hands.

"You on steroids?"

"Judo... yellow belt... using your opponent's size against them..."

"My size?"

"Oh... uh, sorry again."

"Why did he tape you up, Iris?" I asked as I walked over to her dining room chair.

"Mom taped me up," Iris said.

"Why?"

"I don't know. She just... she lost it, Seffy. I came in here to check on her and she grabbed me."

"So then your father came in and taped her up?" Lucas asked. "Without cutting you free?"

"And taped her up in the exact same way?" Jetta asked.

"Who are these people?" Iris asked. "I told you not to talk to strangers, Seffy."

"They're casual acquaintances," I said. "Acquaintances with some good questions."

"If I was infected, would I be talking to you right now? Wouldn't I be moaning and asking for some parboiled brains?"

"They don't run around eating brains," Lucas said. "Not these zombies."

"What do they eat?" Jetta asked.

"I don't know. Seen some take bites out of people… but that's about it. Not sure how much they eat of a person…"

"Well, I don't like the sound of any of it," Iris said. "I mean, some gentle nibbling on the ears…"

"We can figure out what they eat later," I said.

I heard Iris grumble a little as she pulled the tape off her ankles.

She stood up from the chair.

She held out her arms for a hug. "Bring it in, slightly-bigger sister."

I stepped back.

"She's not infected," Lucas said.

"I don't know," I said.

"It's okay," Iris said. "I understand. You're exhausted. Stressed. Probably completely insane." She turned to Lucas. "Thanks, bud," she told him. "I really appreciate you sticking your neck out for me."

I recognized that tone, the one that gives Iris everything she wants in life. A tone that would just sound ridiculous coming from me. Or even from Jetta.

It just works from girls like Iris.

"You know," Lucas said with a grin, "I'm getting pretty good at this rescuing stuff…"

She reached out and pulled him toward her.

She went in for his neck.

Lucas started jabbing his hand at her.

She fell back, knocking over the chair, and nearly hitting me. She landed on her knees.

Blood was pouring out from her neck and the left shoulder. I heard her gasping for air.

Lucas stepped toward her.

I shoved him.

He tripped and fell down to the carpet.

"That's my sister," I screamed.

"She's a zombie," he said. "And a crazy bitch."

I grabbed Iris' arms and pinned her to the floor, pushing her face into the shag.

"Find the tape," I said to Jetta.

I heard the front door open. Heavy footsteps moving through the house, toward us.

Jetta knelt down beside me, a roll of silver tape in her hand.

"Tape her wrists," I said.

Iris didn't fight as Jetta wrapped the tape around her hands. She was still gasping.

"Make sure she doesn't bite you," Lucas said. He was cold, distant… it sounded like he was giving me some casual advice on home repair.

Jetta taped Iris' ankles, then pulled up her legs and ran tape across to her wrists. She helped me roll Iris onto her side, both of us keeping as far away from her mouth as we could.

The bedroom door opened.

"What's going on?" my father said. "Oh, my god… what have you done?"

He knelt down beside us, placing his rifle on the carpet.

"Iris…" he said, quietly. "My god…"

Her gasping was getting quieter, more like regular breathing. Her pajama top was soaked in blood, as were my clothes… but her stab wounds had started to close. Her eyes had already gone from glassy to angry.

She tried to talk, but it was too quiet and raspy for me to understand.

"The bots are healing her, Dad," I said. "She's okay…"

"Put the sock back in," Lucas said as he finally stood up, "unless you want this to happen again."

"She doesn't need a sock."

"No," Dad said, "she needs the sock. She can lunge…"

"No sock," I said.

"I don't get it," Jetta said. "She was talking… just like a normal person…"

"How normal?" Dad asked.

"I couldn't tell," I said. "I honestly couldn't tell."

"The longer they're infected…"

"Yeah. Whatever it is takes over… controls them…"

"That's why the government's shut everything down," Jetta said. "Because they knew this was coming. They knew they wouldn't be able to tell who had it…"

"I don't know about that," Dad said.

"Beth doesn't seem as far along," I said. I could see it in her eyes.

"Beth thought Iris was okay," Dad said. "She thought I was losing my mind, taping her up and shoving that sock in her mouth. So the moment I looked away, Beth let her go. And Iris took a chunk out of her neck."

"But it's not there, now," Lucas said. "No neck wound, just some dried blood." He was circling around my stepmother like she was a museum piece.

"Iris lied to us," I said.

Lucas scoffed. "Yeah… she said she wasn't infected…"

"No… about her mother taping her up. She honestly tried to trick us. She pretended she wanted to hug me… she even started coming on to Lucas…"

"Gotta be some kind of brain disease," Jetta said. "Especially that last part."

"I'm sorry," Iris said.

I looked over at her. "What?"

"I'm sorry, Seffy. I had to. But I'd never bite you."

"What the heck is going on?" Dad said.

"What's going on in there, Iris?" I asked her. I wanted her to tell me that there was still a fight inside, the real Iris trying to regain control.

"I'm fighting it, Seffy…" she said. "I really am. I just… I just need to keep fighting. Just… just… don't leave me like this. We need to find some way to fix this. Maybe together we can figure it out."

"I don't want you to bite me, Iris. You understand that?"

"I said I wouldn't bite you… you're my sister. I can hold back."

"Like you did with your mother?" Dad asked.

"That was before, Dad," she said. "I'm… I'm more in control, now. I can fight it. Just keep those two idiots away from me… then

I'm sure we can work this out."

I'm sure that's exactly what the infection knew I'd want to hear, as weird as that sounds, that an infection would be some malicious entity, trying to deceive me.

But that's what it seemed to be. And it would keep talking, forcing Iris to lie to me until I finally started to believe it.

I'm not strong enough to hear those lies. I'm not strong enough not to fall for them.

I reached over and grabbed the sock by the chair legs.

I stuffed it in my stepsister's mouth.

6

THE EXPERIMENT

Once Iris was re-gagged, Jetta and I stood up and we all looked at my father.

"I didn't want you to panic," he told me. "I still think there's hope."

"Hope for what?" Lucas asked. "The Apocalypse?"

"You're right, Dad," I said. "I can see it, too. She's still in there. Somewhere. There has to be a way to get them both back."

"I have to get back to the porch," Dad said.

"I'll come, too," Lucas said. "Two sets of eyes."

Dad nodded.

He didn't know who'd stabbed Iris. He hadn't asked.

I don't know if it would be better for him to think it had been me.

Lucas and my father left the room.

Jetta and I looked at each other. We both had blood all over us, but definitely me more than her.

"I have clothes here," I said. "In the guest room, in the basement. Not much, though. I don't stay over very often."

"I think I'd fit your sister's clothes better," Jetta said.

"She's taller than me. By a good three inches. And you…"

"I'm shorter, yeah. It's just…"

"I'm like a size eight," I said.

"I'm a size three."

"Go see what you can find, then."

Jetta turned to leave. She stopped and turned back.

"He tried to kiss me out by the outhouse," she said.

"Lucas?"

"Yeah… went in for the smooch."

"What did you do?"

"I pulled away and... I don't know... somehow I made a bit of an 'ick' sound."

"Ouch."

"Yeah... it just sorta happened."

"Couldn't happen to a creepier guy."

She smiled, then turned and walked out of the master bedroom.

I glanced over to Beth. She seemed a tiny bit more *aware* or whatever, watching me, occasionally testing the tape that held her to the chair. At some point she'd be just like her daughter, looking and acting so normal...

She was even starting to look more like Iris, as if her hair had grown a little softer, her face a little smoother.

I looked down at my stepsister.

"You're still in there," I said. "I know that."

She muttered something.

I was glad I didn't understand.

I walked to the kitchen and over to the basement stairs.

There was a gunshot, from the porch.

And barking. A whole lot of barking.

I turned and ran to the front door.

Another shot. Sounded like a different gun.

I walked out to the porch.

Fender was tied to the railing again.

Dad and Lucas were staring out to the road.

I looked down toward the driveway.

A crowd of people walking toward the house. Maybe the crowd we'd seen at the interstate... maybe a different one... I think it was a different one, over two dozen people.

I didn't see our friend with the axe.

My father called out. "No one come any closer!"

"Stay back!" Lucas yelled.

They both had their guns trained on the crowd. I couldn't tell if anyone had been shot.

Some in the crowd kept walking, a little over a dozen.

They were already just a few meters from Lucas' SUV.

"They're zombies," Lucas said. "No way any of them would keep coming otherwise."

"Then we shoot," Dad said.

74

"I have seven rounds left," Lucas said.

"We can time our reloads… switch off…"

"My shells are in the SUV. Not sure I can reach them."

My father sighed. One of his big ones, the ones that tell you just how much of a disappointment you are.

"Seffy," Dad said, without looking back at me, "can you use my bow?"

"I think so," I said.

I grabbed his bow and quiver pack. I brought them up to the edge of the porch, beside Lucas.

"We don't have enough," I said. "Five arrows, however many rounds…"

"I've got ammo," Dad said. "In my pack. Side pocket."

I felt one of the side pockets, than the other. I unzipped the second pocket and pulled out a box of loose bullets. I found a second magazine at the bottom of the pocket.

"Where's that other girl?" Dad asked.

"Getting changed."

"She needs to get her butt out here."

I stuck my head into the house and called for Jetta.

"Think she'll know how to hand-load a mag?" he asked.

"Probably not."

"Well, she'd better be quick enough to figure it out, because I need you on the bow."

"Yeah…"

"I need you now, Seffy."

I picked up the bow. I loaded the first arrow.

I raised the bow and drew back.

"Remember, guys," I said, "these are still people."

"People or not," Dad said, "we still need to kill them."

He took the first shot.

He hit one of the men in the front row in the chest.

"Hit the men first," he said. "In the chest. Don't aim for the head 'cause you'll end up missing."

"Chest won't kill 'em," Lucas said.

"It'll stop them long enough to finish the job."

Lucas took a shot.

Another man went down.

Jetta came out onto the porch, in new clothes, but with the same stupid silver beaver belt buckle. I guess cleaning the blood off of her belt was considered a major priority.

"See the bullets?" I asked. "You need to load them into that magazine."

"I don't know how," she said.

"You'll need to figure it out."

She nodded.

"Give it a shot, Seffy," Dad said.

I picked a target, the biggest guy I could find near the front of the crowd. I released.

I hit him lower than I'd wanted, the arrow landing not far from his bellybutton.

He fell just the same.

Neither Dad nor Lucas seemed to take notice.

They'd both fired another shot of their own. And kept firing after that. They were missing a few, but hitting their targets more often than not.

I shot the other four arrows. I took down two more of the oncoming, one man and one woman.

I put down the bow.

By the time I'd done that, Dad had taken the spare mag from Jetta, trading it for the one he'd just used up.

He fired another shot. One more down, and only three left approaching, two women and one man. The rest of the crowd had split, a few taking cover behind the SUV, the others standing in their place with blank expressions. Different shades of self-preservation, different stages of whatever this was.

"Good job on the loading," Dad said to Jetta. "You're a keeper."

"I'm out of rounds," Lucas said.

"See that shovel up against the fence?" Dad asked.

"Yeah..."

"Take it down there. Take out any of the downed ones you can reach. Don't getting yourself killed, but finish the job."

"Yes, sir." It bothered me that they almost seemed to be getting along.

"Wait," I said. "You can't just kill them."

"He has to," Dad said. "You know they'll just keep coming once they're healed up."

"We just need to disable them... longer term..."

"We don't have time for that."

"Do you have an axe?" Lucas asked. "Maybe I could chop off their legs…"

"You're psychotic," Jetta said.

"It wouldn't kill them."

"What if we locked them away?" I asked. "Maybe in a grain bin or something…"

"They'll kill us, Seffy," Dad said. He took another shot.

A miss. Three still coming, less than twenty feet from the porch.

"They won't kill us," Lucas said. "They don't seem to feed on people aside from the first few bites. They mostly just infect them. So worst case, we end up a zombie like Iris."

"And then someone else will come along and shoot us in the head," Jetta said.

"It's murder," I said. "Plain and simple. You can't just do away with someone because they're sick."

"Even if we packed them away in a grain bin," Lucas said, "they'd still end up dead. Do you really think the government's going to come along and save everyone? Either they'll starve to death, or cannibalize each other… or freeze solid, eventually…"

"We should save as many as we can," Jetta said. "Even if we can't save all of them."

"Get down there and start finishing off the big ones," Dad said to Lucas. "Or did you want to wait until I run out of ammo… then you'll be on your own for picking 'em off."

Lucas nodded. He jumped down from the porch and moved slowly toward the closest of the three. He slammed the shovel into the woman's chest.

The woman fell onto the gravel.

"You can aim for the head now," Dad said.

Lucas kept walking, toward the next person.

Another swing, again at the chest. The man went down.

Lucas stepped away.

One more to go. A woman.

My father fired.

That last woman kept coming.

I realized where my father had been aiming. He'd shot one of the men on the ground. In the head.

Lucas reached the last woman. He hit her in the chest with the shovel, knocking her down.

"Don't shoot them," he said. "They're down."

"It's not safe until they're dead," Dad said.

"Don't shoot them, Dad," I said. "Please."

I put my hand on his shoulder.

He lowered the rifle and looked back at me.

"We need to save our ammo," Lucas said.

"Why don't you go and get your ammo out of your car," Dad said.

"There are still over a dozen of them left," Jetta said.

Seven were standing completely still, with a handful more cowering at the rear of the SUV.

"They're not a threat," I said.

The ones who'd come at us, they looked the most like what you'd expect from zombies, the humanity stripped out, the bloodshot eyes. Then there were the middling ones, not hiding, but not attacking... zombies transitioning into something... more human. Were the ones who'd gone and hid behind Lucas' car more like Iris?

After a while, you just wouldn't have any way of knowing what they were. What they would do to you if you got too close.

I watched as Lucas creeped up to the SUV, his eyes trained on the infected who were still behind the car.

He opened the back passenger door and pulled out a backpack.

He jogged back toward the porch.

"I've got maybe two dozen rounds," he said.

"Maybe?" my father said. "You mean you don't know?"

"I packed in a hurry, alright?"

Dad sighed again. "We can't stay here," he said as he started looking through Lucas' bag. "This road is too busy."

"We should be bugging in."

"If we stay we have to disable or kill all of these people. And there will be more of them coming."

"You'd think they would head up the interstate," Jetta said. "Why did they come up this way?"

"They came up from the south," Lucas said.

"They're from Embden," Dad said. "Up the road. I recognize most of them."

"You obviously weren't friends with any of them," Jetta said with a smirk.

"Actually, I was, thanks."

Jetta's eyes went as wide as dinner plates. "Sorry."

"There's not much else down that road, is there?" I asked.

"Not really, no. Around a dozen farms between here and the county line."

"So maybe that's it," Lucas said. "We deal with these ones and we're done."

"We don't know, do we?" I said.

"No, we don't," Dad said.

"So we're taking a big chance either way."

"I'd rather be on the move. The people who stay alive are the ones who are ready to pick up and go at a moment's notice. If things go bad —"

"Go bad?" Lucas said. "Are you joking? How is this not what bad looks like?"

"This could get much worse," I said. "And until there's a cure it can't get any better. So instead of some people being infected it might soon be *nearly everyone* being infected. I mean, there should always be a few holdouts... a few people who manage to stay clear..."

"So the zombies will group up together somewhere," Lucas said. "I doubt that place will be here."

I shook my head. "We still don't know what happens when they get hungry."

"What do you mean?" Jetta asked. "They eat people, don't they?"

"They bite to spread the infection," I said. "Either right on the neck, or if they can't reach the neck, anywhere else that'll slow someone down. I'm not sure they bite to feed at all. And if they aren't feeding on people, they'll need to eat something else eventually."

"And we have no idea what that something will be," Dad said.

"It'll probably be the same thing we eat," Jetta said. "They might just end up raiding pantries and biting into tin cans."

"I still think they'll look on us as a food source," Lucas said. "If this infection is something new, it could just be that they haven't gotten to that stage. Too busy biting new people to finish off the last person they took. But once they develop a little more..."

"You mean to Iris' stage," I said. She'd be hungry by now. She'd need food...

"I don't know," Lucas said. "Maybe..."

Iris could show us what she'd eat.

She'd have loved what I was thinking of, another experiment. The one thing we'd always had in common, aside from our blended family of grot, was a love of causing trouble in the name of *Science*. If I'd been the one infected and not Iris, she'd have poked and prodded me from the moment she'd found me taped to a dining room chair.

She'd understand what I wanted to do.

"We should see what Iris eats," I said.

"I nominate Lucas as the first food source," Jetta said.

"Won't work," Lucas said.

"Why?" I asked.

"She'll try to trick us again."

"How do you know that?"

"I don't... but we can't be sure."

He was right.

I knew that, even if I didn't want to admit it.

"So you try it with one of them," Dad said, pointing out at the crowd of zombies who still hadn't moved.

"What's the difference?" Jetta asked. "Can't they lie just as well?"

"No," I said, "not as well. They haven't reached that point." I turned to Lucas. "Want to earn your keep?"

"Funny," he said. "I think I earned my keep the first time I saved your plump little rump."

"Excuse me?" Dad said.

"Grab a little one," I said.

"Like a kid?" Lucas asked. "I think there's one behind the car."

"No... just... petite."

"Or a Norwegian," Jetta said. "I like the Norwegians."

"Grab from the group that's just standing around," I said. "That's the important part."

Lucas hopped back down off the porch.

He walked over to the group of loitering zombies.

Three women and two men.

From a size perspective, it really came down to two.

I was curious to see if Lucas would go for the blonde or the brunette.

He walked over to the blonde. Expectations met.

As he approached, her stance changed, her left leg lifting a little.

"She's going to lunge," I said.

"I see it," Lucas replied.

He leaned in and she came for him, arms out to grab him. He

grabbed each of her wrists and yanked, twisting her body as he pinned them behind her back.

"This feels… wrong…" he said.

"You get used to it," Dad said.

That gave me a chill. I hadn't forgotten needing to hold down my bleeding sister. It's hard to convince yourself that you're doing it for their own good. Not when they're fighting so hard.

The other zombies started closing in.

Lucas shoved the blond woman toward the porch. She was maybe five-foot-two, so it wasn't hard for a guy Lucas' size. He bent her forward as she walked so she couldn't get her teeth near him.

"Do we have that duct tape?" he asked as he reached the porch.

"I've got some rope in my pack," Dad said.

Jetta grabbed the bag and started rummaging. "This is getting to be a pattern," she said. "Women getting shoved around, tied up… I don't like where this is headed."

"Well, the guys are getting shot in the head a lot," I said.

"Don't worry," Lucas said, "I won't tie you up, Jetta. If things go bad for you I'll just bash your head open with the shovel."

"That's not at all funny," I said.

"It's a little funny."

I heard my father snicker.

I rolled my eyes at him. There's not much point in doing anything more.

Lucas had tied the woman's hands with the nylon rope from Dad's pack and pushed her down onto her knees. The way he was treating her… she wasn't anything to him. Not a person, anyway.

Not that I'm sure Lucas thinks of any women as people.

Jetta started pulling out a selection of fine cuisine from the kitchen while I went in to check on Iris and Beth. I didn't know how many flavors of terrible could happen to two people left bound and gagged — and unattended — in a room.

Iris tried to talk to me as I knelt down to check where Lucas had stabbed her.

"Just don't," I said.

She started to cry.

I couldn't stay quiet.

"Don't cry, Iris. It's okay… we'll figure this out…"

She nodded.

She was trying to manipulate me, or the infection was, really. I knew that. But I so wanted her to be Iris again.

I got back up and walked over to Beth.

Iris started whining.

I pretended not to notice.

Beth's eyes had changed… brightened, I guess, not that there was any particular brightness to the expression on her face.

She was pissed.

Or the infection was pissed.

Or, more likely, the infection had taken over enough control of Beth's body to make me think she was pissed.

I'd now seen what seemed to amount to the whole course of the infection. Errol had been newly bitten… and somehow he'd been fighting the infection, fighting the urge to spread whatever it was to me.

And that blond woman tied up on the front porch, she was what came next, when who you were had lost out and the infection had started taking over.

Then it went to those men in the sewer jumpsuits, same as the group that had come at us a few minutes before, mindless and aggressive… just wanting to bite us, and nothing else seemed to matter.

And finally, the "smarter" ones, hiding behind Lucas' SUV… Beth had moved to that next stage, to Iris' stage. The infection was pretending to be them.

That was more terrifying to me than anything else.

I heard seven shots while I was in the bedroom. They were steady and slow. Deliberate. I knew it was my father shooting the infected on the ground.

Maybe they'd started to stir, and he'd decided that he had to put them down for our safety.

Or maybe they hadn't moved and he'd just wanted to get it over with.

I ran out to the porch.

"Some of them were moving again," my father said.

"You didn't—"

"I didn't shoot any in the head, no. They're still alive… or undead… but this had better not bite us in the rear, Seffy."

"Or the neck," Jetta said, as she walked out with a canvas shopping bag. "Seriously."

"We can't win," I said. "Either we risk our lives trying to save them, or we end up murdering dozens of innocent people."

"I've already killed two of them," Dad said. "I can't take that back."

"I know."

I didn't know how I'd ever be able to justify what he'd done. I just hoped he could.

And I was glad that I hadn't been forced to do that same thing.

Test subject: pretty blond lady
First item: banana
Result: she ate it

In any other situation, it would have been funny to be feeding a banana to someone while wearing oven mitts. I'd held it out in front of her and she took the first bite, and then I sort of shoved the rest into her mouth.

She ate as much as she could before a few bits fell onto the porch.

"You're going to clean that up," my father said.

I wondered what a real biologist would think of me. Maybe one day I'd make it into Dr. Jillian Devreux's column on NatGeo… reckless amateur versus the zombie plague.

But I was probably closer to an evil Nazi doctor than a scientist.

The next item we tried was lunch meat. Jetta had brought out the bologna and the ham; I chose the ham because I wanted to test out some meat, as opposed to flour patties with a whiff of pig intestine mixed in.

I held out the slice of cooked ham. The smell made me sick, not just physically… I don't know, ethically, maybe?

The blond woman bit into the meat and pulled.

I almost lost my balance.

"That looked kinda deliberate," Jetta said. "Like she wants to eat you instead."

"I doubt it," I said. "She still seems pretty out of it."

"So she eats fruit and she eats meat," Lucas said. "She eats people food."

"She thinks she's people," Dad said.

"She's still a person," I said.

"Yes, Seffy, I know."

"So that rules out the preferring-to-feast-on-our-flesh hypothesis?" Lucas asked.

"It seems that way," I said. "Not that we can test this theory out to the fullest."

I wondered about Fender. What was he to them? Do zombies care if you cook the family pet first?

"We should cut off one of those zombie legs out there and feed it to her," Lucas said.

"Is that a joke?"

"Not really, no. You said you wanted to know what they eat."

"I don't get it," Jetta said. "So they bite everyone in sight to spread the disease, and then they just go on with their day? They'll just head back home in a few to cook up some supper?"

"Not all viruses kill their host," I said. "And a smart virus wouldn't kill off any potential hosts it encounters."

"Is that what this is?" Dad asked. "A virus?"

"How should I know? It could be that, or a parasite… kinda like those cat poop parasites Mom's always ranting about. When they infect mice, they actually rewire the mouse's brain. Those mice pretty much present themselves to the cats, making it much easier for cats to catch and eat them."

"Why would they do that?" Jetta asked.

"To infect the cats. Because cats are the preferred hosts."

"Hunh," Lucas said. "So how do we know these parasites or viruses or whatever aren't just rewiring people into food?"

"For cats?" Jetta said.

"For something."

"I think the cat poop parasite does rewire people," I said. "Rewires them into wanting more cats. Caring for them, feeding them, allowing for more hosts."

My mother had told me that. We hadn't really taken her seriously back then.

"So you think they'll survive?" Dad asked. "You think this is as far as this goes?"

"I have no idea," I said. "The infection needs to strike some kind of balance with its host… stay alive while keeping the host alive, too… it's not easy to do. Too much one way, and you've got a cold, eventually getting beaten by your average immune system. On the other side, the host gets weak enough that something else gets through. Like with HIV. Without regular treatment, it actually becomes a full-blown anti-immune disease."

"AIDS," Dad said. "There was a time, when I was a kid, when I honestly thought we might all get it. That the whole world would die of AIDS."

"I wonder what it feels like," Jetta said. "Having something else controlling your body."

"I don't know if you'd feel anything," I said.

"I hope they don't feel anything," Dad said.

"So what do we do with this one?" Lucas asked. He pulled on the rope, pulling her body back against his. "Do we cut her loose?"

"I don't know what's better," I said.

"We can't leave her like this," Jetta said. "She's helpless."

"Does that matter?" Lucas said. He pushed her down onto the deck of the porch. He flipped her onto her back, wrapping one hand around her neck.

"Don't hurt her," I said.

"Hurt her? She's a zombie. It's not like she can feel anything."

The way he was looking at her…

I looked over to my father, to see what he was thinking.

I couldn't imagine what he'd think if he'd seen Lucas gripping Iris by the neck.

But I could see it in his eyes, too.

He wasn't making that comparison. To my father, just like Lucas, this blond woman wasn't someone like Iris or me or Jetta, she was just *something else*.

Something other than human.

I was losing the argument.

"She'll free herself eventually," Lucas said.

"And then go home and make dinner," Dad said.

Lucas grinned. "And that'll be the end of it. She's not our problem."

"No," Jetta said. "I agree with Seffy on this." She gave me a nod.

I had not idea what she meant.

So I nodded back.

"We need to keep them safe," Jetta said. "Do what we can to save them, until they find a cure."

"Yeah, okay," I said, "But it's just that I'm not sure we can do that."

"But you said we should…"

"We can't save all of them, Jetta. We do need to focus on our family."

"But this isn't my family, remember? So I guess you guys will be tossing me aside if I get bitten?"

"Shovel to the head, sweetheart," Lucas said with a smirk.

"Shut up, Lucas," I said. I stepped over to Jetta. I put my hand on her shoulder. "I'm sorry, Jetta. That was a stupid way to put things. We're in this together."

"Us versus Them," she said. "Doesn't seem right to me."

I gave her shoulder a squeeze. I felt like a big sister.

"Yeah," I said. "It isn't right. But it's what we have to do."

7

IT GETS WORSE: PART THE FIRST

Dad had to go to the bathroom, so he went inside while we kept watch on the porch.

My father's hunting rifle was there, but I wasn't big on having to use it. Gunplay and vegetarianism don't usually mix that well. Not that it's a universal rule.

Lucas' shotgun was there, too, empty but with the shells for reloading still sitting in his bag.

So he hadn't reloaded yet. Because he'd gotten all preoccupied.

He'd shoved the blond woman off the porch, and she'd landed in a pile of leaves, her hands still bound behind her.

She hadn't moved from that spot, and Lucas hadn't taken his eyes off of her.

"She's like a mannequin," he said. "Just lying there."

"You should untie her," I said.

"You should focus on what's important. You wanted us to play it loose with those zombies on the ground. Now you need to make sure to shoot 'em when they try to get up."

"My dad did that already."

"They'll keep getting up."

"So what's going to happen?" Jetta asked. "Are we staying in or heading out for a night on the town? You still haven't told me if there's anything fun to do on Tuesdays."

"I don't know," I said. "To be honest, I'm not sure who decides...."

"Nothing changes... we take a vote."

"Great," Lucas said, "another vote. All this democracy is a great way to get us all bitten."

"It hasn't worked out so bad, has it?" I asked. "We're still fine, and now we're four instead of three."

"And with more weaponry," Jetta said. "Like at least a level six of badass."

"You haven't seen my badass yet," Lucas said, sticking his chin out in some kind of… chin pout.

Jetta and I both looked at each other. And we both did our best not to start laughing.

"I don't know what your problem is," Lucas said.

To me, it seemed.

"Why does your SUV still run?" I asked him.

"What?"

"Why didn't it shut down?"

"It did. I just happen to have a less-than-legal part that re-activates after five minutes of shutdown." He was proud of himself.

"So the same part they built into Jetta's car?"

"Wait," Jetta said. "What?"

"Your car would have have restarted," I said. "We didn't need to go with Lucas."

"I've kept you safe," Lucas said. "I've taken care of you."

"Are you kidding?" Jetta said. "You mean you tricked us."

"I made the choice for you. For your own good."

Jetta actually made a seething sound. "And that's what's wrong with you, Lucas. You wonder why women don't swoon over you, why we all think you're such a creeper, right?"

"I'm not a creeper…"

"You don't see us as people. Not in the least. You see us as… as interchangeable girl parts." She nudged her head down at the blond woman in the dirt. "That's the kind of woman you want, right there. Zombiefied. Restrained. Under your thumb."

"Okay, Jetta," I said.

There wasn't any need to piss him off.

"Tell me why you're more than that," Lucas said. "Tell me what value you bring to this other than… those girl parts of yours."

"You're a toolbag, Lucas," I said.

"And a prat," Jetta said.

"I'm getting sick of the way you talk to me," Lucas said.

"Why?" I asked. "Because that's how every woman talks to you? Because that's how you *deserve* to be talked to?"

He took a step toward me, puffing out his chest.

I wasn't going to let him intimidate me.

"You need to start treating us with respect, Lucas," I said. "Do you get that?"

"Things have changed, Persephone," Lucas said. "Take a look around, okay? The men are in charge again. Men like me. No more feminist claptrap required, thanks."

"I'm done with this," I said. "Done with you. I'm going to go check on my family."

"I'm coming, too," Jetta said.

"You have a job here, Seffy," Lucas said. "You made this mess…"

"Okay," I said. "If any of them come at you, just wait for me to come back and rescue you."

Jetta laughed. Loudly. Like she wanted Lucas to feel like a piece of garbage.

Probably not the best idea.

"You two idiots deserve each other," Lucas said. "And deserve exactly how things are going to end for you."

Jetta and I walked inside.

Lucas called us a few choice names as we left.

Iris had squiggled her way over to the dining room chair where Beth was taped, and had started pulling at the tape on her mother's ankles.

When we came into the room, she stopped and looked at us.

Her eyes were red, but a different kind of red. It looked like what you'd get from at least twenty minutes of solid crying.

"I don't know how you can handle this," Jetta said. "She's your sister."

"That's why I have to keep her safe," I said.

Iris muttered something through her sock. I was pretty sure she wasn't telling me to *punt*.

"I still wonder what it's like," Jetta said as she knelt down beside Iris. "Does she know what's happening?"

"Errol knew," I said.

"Errol… he's your boyfriend."

"More like a boss of sorts."

She nodded. "Sugar daddy?"

"What? Gross."

"The concept, or Errol?"

"I hope she's asleep or whatever in there," I said. "Like a coma… and once they find a way to get the infection out of her, she'll just wake up with a headache and a less hairy moustache."

"Hopefully." Jetta ran her fingers through my sister's hair. "She's beautiful."

"That's not really a compliment for me," I said. "We're just step-sisters, so it's not like we share any genes."

"You're cute, too… don't worry. And you do look alike. Your eyes are the same, aside from the color. But anyway, I mean, most women are beautiful, aren't they?"

"Yeah…"

I realized that Jetta hadn't stopped playing with Iris' hair.

"Why are you doing that?" I asked her.

"I don't know. It's kinda like the faucet, I guess. Sometimes I touch people… uh, inappropriately… you know, when I'm nervous."

"Well, you should probably think about not doing it anymore."

"Sorry… I didn't realize it upset you."

"It's not that… but, I don't know… it's kind of like messing with someone who's passed out drunk."

"Like we should paint her toenails black or something?"

"Is that what you people do up in Canada with pass-outs? Paint toenails?"

"We tried that hand-in-cold-water thing once… the results were expected and unpleasant."

I laughed.

Iris didn't.

"We used to pile things on top of them," I said. "Like building a tower of crap. Then when they'd wake up it was a *crapavalanche*."

Jetta grinned. "I should be writing this down."

"You're still touching her hair."

"Oh… sorry." She pulled her hand away and held both up in the air. "I guess I'm a fidgeter."

"We'll have to ask her about this," I said. "When she wakes up."

"Yeah… hey, Iris, do you remember when that creepy girl with the nose ring was playing with your hair?"

"Need to be more specific. You're assuming this kind of thing isn't a regular occurrence."

"So there are more weirdos like me?"

"There's something about Iris," I said. "Maybe it's how she looks, or how she smiles, or just the bot-hot blonde factor… people are pretty touchy with her."

"I'm glad I'm not blonde," Jetta said. "Brings out the creeps."

"Yes… creeps…" I looked at her pointedly.

She laughed.

I heard the flush of a toilet.

"We'll want to head outside before the door opens," I said. "Old man bathroom smell…"

Jetta leaned in and kissed Iris on the forehead. She looked over to me.

"That was weird, wasn't it…" she said.

"Yes. That was weird."

"Sorry."

We left the bedroom and walked down the hall toward the front door.

A car door closed.

"Someone's here," Jetta said.

I looked out through the front door.

Fender was back to growling, from his place next to the railing, pulling hard against his leash.

Lucas was climbing into the front seat of his SUV.

"What the heck is he doing?" Jetta asked.

The guns.

He'd taken them off the porch.

The shovel, too.

I ran out.

"Lucas," I called.

He started the engine.

He turned and gave me a smile and a little wave.

"Lucas!" I shrieked.

He rolled down his window.

"This is what you get, Persephone," he said. "You get burned."

"What did I even do?" I asked.

"I'll see you girls around, alright?" He looked over to Jetta. "Offer still stands, Jetta. Once they bite you… I've got the shovel loaded up in the back. Just come and find me, sweetheart."

He drove off.

"He left the bow and arrow," Jetta said. "That's something."

"That's the bow," I said. "The arrows are still lodged into those guys on the ground."

I saw one of them stirring. One of the men I'd hit.

"That blond girl," Jetta said, "she's gone."

"What?"

"She's not here."

I looked down to where the petite blond woman had been lying in the dirt.

No infected blonde. No nylon rope left behind, either.

"Do you think he took her?" Jetta asked.

"I don't know… but that's not our problem right now."

The zombie who'd stirred had climbed up onto one knee.

He was looking right at me.

"N-no more guns," he said. "I saw."

"Don't move," I said. "I don't want to kill you."

"You… you w-won't."

"Let's go inside," Jetta said. "Board up the doors and windows or something."

"I don't think that's realistic," I said.

"Neither is hand-to-hand combat."

I nodded, agreeing with her on that.

We slowly stepped back toward the front door.

There was more movement.

The infected who'd been just standing around… they started moving forward. They could tell that the threat had ended. I saw a group coming out of the tuft of trees on the far side of the drive. They'd been the ones hiding behind Lucas' car… they saw no reason to hide anymore.

The sewer sludge was hitting the fan…

"This is it," Jetta said. "We can't beat this."

"You two get inside," my father said.

I turned to see him standing in the doorway.

Jetta went first, slipping past him and into the house.

I followed after.

He ran out for Fender, unclicking the leash.

Dad stepped in after me. He whistled for Fender, who took his time getting inside.

I suppose he was feeling conflicted about everything. Attack the weird zombies, maybe get a treat on the inside…

"I should have seen this coming," Dad said.

"It's not your fault," I said. It was probably mine.

"We're not packed to go… and we don't have much time."

"I'll grab what I can," Jetta said, already halfway to the kitchen.

"But my wife," Dad said. "And your sister…"

"What is it, Dad?"

"I don't see how we can bring them… we'll have to leave them here."

"Will they be okay?" I asked.

"I don't know…"

I didn't know the answer, either, but I had a feel for the odds. Did I honestly think I'd ever see my mother again? Or Errol? Would Jetta find Leona after all this?

"We can't leave them," I said. "Even if that means we carry less of everything else. We need to find a way."

Dad nodded. Then he gave me a hug.

And kissed me on the forehead.

"I love you, Seffy," he said.

"Thanks, Dad."

He knows I love him, too. That's just science.

I didn't want to have to say it.

It took less than five minutes for the infected to surround the house completely. There were at least a dozen on the front porch, and another half dozen waiting at the back door. Others were just… milling around.

They reminded me of college students after a Bisons game, wandering around the parking lot, wondering where the action was going to be.

No one was smashing through windows or even banging on doors.

They were just waiting.

They knew what Lucas had done to us.

They knew we were screwed.

Somehow… they just knew all of it.

We needed to move quickly.

Dad and Fender were going to cut over to the machine shed for the tractor. Dad couldn't remember if he'd left the trailer hitched on from the last dump of manure, but he was confident he could get inside and get it hitched up before they took him down.

I got the sense that he expected some kind of martyrdom; I made it clear that I wasn't about to tie up and drag his wrinkly old butt around, too.

Jetta was in charge of bringing the supplies out, and she managed to sling four backpacks around her body for the trip outside.

My job was handling Iris and Beth, and bringing them out to the tractor and trailer once Dad drove out of the machine shed.

Once the trailer was filled with supplies and my zombie relatives, Jetta and I would head for the horses. I wasn't sure we'd even have time to tack them up.

I grabbed a kitchen knife, a fifty-foot extension cord, and a fresh roll of duct tape, red instead of silver. I went back to the bedroom.

I started with Beth.

I cut her ankles free from each of their corresponding chair legs. I tried to fashion a hobble for her ankles from the tape, but after two attempts — and some angry groans through her sock — I gave up. I didn't know if they'd try to "make a run for it" when I brought them outside, but I knew it would be way worse if they tripped on some half-baked restraint.

So I cut her loose from the chair, keeping her wrists bound behind her back. I wrapped two new loops of tape, one at elbow-level, the other just below her shoulders.

I sat her back down in the chair.

She didn't try to get back up.

I went over to Iris, making sure to swing around so I could see Beth at the same time. I cut Iris' ankles free and added her two loops.

I helped her up.

She muttered thank you through her sock.

"Understand this," I said. "If either of you try something, I won't hesitate to use this knife."

Iris managed a pretty skeptical sigh.

Zombie Iris wasn't stupid.

I tied one end of extension cord around Beth's wrists, then

brought it over to Iris. I attached her wrists the same way, giving me maybe twenty feet left to serve as a leash.

I walked out the bedroom door and into the hallway.

I pulled on the cord.

My prisoners followed, reluctantly at first, but soon they were walking at a normal pace.

I had a feeling they wanted to lure me into thinking it'd go this easy on the outside.

We all gathered at the back door.

"If anything goes bad," Dad said, "you climb onto the back of a horse and go."

"We need a place to meet up," I said. "Jetta, do you have your phone?"

She juggled her load of backpacks, and pulled out a small pink tablet. She handed it to me.

There was still no connection.

I tried pulling up a map. Everything south of Grand Forks was nearly bare, with little more than the interstates.

"No connection means no data," Dad said.

"It should have updated when she came down here," I said.

"I guess it doesn't. But I've got my tablet."

"You'll have to give it to Jetta, then. Because she won't know where she's headed."

"I don't know where *I'm* headed…"

He pulled a tablet out of his pocket. He brought up the maps and handed the tablet over to me.

I held it up for Jetta to see. "Iris and I would take the horses down the old rail bed to this village… Alice. That's where David — he's Iris' boyfriend — that's where he lives. See this big lake?"

Jetta nodded.

"That's Lake Bertha," I said. "Now the track runs just north of the lake, and you can see this causeway…" I traced the line of the track as it crossed a smaller lake. "You can see that rectangle there… an old signal tower. We used to stop there sometimes, just sit and enjoy the nothing."

"North Dakota's a whole state of nothing," Jetta said.

"Well, there's even more nothing along there. And we'll see anyone who's coming a mile away."

"So that's where we meet?" Dad said.

"If we get separated," I said. "And we're not going to get separated, right?"

"Right."

I turned to Jetta. "Are you ready?" I asked her.

She nodded.

She was pretending she was.

Me, too.

Dad opened the door.

He ran toward the machine shed, Fender on his heels.

I slammed the door behind them.

We watched through the lightly glazed window on the door. Seven of them were chasing them toward the shed.

Some would still be at the front porch, and might not even notice the flurry. Others might be waiting to see who else comes out of the house.

I didn't know.

I saw my father reach the machine shed. He went through the door, Fender following behind.

I hoped that he'd find a way to barricade it shut.

Within ten seconds, one of the infected started trying to open the door.

He wasn't getting in.

I counted ten seconds more.

I couldn't hear the tractor.

The overhead door stayed shut.

"He's probably hooking up the trailer," Jetta said.

"Yeah…"

"They can't get in…"

"Yeah… I know, Jetta."

"Okay."

I counted another ten seconds.

Nothing.

Then I heard the tractor.

A few seconds later the overhead door opened.

"You're next," I said to Jetta.

She nodded.

I opened the door.

She ran.

Dad drove the tractor to meet her.

The seven followed behind.

And three more from around the side of the house.

The three would reach her first.

My turn.

I opened the door and stepped out, yanking on the extension cord.

Iris and Beth didn't move.

"Come on," I said.

Iris sweared at me through her sock.

I pulled harder.

Beth took a step forward, but Iris turned to glare at her mother.

No one took another step.

The three who'd been moving toward Jetta had taken notice of me.

I was closer.

So they changed direction.

I stepped back into the house.

I pushed past Iris and Beth.

I put my full weight against Beth and shoved.

She fell forward two paces, bumping into Iris.

Iris held firm.

So I shoved Beth again.

And then I shoved Iris.

There wasn't enough time to get them out.

I left them in the hallway.

I pushed past them again, back out the door.

Dad had reached Jetta with the tractor. She'd thrown herself into the trailer where Fender was standing, packs still wrapped around her; Dad hadn't even slowed down.

I ran to meet them.

Dad turned the tractor, driving it toward the belt of trees at the west end of the yard site. I understood why; the tractor was moving more slowly than I could run, and some of the infected would catch up to him soon as it was.

"There's a rake in the trailer," he said to Jetta. "That's the best I could do."

Once she'd pulled off the last of her packs she hopped out of the trailer.

Fender jumped down, too.

For a moment I was worried he'd try latching onto her ankle or something, like she was the biggest threat.

But he milled around her, watching out for the infected who were coming their way.

Jetta pulled the rake out, more of a soil or sand rake then something you'd use for leaves. It looked pretty hardcore.

Not a bad thing to have.

She held the rake with two hands. She held it a little like I'd expect someone to hold a hockey stick, her left hand low down near the base.

She walked up to the nearest pursuer and swung the teeth at his face.

That was enough to bring him down.

She moved on to the next one.

I reached the trailer.

"We need to go back to the house," I said to my father. "Grab Beth and Iris."

"We won't make it," he said. "We'll have the whole bunch to deal with."

"There's got to be more stuff in that machine shed… a shovel, or an axe…"

"There's at least another shovel, yeah… not as good as the one Lucas stole…"

"Well I'm not worried about ergonomics or handling… just something with a heavy blade."

He nodded. "Take over driving, and I'll run back to the shed and get it. Don't turn back for the house until we've thinned out the herd."

"You keep driving," I said. "I can run faster than you."

"Seffy…"

I didn't argue.

I just ran.

I looped around, along the grain bins, trying to keep as much distance as I could between me and anything that moves, Jetta and her rake included.

Fender came running after me.

I reached the machine shed; Dad hadn't bothered to close the overhead door.

I found the shovel but took a quick survey; nothing that seemed any better for hacking and slashing, so I grabbed the shovel and headed back out, Fender trying to keep between me and everything else.

I appreciated the sentiment, but was a little worried he'd end up tripping me.

I came up behind the horde of infected, the four who were still coming up on Jetta and the tractor.

I started whacking them, slashing at their spinal columns, hoping that a good shot might slow them down for longer.

I wasn't about to kill anyone.

I wanted to be able to live with myself once it was all over.

With help from Fender pulling on legs, I took three of them down while Jetta met the fourth.

We saw six more moving toward us.

Dad turned the tractor back toward the house.

"We should grab the horses," I said to Jetta.

We ran to the stable.

"Can you ride bareback?" I asked her as I opened the stall for Iris' little light brown quarterhorse, Arkham.

"I can ride western, I guess. But that's it."

I grabbed Iris' blanket and saddle, throwing them up onto Arkham in one haphazard toss.

It wasn't perfect, but it was quick.

I cinched the girth and went back for the bridle.

Jetta adjusted the stirrups and climbed on.

I slipped the bit into Arkham's mouth and snapped together the bridle. I handed the reins to Jetta.

Then I passed her the rake.

"I can't do this one-handed," she said.

"You have two hands available," I said. "Arkham knows what he's doing. When you need to, just drop the reins."

I pulled Star out of her stall.

I decided to grab my tack, too. And Iris' grooming kit, in the cute little pink bag.

For all I knew we'd be living on horseback for a while.

I tacked her up and climbed on.

I brought her around and reached down for the shovel.

"It'll be like jousting," I said.

I led Star out of the stable.

Dad was almost to the house, but there were two of the infected less than ten feet from the back of the trailer.

I squeezed Star into a gallop.

Fender had no problem keeping up to us.

I dropped the reins and held out the shovel.

Two swipes, one for each of his pursuers. To their backs.

Both went down.

Dad stopped the tractor just off the back door.

Beth and Iris had come out to see what was happening, dragging the extension cord behind them.

I guess zombies get curious, too.

I climbed off Star.

Dad grabbed Beth and I grabbed Iris.

We pushed them over to the trailer, while Fender did his best to be in the way.

Dad counted us down.

We lifted Beth and threw her into the trailer.

Then we did Iris.

Jetta caught up to us on Arkham.

I climbed back onto Star, and Dad onto the tractor.

We cut toward the southwest corner of the yard.

I mowed down two more of the infected who came to close.

We passed through the snow belt and out into the fields.

The horde didn't follow.

They'd turned back toward the house.

"I think they're moving in to our old place," Dad said, over the sound of the tractor engine.

"Or hoping we left someone behind," I said.

"Or if there's a God," Jetta said, "they'll keep moving, maybe run into Lucas just up the road… with a flat tire…"

I grinned, but I knew that I wouldn't actually wish that on anyone. Even Lucas.

I didn't know what Iris was going through.

I didn't know if she was watching it happen, knowing she'd lost control of her own body.

Knowing that if it saw a chance, that infection inside of her would force her to tear into every single one of us.

8

THE ABANDONED RAILBED OF OUR DISCONTENT

We didn't stop moving.

With nowhere else to go, we decided that the little fill-in causeway near Lake Bertha was as good a place as any for a little wait-and-see.

Maybe when things seemed calmer, we'd scout out the town of Alice, to see if they'd made it through. We'd see if David and his parents were still okay.

We followed the creek across 40th Street, to where the water widens out into a sloughy little pond. We followed the roads from there, moving due south on 144th until we reached the far side of Embden.

There we met the old track bed, which cut a diagonal line across the acreages, moving southwest toward Lake Bertha. This was the route Iris and I had always taken to Alice, the most direct, and the least likely to have pickup trucks spooking the horses. There'd been an understanding with the neighbors that this is just what we did, and that there was no point in getting angry with us for it.

At least we weren't barreling through on snowmobiles, leaving a trail of empty beer cans.

We passed by the abandoned yard site; I sometimes think back to the time we went there on a "double date", not long after Iris and her bots were released from hospital. She'd wanted to go somewhere "spooky" with her latest boyfriend, but was too creeped out to go with him alone. I'm still not sure whether it was the setting or the company that was providing the creepy bit. So she asked me to come along, and I brought Errol to turn that rickety third wheel into a possibly-less-rickety fourth.

The place has gotten worse since then, with more and more broken bottles and potato chip bags littering the long grass as the walls themselves start peeling away with the wind and rain.

And it's even spookier if you consider the rampant spread of a mind-controlling infection.

Or guys like Lucas running around with stolen rifles and zombie slavegirls.

I saw something moving by a stand of trees.

I pointed it out to Jetta, then steered Star toward it. I wanted to meet whatever it was head on.

A young man stepped out in front of me.

It was David, Iris' boyfriend.

He'd been her boyfriend for near six months. A personal record for her.

His hair was disheveled, his clothes were filthy and his backpack was held together partly with duct tape, but he looked okay, otherwise. Good... like a younger version of a Hemsworth brother good, actually. Just like how Iris' boyfriend *should* look.

Like a guy who'd just gotten some bots of his own.

It was weird, but I tried to remember the last time I saw him, if he looked as good as that. Because our lives could depend on how well I could compare those two Davids.

"Where's Iris?" he asked me. He took a step toward me.

"Don't come any closer," I said.

"I'm not infected."

"Iris is infected."

"Oh my god... where is she? You didn't —"

"We've got her," Dad said. "She's safe. But you still haven't proven that you're not infected."

"What are you talking about? I'm standing here talking to you, aren't I?"

"That doesn't mean anything," I said. "The infection... it changes people who get bitten. They don't stay like that... like zombies."

"Well, I didn't know that," David said. "So I guess that means I'm not a zombie."

I shook my head. "We have no way of knowing for sure."

"So what, then? You just pass on by?"

"There's got to be a way to know," Jetta said.

She climbed down off Arkham and started walking over, rake in her hand.

"Don't, Jetta," I said. "Don't get close to him."

"How long can a zombie resist?" Jetta asked. "If I dangle some fresh and hot neck meat in his proximity?"

"I'm not a zombie," David said.

"If he's infected," I said, "he'll wait until you drop your guard. He'll be smart enough to wait…"

"Yeah, now that you've given him such good advice," Jetta said.

"We should restrain him," Dad said. "Like with the other two."

"Other *two*?" David said.

"My wife is infected, too. Iris' mother."

"I'm sorry, Mr. Schmidt."

"So do what's right, David. Get down on your knees and put your hands on your head."

"I can help… I have a gun."

"Where's this gun?" Dad asked.

"Over there." He pointed into the trees.

"Not with you?"

"I didn't want to get shot. You can hear that tractor of yours coming from a mile away."

Jetta walked over to check.

"It's here," she called out. "A rifle or shotgun or something."

"A shotgun," David said. "I can go get it."

"Don't," I said.

"Come on, guys… you can trust me, alright?"

"The last guy we trusted ran off with my rifle," Dad said.

"And now you've got a new gun, Mr. Schmidt. You're much better on it than me."

"Yeah, I've got a new gun. So get on your knees, hands on your head. There's still room in the trailer. Smells like horse droppings, though."

"Please, David," I said. "Just do it. We don't know any other way."

"Can I see her first?" he asked.

"Why does it matter?" Dad said. "She's in the trailer. We had to tape her up and stuff a sock in her mouth so she wouldn't try to lunge. Her mother, too."

"She's alright," I said.

"I need to see."

"Jetta," Dad said, "get the shotgun and bring it here."

"I've never picked one of these up," she said. "I'll be really sad if I accidentally shoot someone."

"It happens to all of us," I said.

She looked at me, confused.

It's always such a fun story to tell at parties, but I'd never told it while running for my life.

I wasn't sure how I'd even start...

Jetta gingerly picked up the shotgun and carried it toward the tractor, pointing the barrel up.

"Should point it down," Dad said. "People don't need feet as much as they need heads."

"That includes zombies, too, eh?" she said.

She handed the shotgun to my father, barrel first, naturally.

"I'm lucky to be alive," Dad said. "But thanks, Jetta." He checked the chamber, then pointed the gun at David. "Come and take a look," he told him, "but don't be an idiot."

"Okay," David said. "Thanks."

"Is this birdshot?" my father asked, pulling a shell out from the chamber.

"Yeah. Easier to hit things."

David walked to the back of the trailer.

"My god," he said.

"There's no surprise there," Dad said. "I told you what we had to do."

"Take the socks out... there's no reason for those."

"You don't understand," Jetta said. "They can get all in your head, make you feel like you should cut them loose."

"They're okay as they are," I said. "There's no need to do anything else."

David looked back to me. "She's terrified, Persephone. Do you get that?"

"Don't explain my sister to me, okay?"

He wanted to argue some more. I could see it.

But he didn't.

He unslung his beat-up backpack and placed it on the ground beside him.

He slowly got down on his knees. He put his hands on top of his head, lacing his fingers.

"Not your first arrest," Jetta said.

"I've watched a few movies," he said.

I untied the extension cord from Iris and Beth, then used it to bind David's wrists. It didn't feel as tight as I'd wanted, but I hoped the extra loops would counter that slack.

"Where are your parents?" I asked as I lifted him to his feet.

"Bitten," he said. "I didn't even think of bringing them with me. I'm lucky I got out at all."

"I know… it's okay…" I put my hand on his shoulder.

Probably a pretty stupid thing to do.

But he didn't come at me.

"Still not a zombie," he said as I helped him into the trailer.

"Uh, okay… but still no way to tell."

Fender climbed over and licked David on the cheek.

David did his best to shove the dog away.

He nuzzled in next to Iris. She laid her head against his shoulder and let out a plaintive whine.

"The socks, Seffy… please…"

"Think about it, David. If you're not a zombie and we take that sock out of her mouth, what do you think will happen?"

"More than a hickey," Jetta said.

He seemed to think it over for a moment.

He kissed Iris on the cheek. "I love you, Zombie Iris," he said.

I'm pretty sure he was crying.

It was almost dark by the time we reached the old stone block foundation of the signal tower.

Jetta and I climbed down from the horses, and made sure they got a chance to drink from the lake.

Dad stopped the tractor and gave out a long Dad sigh.

"Can't see much," he said.

The tractor had headlights in theory, not that I'd ever seen them.

Dad flipped the switch.

One came on.

"I'd call that a blessing," he said.

"So that'll light up one way," Jetta said.

"Might be better not to have them at all," I said. "Moon's out. No headlights means no weird shadows."

"Weird shadows?" Dad said.

"We'll see movement enough in the moonlight."

Dad nodded.

And turned the headlight off.

"It's getting cold," Jetta said. "Did anyone think to bring a blanket?"

"Blanket wasn't on the priority list," Dad said. "We went with food and water instead."

"So when we freeze to death…" I said.

"Don't be negative, Seffy…"

"Yeah… *don't be negative… be more like your sister…* I know how that all goes."

"We're staying here overnight?" David asked from his place in the trailer.

"Looks like," Dad said. "Better than getting bit."

"Being warm might be even better, though," Jetta said.

"You want to leave? You can go ahead. It's not like you were invited."

"Whoa, Dad," I said. "It's not like she did anything to deserve that."

"Look… I'm just tired, alright. And sick of the complaining."

"I wasn't complaining," Jetta said. "I was just… talking. Leaky faucet."

"It's okay," I said. "He gets grumpy when he's tired… just like his daughter."

"So how long is this going to take?" David asked.

"We'll revisit the situation at sunrise," Dad said.

"No… I mean with the zombie test. Or are you going to leave me in the poop trailer all night?"

"Iris is stuck in the poop trailer," I said. "So at least you'll be together."

"This is ridiculous. I'm not a zombie. Or what, do you need to kill me to find out?"

"That's it," I said.

"I was kidding."

"No… I mean, you don't have bots, right?"

"No."

"Not that it would matter if you did, I guess, since regular bots don't work like this."

"So wait," he said, "are you saying that this disease is caused by botshots? Is that why Iris is infected?"

"Someone probably bit her," Dad said.

"I'm not sure," I said. "When did you realize she was infected?"

"I was just about to head in to work for the afternoon. Maybe 11:30? I came in and found them… she'd just bitten her mother."

"So who bit her?" Jetta asked. "Someone snuck into your house for a nibble?"

"It might be the bots themselves," I said. "The ones she's had in her the whole time."

"I thought you said it wasn't possible," Dad said. It felt like he was jeering a little. "Bots being transmitted from person to person."

"I think something got into these bots. Something's… affected them."

Or *infected* them, if that could happen.

"How is that possible?" Jetta asked.

"Bots respond to biological responses," I said. "They're designed to be sensitive to the changing needs of the body. Like if a woman gets pregnant. It's not like the bots would try and kill the embryo."

"So if the body gets infected by something…" Dad said.

"The bots may have responded as though that infection was a valid physiological behavior. Maybe the infection tricked the bots."

"And the bots adapted to the new normal," Jetta said.

"And I'm not a zombie," David said. "Remember? You were starting to move in that direction before…"

I reached into my pocket. I still had the kitchen knife.

I pulled it out. I grabbed his bound hands.

"Thank you, Seffy," he said. "So much."

I cut into his palm.

"Ouch! What are you doing?"

"Cutting you loose," I said. "Knife slipped."

I watched the skin as the blood came out of the cut. It wasn't much, but it was there.

"Then cut me loose," he said.

"Just a second… you're bleeding…" I turned to Jetta. "Did you bring the first aid kit?"

"I don't think so," Jetta said.

I kept my gaze on the cut, watching it bleed.

"It's fine," David said. "Don't worry about it. Just cut that cord."

"Might need something else to cut it," I said.

"Just saw right through it."

"I don't want to cut you again."

The blood hadn't stopped. I couldn't see any scabbing yet, but what was more important was that the cut hadn't gotten any smaller.

I dropped his hands and hopped out of the trailer.

"What's going on?" David asked.

I walked over to my father. "He's bleeding," I said. "No repair work."

"No bots," Dad said.

"Are you serious?" David said. "That's the test? Why didn't you just tell me that?"

"*Probably* not a zombie," I said. "Congratulations."

"So why didn't you tell him you were going to cut him?" Jetta asked.

"If this infection controls a person's body and the bots inside… it's possible that the bots might delay healing… to manipulate us."

"Sounds a bit like a paranoid delusion," Dad said. He laughed. "But I guess that's not a bad thing to have on our team."

And in your family, I wanted to say. I don't know why that matters so much to me.

"But it's possible he's still tricking us," Jetta said.

"I know," I said. "But I don't think he is."

"And that's good enough?"

"It has to be," Dad said "We need more eyes and ears."

"I'd like my backpack," David said.

Jetta looked over to me.

I nodded.

She walked over to a pile of bags she'd stuffed under the trailer. She pulled out David's backpack, to show him.

He held out his hands.

She brought it over to him.

"This is quite the pack," she said. "Hobo chic?"

"It was my father's… he never threw anything out, and it was the first one I could find. Not sure he needs it now."

"Oh… well, it's lovely."

She looked over at me, like she expected me to change the subject.

I didn't really feel like talking.

"Something's happened to Mrs. Schmidt here," David said.

"I know," Dad said. "She's getting younger. The bots…"

"They look like sisters," Jetta said.

"Iris always wanted a sister," I said. "You know, one that looks like her."

Jetta smiled. "You look like her. You two have the same eyes. Other than the color…"

"Yeah, you told that one already. And I doubt it."

"Don't doubt it," Dad said.

"What does that mean?" I asked him.

"Just take the compliment."

"Compliment?"

"Or whatever."

"I think you're beautiful, Seffy," Jetta said. "I would totally stalk you and steal things from your garbage."

"Thank you, Jetta."

"You two are messed up," Dad said.

I smirked. "I know where I get that from."

When I was seventeen I went with some girlfriends of mine to a cabin near Bemidji, Minnesota. It was meant to be one of those martini and gossip type of getaways, but Anna Kellum messed up and forgot to get her big sister to buy us the booze. But I still had high hopes.

It was Labor Day weekend, and it was cold as… well, Bemidji. And the cabin didn't have any other heat than the wood-burning fireplace.

We went to bed at around 2am — not much of a girls' night — and let the fire die out.

Even sharing a bed with hot-blooded Martina Rojas didn't keep it from being the coldest night of my life. So cold that you start to wonder if that's what it feels like to freeze to death.

That is the only thing in my experience that compares to our night on the old rail causeway near Bertha Lake.

Add to that the fact that Jetta kicks in her sleep. Like a frickin

Canadian mule.

But I probably felt better than David, who was cuddled up to Iris. No one's said anything about it, but he's pretty much cuddling with Beth, too, by default. I'm not saying that could cause issues in the future, but... it's just kinda weird.

My father woke me up while it was still dark.

"Incoming," he said quietly.

Not the smartest thing to say to someone who just got up. For whatever reason I assumed he was about to cannonball on top of me.

"Four of them," he said. "Coming up from Alice."

"Infected?" I asked.

"Don't know... can't see who else would be on foot in the middle of the night."

I was thinking the opposite. It took some kind of awareness to follow an old rail bed that's barely noticeable these days in some of the fields it crosses. Not that zombies couldn't be aware, but that I didn't see a reason for some bright-eyed, clever zombie to follow the rail bed in the first place.

If you're looking for someone to infect, that seems like the last direction to head. But if you were looking to run away from all the people trying to bite you in the neck...

"I don't see infected coming this way," I said.

"I saw them already. You haven't even gotten up to look..."

"No... I mean that I think they might be clear."

"Clear... as in uninfected..."

"Yeah."

"I don't see that," he said.

He left me and started walking toward the west, to where they'd be.

I got up and followed.

"We'll have to shoot them," Dad said. "Same test you did on David... just a little more rigorous."

"There's nowhere you can shoot someone with a shotgun and expect them to heal up on their own."

"Unless they're infected."

"We'll do the same test I used," I said. "The knife."

"You said it yourself, Seffy. They might be able to fake it. It's not like they won't clue in to what you're doing after the third or fourth one."

"We should run," Jetta said. She hadn't gotten up, but she seemed fully awake.

"We need to figure this out," I said. "We can't just keep running."

"Take a step back from this, Seffy," Dad said. "Here we are trying to survive, and you're hoping to find a new way of doing things when the old way works just fine. You want to risk all of our lives just in case these four strangers happen to be upstanding citizens?"

"They could be having the same discussion about us," Jetta said. "Right now. Thinking we're a bunch of zombies. Trying to figure out how to know what's up."

"We've got horses and a tractor," Dad said. "How does that look like zombies?"

"You better believe Iris could hop on a horse right now if we cut her loose," I said. "If we know that, they probably know that, too. Anyone who's lasted this long should have a good idea what they're up against."

"I need everyone behind the trailer," Dad said.

I shook my head. "I'll stay with you."

"You're what matters, Seffy… you and Iris. So you hide behind the trailer, and bring the horses with you, and if things go wrong, grab Iris and lift her up on Star and you two get out of here."

"I'll come, too," Jetta said. "Even if I don't matter or anything."

I heard David climbing out of the trailer.

"I'll stand with you, Mr. Schmidt," he said.

Dad nodded. "Tie up the dog, alright?"

I guess David mattered about as much as Jetta did to him.

Expendable people.

And somehow I wasn't considered one of those.

I guess that felt good. Kinda.

Jetta and I went over to the horses, right near the front of the tractor.

They were both lying as best they could on the narrow sliver of grass between the dirt and the water, looking more like puppies sharing a nap. I gave Star a pat and stepped back as she stood. Arkham followed her lead.

We'd never needed to worry with Star on a normal day; she'd stick around, and as long as she was there Arkham would be, too. But if Dad had to use David's shotgun, Star might spook. I didn't have their halters, so after tacking them up we had to lead them by their reins over to the trailer.

"You'll need to hold on," I said to Jetta. "As long as you're holding him and I've got Star, he should be okay... he'll be jittery, but hopefully he won't bolt."

"Hopefully?" she said.

"That's the best I've got."

Dad climbed up onto the tractor.

He flicked on the headlights, lighting up the abandoned railbed in front of it.

I could see them. Four people, two of them short enough to be children. I watched as they approached.

Maybe a family... maybe needing our help.

As they came closer, I could see that there was a man and a woman, and yes, two kids, both under ten. I couldn't tell if the kids were boys or girls in their gray fall jackets.

"That's far enough," my father called out once they were maybe a hundred feet away. "Names."

"What was that?" the man yelled back. He sounded confident, maybe even a little aggressive.

"Tell us who you are."

"You first."

My father raised the shotgun. "I'm Adam Schmidt," he said, "with some family and friends. Now tell us who you are so I don't have to shoot you in the face."

"Chris Brager," the man replied. "And family. Kids are frightened, and you're not helping."

"Don't try and guilt me. I've had a rough day. Where are you headed?"

"We were walking the dog out at Little Yellowstone... car shut down on the way back home."

"Where's home?"

"West Fargo."

"Where's the dog?"

"Gone."

"You armed?"

"Nope."

Dad turned to David. "What do you think?"

"I doubt they're infected," David said. "Like Seffy said... this isn't where you'd go if you wanted to find people to bite."

"I think she's right," Dad said.

I hadn't expected that.

"We'll need to check them for weapons," David said. "I can do that."

"You sure?"

"Yeah."

Dad nodded.

David started walking toward them.

"My friend is going to check you for weapons," Dad said. "So tell us now if you were lying a minute ago."

"No guns," the man said. "Just a bread knife from our picnic bag."

"Put that knife on the ground in front of you."

I saw the man pull something out of his pocket. He knelt down and threw it into the dirt.

We waited for David to reach them. He was walking almost at the edge of the water, leaving a clear sight line.

Dad hadn't lowered the shotgun.

I wondered if birdshot was better than a regular slug. Would Dad be more or less likely to shoot David by mistake? What kind of spread is there at a hundred feet? Does my father have anywhere near the aim to pull that off?

I had a feeling he wouldn't fire. The cure would be worse than whatever David could catch.

David said something to the man once he was within twenty feet or so; I couldn't hear it from where I was standing, behind the trailer.

The man spread out his arms, while the woman and kids took a few steps back.

David patted the man, from one side to the other, going up and down his legs. With all the technique of someone who'd never patted anyone down before.

It wouldn't have been hard for him to miss something.

David said something else I couldn't hear, and the man and woman switched places.

David's pat down on her was even less thorough.

I wanted to ask my father what he was thinking, but he was too far in front. I wasn't about to shout at him.

"This seems okay," Jetta said. She gave Arkham a pat on the neck.

"I hope so," I said.

David took a step back from the woman.

The man and the kids walked a little closer.

David leaned down to pick up the bread knife, or whatever the man had placed on the ground. He leaned down with his back to them.

That would have been the moment.

David stood back up.

He handed the knife back to the man.

And then they started walking toward us. The man, and probably his wife and their two little boys. Along with David, who looked proud of himself.

Dad lowered the shotgun.

"Are we good?" Jetta asked me.

"I don't know," I said. "Let's just stay where we are for now."

So we waited.

And watched.

As the man, Chris, held out his hand.

As my father took it.

"Persephone," the woman said. She waved to me.

"You know her?" Jetta asked.

"I don't know," I said. By that I meant that I had no idea.

She was late twenties, long dark hair and bulgy eyes, and a little bit thicker than she ought to be. She looked like a lot of people I knew, but no one specific.

I smiled at her anyway.

"I know your mother," the woman said as she walked over to Jetta and I, the two kids staying with the man. "I used to work with her at the hospital." She frowned. "She isn't here, is she?"

"She was in town," I said. "I wasn't able to get to her."

Iris kicked the side of the trailer.

The woman turned around to see.

"What the heck is going on here?" she asked. "Oh my god…" She stepped back from me. She stuck out her hands in front of her. "Just… we don't want to be involved with this…"

"They're infected," I said. "That's why we had to tie them up."

"Get back here, Julia," the man said. "Stay with us."

"Mom…" the older boy said.

"It's alright," I said. "Everything is fine."

"They don't look infected," the woman said.

"That's what infected looks like… after more than a few hours."

"How do we know you're being honest with us?"

"Why would I lie? Why else would we have two people tied up?"

"I was tied up, too," David said. "For a while."

"What are you talking about?" the man asked.

"They thought I was a zombie."

"What's wrong with you people?" the woman said.

"We need to keep going," the man said. "Find somewhere that's safe."

"It's not safe up the rail line," I said. "There are more people infected up there. We were chased out of our house."

"We're going to keep going," the woman said. "Thanks."

"You'll get bitten," Dad said. He still had the shotgun in his hands, pointed toward the dirt. "It's safer here."

"Is that your way of handing out an invitation, Dad?" I asked him, hoping to make us seem a little friendlier and less psychotic.

"Just let us through," the man said, "okay?"

"Yeah," Dad said. "Go on through. Doesn't matter to us."

Jetta and I pulled the horses to one side of the causeway.

The older boy patted Star as he and his family walked by.

The woman — Julia — looked back at us for a few seconds, right after they'd passed. I wondered if she knew how bad their chances were, trying to bring two kids into all of that…

"We must seem like a bunch of psychos," I said once they were clear. "She even knew me and she didn't want anything to do with us."

"I understand that," Jetta said. "It's hard to believe it if you haven't seen it… how they change…"

"I'm still not sure I believe it," David said.

"You really want to be part of a demonstration?" Dad asked him. "Because I'm sure Iris would be willing."

"A whole new meaning to sucking on your face," Jetta said.

We all just glared at her.

"I'm not sorry," she said with a smirk.

I laughed.

No one else did.

"Do you really think they'll get bitten, Mr. Schmidt?" Jetta asked.

"I think we're all going to get bitten before this is over," Dad said.

"That's optimistic," I said.

"Things aren't getting better, are they?"
I couldn't argue with him about that.

9

IT GETS WORSE 2: THE WORSENING

I didn't get a chance to go back to freezing to death.

Before the Brager family had reached the far side of the little lake, we heard the sound of airplanes.

It wasn't like there weren't airplanes around, or that there hadn't been a few flying overhead the day before. I'm sure there were even a couple of redeyes that had flown over while I'd been shivering beside Jetta, her mule feet, and her overly cuddly hands.

But these airplanes didn't sound the same.

"Military," Dad said as we all looked toward the lights coming from the southwest. "From Ellsworth, maybe... in South Dakota."

"Airdrops?" I asked.

"Drops of what?"

"Something to treat this infection, maybe?"

"Maybe," Dad said. "But we need to be prepared for the worst."

"There's something worse than this?" Jetta asked.

"Might just be reconnaissance," David said. "Counting zombies."

"Before sunrise?" I said.

"I think we'll be safe," Dad said. "We're a long way from any targets."

"Targets?" Jetta said. "You're not serious."

"Always be prepared," I said. "My father, boy scout and serial monogamist."

"Mind your mouth," Dad said.

I didn't have a chance to respond before a flash of flame from the west. The sound came not long after.

A bomb.

"Where did that hit?" I asked.

"That's long past the county line," Dad said. "This infection reaches farther than I thought."

"You think that's for the infection?" Jetta asked.

I understood the question, but it wasn't like there could actually be a different answer.

"Makes sense that it's more widespread," David said. "That family came up from where, Ransom County? Or at least right by the county line."

"They shut down all cars in the general area," I said. "It's not like it's precise enough to follow the county line. I'm sure they'd rather overdo it than the alternative."

"What are they bombing?" Jetta asked.

"Probably a horde of zombies," Dad said. "Maybe that's how they hope to hold the quarantine line."

"Assuming there is a quarantine line," I said. "Or an isolation line, probably, since they're assuming we're all as good as infected. And if this infection is so widespread…"

"They wouldn't be dropping bombs if they weren't holding a line," Jetta said.

"Why do you say that?"

"Well… would you bother with the middle of nowhere if there were zombies running around New York City or LA?"

"Good point," Dad said. "Smart, Jetta…"

He'd given her more compliments in less than twenty four hours than I'd gotten in three years.

But that wasn't important. Not important enough for now.

I could be all mopey about it later.

"But what does this mean?" I said. "If we can't tell who's infected on the ground, it's not like they'll be able to tell from ten thousand feet in the air."

"One of two things," Jetta said. "Either they don't know about people like your sister, or they're cutting their losses."

"Cutting their losses?" David asked.

Jetta sighed. "What would you rather do? Kill two hundred thousand people who are all about to get bitten, or lose the whole country?"

"I'm not about to get bitten," I said.

"Then you should probably write your congressman. Assuming he's not the guy who's gonna bite you."

"We'll be okay here," Dad said. "Middle of some wetlands, no buildings for over a mile in each direction."

"Until they drop the nukes," David said.

"So we're in isolation," I said.

"That's been mentioned, yes," Jetta said with a smirk.

"That means they've drawn a line somewhere and they're going to hold it. I'll bet the bombing has to do with that, like you said, Jetta. Holding the line. If they were doing something more *mass-murdery*, those bombers would probably be flying over Fargo, trying to take out as many current and future zombies as they could."

"So we hunker down and wait," Dad said. "We stay away from wherever that line might be, and we keep away from the populated areas."

"We wait for what, Dad?"

"What do you mean?"

"They're not going to show up to rescue us. Do you remember what happened in Idaho?"

"Yeah... I do. Every man for himself."

"Anarchy," David said.

"Something like that happened when I worked down in Houston, too," Dad said. "A hurricane flooded New Orleans. Katrina. They had a stadium, tens of thousands of people stranded. The official story was that they found ten bodies in the mess after they bused everyone out. That's just the official story. When you cram desperate people together, in a confined space... bad things happen."

"Bad things have already happened," Jetta said.

"It'll get worse for most people."

"I don't see how this gets better," I said. "Since they're not air-dropping some miracle cure, I doubt they'll be coming by to rescue people anytime soon. We could be trapped out here for weeks."

"Idaho was weeks," Dad said. "This could take months."

"We have maybe a few days of food and water."

"We can get more."

"By staying right here?"

"I can look for some. Or David."

"While we womenfolk sit on our little lady rumps."

"You like biology, don't you, Seffy?" Dad said. "Isn't that your big deal?"

"I don't want to hear it, Dad..."

"Tell me, *biologically*, what happens when a 250-pound man with a gun decides he wants to hurt a hundred… a girl your size?"

"He's right," Jetta said. "It sucks, but he's right."

"David isn't more than one-sixty," I said.

"One-seventy," David said. "Protein shakes."

"You should have saved your money and just hit up the donut shop," Jetta said.

"No one wants to rape David," Dad said. "Or at least, not every second guy out there."

"Do you really believe it's that bad?" I asked him. "Honestly?"

"It's that bad, Seffy. Or at least it might be. And I'm not going to risk it."

"That girl," Jetta said. "Out in the field…"

"What girl?" Dad asked.

"It doesn't matter," I said. "I know it's not safe out there. And it's less safe for Jetta and me over you guys."

"We need more than food and water," David said. "We need heat. I doubt November will get any warmer than this."

Dad nodded. "We're better off camping out here than moving somewhere more populated. We can figure it out. You got a brush for the horses, Seffy?"

I pulled Iris' grooming kit out of the trailer. I tossed the little pink bag over to him.

"So that's our plan?" I asked. "Camping out until we get buried alive in snow? Or just plain old get hypothermia and die?"

"Just say what you want to say, Seffy." He walked over to the horses with the kit. It was like he had a little pink purse.

That was the Dad I remembered. Things got stressful? Don't stick around. Check out. Find anything else to do, anywhere else to be…

It didn't matter. I'd long gotten past needing him to make my decisions.

"I don't know what I want to say about it," I said. "I just don't want *this*."

"I want to know what started this," David said, as he leaned up against the tractor tire. "Why here, why now…"

"Does it matter?" Dad said as he untacked Arkham.

"It matters to whoever wants to find a cure," I said. "David, you said your parents were bitten…"

David nodded.

"Are you sure?"

"I know they were infected, yeah."

"No, that's not what I mean. Did you see them get bitten, or notice bite marks?"

"I saw my mother bite my father."

"Then who bit your mother?" Jetta asked.

"Same phantom who bit Iris," Dad said, apparently paying enough attention to butt in occasionally.

"She was fine when she came home," David said.

"Came home from where?" I asked.

"From visiting a friend in Enderlin."

"They turn faster than that," Dad said. He'd untacked Star, too, and was giving Arkham a once-over with the curry comb.

"Turn?" Jetta said.

"Once they're bitten," I said, "they don't have long before the bots take over... and the infection goes along for the ride. Remember that old lady at the gas station? And the clerk? They changed pretty much right away. The clerk was... he was *aggressive* within a few minutes."

"So she wasn't bitten," David said. "What does that mean?"

"Did you mother ever get treated with botshots?"

"Yeah. For Type II Diabetes. She was part of that trial out of Sanford Federal. Still needed insulin after that, though. So I guess it wasn't that good of a trial."

Or she was just part of the control group. Maybe no bots at all.

"Two patient zeroes, right there," I said. "Along with one or both of those guys from the sewer company, and maybe one near where Errol was bitten. Something in the water. Mixed with the bots."

"So that's the infection," Dad said, without taking his eyes off his brushing.

"I think so."

"So if we know the source," Jetta said, "they must know the source, too, right?"

"Who's they?" David asked.

"The government..."

"Oh... you mean the guys with the bombs."

"We can't be sure they've studied it at all," I said. "You'd hope so... but right now they seem to be putting a lot more effort into containing it."

"I'll bet they know," David said, pushing himself off the tractor tire. "If the water table's infected with some kind of parasite or some-thing... they know it's all over the area."

"I wonder," I said.

"What?" Jetta asked.

"If the bots are a big part of the problem... maybe we just need to kill the bots."

"Kill the bots?"

"Iris and I have done it before... an electromagnetic pulse can disable them."

"Disable them, or kill them?"

"They're not alive," I said. "So all we can do is turn them off and hope that whatever this infection is, it doesn't have the ability to just flip them back on."

"How do you know this?" David asked.

"I don't," I said. "Iris does. Didn't she ever get into it with you? Those bots of hers are the most exciting thing in her life."

More exciting than David, anyway...

"I don't really remember..."

"So they can recover from one of those pulses?" Jetta asked. "Shouldn't it fry their circuits or something?"

"Bots aren't made the same way as other electronics," I said. "They feed off the body, for energy and self-replication, so they use very little ferrous material in their construction. Just enough that they can be controlled from the outside by molecular MRI or whatever else... you know, just in case."

"In case of zombie apocalypse," Jetta said.

"So you honestly think it's as easy as zapping someone with an EMP?" David asked.

"Maybe," I said.

"Even if that's the case... where are you going to find the equip-ment to do that? It's not as easy as smashing a hole in a microwave oven."

It wasn't as easy.

I knew that, because I'm not an idiot. Well, not most of the time. And because I know how to read pamphlets.

"My Mom's treatment," I said. "rTMS. At the clinic on 3rd Ave-nue North. Apparently it can disable bots. When Iris and I messed around with a Tesla coil, we managed to drop her active bots by al-most twenty percent."

"How could you even know that?" David asked.

"An educated guess based on a blood sample."

"Well, dang," Jetta said. "You guys were pretty thorough."

"Iris doesn't like uncertainty," I said. "If she could have snuck into Sanford Federal for a bot scan after running that coil, she would have."

"So you want to head back to some clinic in downtown Fargo to see if you can zap away the bad bots?" David asked.

"I don't know," I said. "We don't know what that would do."

"Well," Jetta said, "what do we think the bots are doing now?"

"Repairing tissue," I said. "Not just injuries like shotgun wounds, but even just reversing wear and tear. At a very high rate. It probably isn't sustainable... like long term."

"So what happens if the tissue isn't repaired?" Dad asked. "Does that actually do anything to help cure someone who's infected?"

"We have no way of knowing... if this virus or parasite or whatever is actually taking control over nerve endings, over muscle control... disabling the bots might not cure anything... it just might make the infected easier to kill."

"Which isn't so great," Jetta said, "because we don't want to kill them."

"And it's possible that the bots are what's keeping their bodies alive," I said. "If we disable the bots, it's possible that the resulting imbalance would kill the host."

"So Iris dies," David said. "Still not a great plan."

"Nothing's solved, then," Jetta said. "We can weaken the infected, but can't touch the infection itself."

"Not with rTMS," I said.

"Someone else must be working on this," David said. "Someone... qualified."

"Oh, good," Jetta said. "So then let's just sit back and do nothing and hope you're right, instead of, you know, talking this through."

David scoffed. "Talking what through? Are we going to ride in and save the world? Are we superheroes now?"

"We're just talking it through," I said, "like Jetta said."

David scoffed again. He was becoming incredibly punchable. "Oh, good," he said. "So let's talk it through. It's not like we should be focused on finding food or water."

"Shut up, David," Jetta said. "Please."

She stepped away from us, heading to the back of the trailer. I found it funny the way she would get angry. So sudden, so quiet, but so... alarming.

"Look," David said, "we don't have the know-how to treat some mystery disease... you're not a real biologist, Seffy. You're not even a biology *student*."

"No," I said, "you're right. I'm nothing. It's a good thing finding a cure isn't up to me. That's not my job."

"I think you're it, Seffy," Dad said.

I looked over to him. David did, too.

I hadn't even been sure my father was still following the conversation.

"Everything we need is at the hospital," he said. "They would have an rTMS machine there, too, just like the clinic. And they have the bot scanner, to check if the bots have been disabled. And they have the printers there, don't they?"

"They don't have the most advanced printers at the hospital," I said. "Those are at least five years behind the times. The newer ones are probably at the biomedical lab on Broadway."

"Printers?" David asked.

"If this virus or parasite has ever been studied before, there's probably a treatment on file."

"But don't these things mutate?"

"I'm sure that's how this happened," I said, "but mutations happen all the time, mostly in viruses. The printers can hopefully adapt the remedy to match."

"Hopefully? And what if it can't?"

"Then the infection runs its course... and if the bots are what's keeping the infected person alive..."

"There's no way you're testing this out on Iris."

Jetta clucked her tongue from where she was standing, at the back of the trailer.

David shot a glare at her.

"I just want to mention something," Jetta said. "About Iris."

"What is it?" I asked.

"You said something a minute ago... about how you don't think it's sustainable... the bots..."

"Yeah... they're working too hard. Probably replicating too quickly, too. And they run off the body, feed on whatever nutrients the body takes in. Eventually, those nutrients will run out."

"They're overclocked," Dad said.

"I think that's happening," Jetta said. "To Iris."

David and I both rushed over to the back of the trailer.

Iris' face was sallow, her eyes glazed over.

I wasn't sure she was conscious.

"What's going on?" David stammered.

"It looks like a new phase," I said. "Some kind of oversaturation, maybe."

"What are you talking about?"

"Too much infection. Or too many bots. I think the infection is feeding off of her, now. Taking more than her body can afford. We should try getting her something to eat."

"Like what?" Jetta asked.

"Same thing we gave to that blond woman. Any food that we'd eat."

Jetta ran to the packs. She pulled out a loaf of bread. "Took this from the house," she said. "Will this work?"

"I don't know."

She handed it to me.

I unwrapped the tape from my sister's mouth.

She didn't make any kind of noise.

I looked into her eyes. I couldn't see her in there.

I was starting to panic. But I couldn't let anyone see that. I couldn't let things fall apart.

Iris was breathing.

She had a pulse.

But that was it.

"She won't be able to chew or swallow," I said. "She needs a feeding tube."

"I'm guessing we don't have that," Jetta said.

"Without a tube the best we can do is try to get some liquid into her… but it won't be enough. We can't get enough nutrients into her to keep her alive."

"You talk like she's your patient," David said. "Do you even care that she's your sister?"

"The infection is killing her," I said. "Iris is going to die."

"What the heck is wrong with you, Seff? She's your sister, you know?"

I didn't answer him.

I just felt numb.

The infection hadn't found some kind of balance with Iris; I was sure it had always been sucking the life out of her. I hadn't seen it before, and now...

I felt an arm on my shoulder. I assumed it was Jetta.

It wasn't.

Jetta had already moved on to Beth, taking out her gag and feeding her the bread. Beth was taking it.

"We'll figure it out, Seffy," my father said. He gave me a hug. "We'll go into town, we'll get to that lab on Broadway and you'll find a cure."

"I don't know if we can pull this off," I said. "I don't know if they even have an rTMS machine at that lab."

"They do... or they did... your mother used to go there, back when they still had a clinic attached. Before they opened up that new outpatient place on Third. You don't remember back then, do you?"

"Then they probably moved the equipment when they moved the clinic."

"So worst case, we have to make two stops. Look, Seffy, I know we can pull this off. I know *you* can. You and Iris are the smartest girls I've ever known. You two are the best thing I've ever done."

"Well, technically," I said with a smirk, "Iris is the best thing Beth's ever done."

He shook his head. "I don't see how you can't see it."

"See what?"

"Iris is your sister, Seffy. I'm her father, too."

"Hold on..." I pulled away from him.

"I didn't know how to bring it up."

"What?"

"I met Beth not long after I married your mother. She was young, she was kind... and she really liked me for some unknown reason."

"You married Mom because she was pregnant," I said. "She told me that. Even before she lost her mind."

"Yeah. I could only marry one of them at a time. And since Beth was only seventeen..."

"God, Dad. This is a really stupid joke."

"She's my daughter, Seffy. And I've never told her that."

"And you never told me that you've started ruining my mother's life before I was even born. What is wrong with you?"

"That was nineteen years ago, Seffy."

"No... it's running straight through until today, since today is the first time you've bothered to stop lying to all of us."

"She doesn't know," he said. "I still haven't told her."

"It's still about her... it's always been about her. How does it affect Iris? Oh, no... *poor Iris*..."

"She's dying, Seffy."

"I know. And we need to help her. And then I need to tell her all of this, so she and I can hate on you together. One big happy frickin family."

"I wish I was a part of your family," Jetta said. "Always something happening."

I stopped being angry long enough to give her a little smile.

I appreciated what she was trying to do.

"So how do we get to Fargo?" David asked. "We can't drive forty miles on a tractor, can we?"

"We could," Dad said. "if I had the fuel. But I don't, and even if we get some... it's not the best idea. We need a car."

"We had a car," Jetta said.

"We had two of them total," I said, "if, you know, we're keeping count."

"Do you think we could go back to your car, Jetta?" Dad asked.

"It's sitting out on the interstate," she said. "So it's probably royally messed by now. If someone hasn't figured out a way to restart it."

"And I don't think Lucas will feel the urge to drive us into town," I said. "Assuming we could even find him."

"We need a classic car," David said.

"What?"

"Something that wasn't forced to be retrofitted with autonav."

"That's a good idea," Dad said. "But that might not be too easy to find."

"Mechanic's shops, maybe," I said.

"I know where to find one," David said. "Old guy in Enderlin tools around in a '93 Cobra R."

"A sports car?" Jetta asked.

"No... something better. A friggin race car."

"Enderlin's where your mother was, David," I said. "If she caught the infection from there…"

"It could be ground zero," Jetta said.

"This whole area is ground zero," Dad said.

"But there are more potential hosts in Enderlin," I said. "Probably close to a thousand people living there. So that could make for a buttload of zombies."

"We could go all the way into town and find out the car's not even there," Jetta said.

"It'll be there," David said. "It's the second week of November. You don't drive a Cobra R in November."

Jetta shook her head. "I'm not sure what things are like here, but up in Winnipeg they drive their fancy cars until the snow flies."

"It'll be there, okay?"

"Yeah, okay," I said. "We get it. You really believe in the Cobra R."

"Your car's probably closer, Jetta," Dad said. "We could check on it first. Eliminate the options one at a time."

I shook my head. "The interstate is too busy. Even if Jetta's car is still ready to go, we won't be able to get to it. We'll die trying."

"So it's the Cobra R," Jetta said.

"We won't all go in," Dad said. "David should go. Maybe bring Jetta."

I laughed. "So everyone but you and me? That's ridiculous."

"David will have the shotgun… whoever stays here will have to use the shovel and the rake against whatever shows up."

"No zombies have shown up," Jetta said. "If anything, it's un-infected people you have to worry about along this old trail."

"I don't want the shotgun," David said. "It's not like I'm going to be shooting people from horseback."

"You'll need it," Dad said.

"You keep it."

"I'm going with David," I said. "I doubt Jetta's ever been to Enderlin, North Dakota."

"And you've been what, twice?" Dad asked.

"Something like that, yeah." I turned to David. "We'll take the horses. That's our advantage. You're okay with that, right, David?"

"That's good," David said. "You and I should be able to move pretty fast on horseback."

"I don't want you to go, Seffy," Dad said as I picked Star's saddle off the siderail of the trailer.

"I don't care what you want," I said.

"You can be mad at me. But don't go."

"I am mad at you. And I'm going. Idiot."

"Your mouth…"

"We'll be quick," I said.

"Don't be quick… be careful."

"Yeah, whatever."

He walked over and tried to give me another hug. I didn't stop him.

He kissed me on the cheek.

Then he went and grabbed Arkham's saddle.

"I'm sorry, Seffy," Dad said. "This isn't how I'd wanted this to go."

"Whatever."

It was probably better that way. I wouldn't be able to waste time being angry. I'd have to pretend it didn't matter that much, that we were okay, because that was how we'd get through it alive.

"I'm sorry," he said again.

"Yeah," I said. "I know."

He nodded.

"One more thing, Dad," I said.

"What is it?"

"Jetta's not much older than seventeen, so you know… try not to get her pregnant, too."

Jetta laughed at that.

Somehow, so did David.

My father blushed.

I don't think I'd ever seen him blush before.

But it didn't make me any less angry.

10

ENDERLIN IS FOR LOVERS

David and I took the horses along the old rail line until we reached the first road that could take us south toward Enderlin, leaving the shotgun and the ankle-biting hunting dog with my father. David led the way, since he's hung around there since the moment he was conceived. And he's familiar enough with horses, not that I've ever seen him happy to be on the back of one.

From what I knew, he'd only ridden when Iris had asked him to.

I think that horse-hate comes from living on a farm. Townies like me think they're these exotic creatures, with graceful manes and powerful legs. Country boys like David really just see the hard and smelly work with very little payoff.

Aside from getting and possibly keeping girls like Iris.

I guess that counts for something.

That might be the only reason most country boys don't chop those horses up into delicious horsey steaks.

"I'm sorry about how I acted back there," David told me as we passed along the side of a large slough. "I know I've been really hard on you, Seffy."

"I get it," I said. "This isn't fun. We're all barely hanging on."

"You're hanging on just fine. I've never really seen you like this."

"Like what? Exhausted and cranky? Because that's most Wednesday mornings."

"Taking charge. You've always been so quiet around Iris and me... like you're just some kind of chaperone."

"Iris has always been the center," I said. "The bright and shiny object in the middle of it all."

"Yeah... too bright sometimes. God, Seffy... I can't handle

this…"

"We focus on what needs to happen. That's how we handle it."

"Yeah… I guess."

We passed by a yardsite. Old farmhouse, forgotten sheds… I'd say three out of four farms are like this, the current owners only worried about the fields. Those new owners would obviously rather not have those layers of someone's family history and various household toxins lying on top of a half acre of arable land. But it's not worth the money to tear it all down and clean up the plot.

It makes me think of *Little House on the Prairie*, of families settling a new place and another, and another, and scraping by and working hard, but working together.

I'll bet Charles Ingalls didn't have a secret family. And his wife Caroline probably never tried to cook a fishbowl in the oven, goldfish included.

We don't have to worry about the material hardships as much, or didn't, before sometime yesterday morning. I guess messed up families had to take over for a while.

"This might be a good place to end up," David said. "If things don't work out in Fargo."

"Not a vote of confidence," I said.

"Having a Plan B doesn't say anything about the worth of Plan A."

"There won't be a Plan B, David. You know that, right?"

"No, I don't."

"Do you even know what it's like in town right now?"

"Again… no…"

"Imagine what happens if you have a thousand infected people who don't even look infected running around a city of a hundred thousand people… you end up with a hundred thousand infected people soon enough."

"And we want to drive right into the middle of that."

"Yup."

"Good thing we can't all go… some of us might be able to get out of this unbitten."

"What? Why can't we all go?" I asked.

"It's not a minivan, Seffy. The Cobra R only has two seats."

"That's a pretty important piece of information, David. Like something you should have mentioned before we started riding down to Enderlin."

"We can put Iris and Beth in the back seat. Might be room for one other person to cram in, maybe someone small like Jetta…"

"So who stays behind? You or my father?"

"Probably you, Seffy. I guess if we can fit your Dad in the car, you and Jetta could stay here… maybe hide out somewhere like this."

"I'm the one who came up with the plan."

"Your father's by far the best shot out of all of us. And I've got a good twenty or thirty pounds on you, not to mention upper body strength…"

"I'm not going to cower in some abandoned farmhouse while you guys go off and try to save my sister. I know this stuff better than you do, David. I know how to disable the bots. And I sure as frick know more about printing antivirals."

I realized how pointless the argument was. We didn't have the car. We hadn't even reached Enderlin. For all we knew, we'd end up with a couple of neck bites just up the road.

"Let's just find the car," I said.

"Sounds good."

And we kept riding our horses along the edge of the road.

❧

We approached a second farm, but this one hadn't been abandoned. I could see a large gray pickup out in front of the farmhouse.

"Might not be safe," I said to David.

"Not sure what's safer," he said. "We could come up straight on or we could be just as visible skirting around in the fields."

"We should skirt around… they'll see us, but that way we'll see them, infected or not."

"Or they'll pick us off with a shotgun as we head by," he said.

"People don't have the kind of aim you think they do. And their guns don't have the range." I pointed to the left. "We wrap around that way… we may want to stick to the middle of fields from here on in."

He nodded, and led Arkham hard to the east.

"I'm going to be so pissed if I get shot," he said.

"I can live with that."

He laughed.

I wasn't really joking.

∽

We crossed a road and kept going, through cut stalks of barley. It was still at least an hour or two to Enderlin, and I was starting to remember that I hadn't eaten since my short stop-in at Lucas' house of zombie paraphernalia, almost twenty-four hours before.

I had this vision in my head, of the kind of father who would remind his daughter to eat something, but I knew that not only was it not really Dad's fault, but that I'm pretty sure most dads wouldn't be on top of something like that.

"I've got snacks," David said.

"Yeah, good," I said. "How did you —"

"You and Iris have that same 'so-hungry-I-might-kill-someone' look."

"That might be all women."

"Well, I think it's cute. When it's not endangering my safety."

I think he was trying to be funny, but it felt like a dig.

He tried to reach behind his back, to his beat-up backpack. "Not sure I can do this on horseback," he said.

"You're kidding…"

"Okay… I just want a quick break."

I smiled. Not sure why that's so automatic with me.

He slowed Arkham down.

"We should loop back to the water back there," I said. "Get the horses something to drink."

"Good thing they don't have to worry about what's in the water."

I took the lead, pointing Star toward the patch of wetlands. I brought her up on the gravel road to spare my feet from what generally happens when you dismount in a marsh.

I climbed down.

Star made her way to the edge of the pothole and started to drink.

David and Arkham joined us.

David and I sat down on the edge of the road, our feet dangling into the brown grass. He pulled out a couple of homemade granola bars and handed one to me.

I didn't ask who'd made them.

"It's still peaceful out here," David said. "So beautiful."

"So flat and uneventful."

"Is that really what you see?"

"It varies. You see what you want to see out here. You can see this place as the most boring part of flyover country if you're in the right mood."

"The right mood?" He gave me a funny look.

It made me giggle. A little. "You know what I mean."

"I guess I'm always in the wrong mood," David said. "I just see perfection. I always hoped that Iris would see it, too."

"She doesn't?"

"You know your sister…"

"Not as much as I like to think I do."

"She doesn't want to draft tractor parts in Fargo, Seffy. She wants to get far away from here."

"That's what I thought I wanted, too," I said. "But this place grows on a girl, you know?"

He nodded. "I just want Iris to be okay."

"We'll fix this, David. We will."

He reached over and put his hand on my knee. He gave it a squeeze.

I didn't like it, but I didn't want to cause a scene.

And so for some unknown reason I smiled again.

Then I got up.

"Time to go," I said.

"That's it?"

"We've got somewhere to be."

He nodded.

But he didn't get up until I was already climbing back onto Star.

We passed by several larger sloughs, until the last one brought us right near another abandoned yardsite. By the time I'd realized how close we were getting, it seemed too late to skirt around without having to go back half a mile.

But it looked quiet, so I hoped for the best.

The belt of trees that encircled it was filled with pieces of garbage: some scrap metal, some old tires, and the occasional gas station sign with a hole in the middle.

"Hoarders," David said. "Filling old farms with crap. Should be a law against it."

I shushed him.

He glared at me.

I needed to know if there was anyone around.

And I didn't need more advertising for us on top of the sound of the horses' hooves.

A gun went off.

I held Star steady, but Arkham spooked.

David lost the reins.

Another shot.

Arkham bolted.

I tried to catch up, to reach the reins, but I couldn't get there.

And David came off the back of his horse.

He'd rolled backward, not on purpose, his head smacking hard against Arkham's hip. He then fell to the right side, landing on his rump in the dirt.

I couldn't tell if he was okay.

He wasn't moving.

And we had to keep going, away from the gunshots.

I had to let Arkham keep running.

I jumped down from Star, keeping one hand on her reins.

"David," I said, "we gotta go. Are you able to get up?"

"I… I don't think so," he said, gasping as he spoke. "I'm having… I'm having trouble doing anything…"

I thought the worst. His head slamming so hard, his neck, his spine…

"They're shooting at us," I told him. "They want to kill us. You need to get up."

"I can't."

"I can't carry you, David. If I let go of Star, and they fire that gun again…"

"Just keep going, Seffy. I'll be alright."

"They want to kill us."

"I can't get up."

He wasn't going to budge, whether he could or couldn't. He

136

wasn't going to.

I scanned in the direction of the yardsite.

I'd thought the gunfire was coming from there, but I wasn't sure... somewhere to the east, at least... but there was no one moving toward us through the field of wilted wheat stalks.

No movement at all.

And no more gunshots.

"What are they doing?" David asked. "They shoot, and then nothing?"

"Maybe they just wanted to scare us off," I said. "Maybe they didn't mean to hurt us."

"They could have just left us alone... we weren't heading toward their farm. They must've known that."

"I don't know."

"So what do we do now?"

"*I don't know.*"

He gave me a sad little smile. "So I guess you're not leaving me behind?"

"Iris would kill me if I did," I said.

He nodded.

"Can you move your hands?" I asked.

He looked down at his right hand. "I'm scared."

"What? Why?"

"I'm scared that I'll try to move it and nothing will happen."

I took a step closer to him, bringing Star with me.

I stepped on his hand.

"Holy hell," he said. "What was that?"

"You feel that?"

"Yeah."

"Good sign. Now wiggle your feet before I get Star to test those out."

He scuttled a foot or two away.

"I'm okay," he said. "I'm okay."

I tried not to roll my eyes.

"I'm not sure we'll catch up to Arkham," I said. "He bolted in the right direction, but that doesn't mean he kept to it."

"Around here you can watch your dog run away for three days," David said. "Can't you see the horse?"

"No... I can't."

"Then I guess we have to move on without him."

"That's Iris' horse, jackass."

"Maybe we'll see him on our way."

"Whatever. We should walk Star at least partway to the road. They stopped shooting once we came off the horses, so maybe they won't start up again."

I knew it was wishful thinking. But I didn't have anything better to run with.

I started walking.

"I'm sorry, Seffy," he said.

I didn't respond.

"I'm sorry I messed this up, that I lost hold of Arkham."

"Let's just keep moving, okay?"

"Sure, okay."

I was tempted to just hop onto Star and ride away, leaving him behind. So far he hadn't done much, if you don't count those granola bars.

⁊

We reached the road and crossed it, and I climbed onto Star before helping David up to sit behind me.

"I feel like a biker chick," he said as he wrapped his arms around me. He'd placed them a little low, just south of my navel.

If I'd thought for an instant that he'd done that on purpose, he'd have fallen off his second horse of the day.

I squeezed Star gently with my feet.

There hadn't been any more gunshots; it seemed like my theory was holding up. Someone was holding out in the abandoned farm-yard, and when they saw us coming, they decided to show us just how tough they are.

They probably hadn't even meant Arkham to bolt.

They were probably just as frightened as we were.

Not that it would make much difference in getting Iris' horse back.

I led us down a line between two farms, trying to maximize my distance from both.

"There's a corral over there," David said.

138

"Where?"

"On our left."

I looked over.

Horses. At least half a dozen.

"Would Arkham have gone that way?" he asked.

"Good chance, I'd say."

"Then we should get closer."

"I don't see any horses on the outside of the fence."

"Too far to know for sure, isn't it?"

"Yeah."

I wanted to check the corral, see if Arkham was milling around it, or if he'd managed to hop the fence and join the party.

Iris would be devastated if Arkham didn't come home.

Not that we had a home, or the real Iris.

Arkham didn't matter as much as that.

"We should keep going," I said. "If he did end up there, he'll likely be there when we're on our way back. So we can stop in and check."

We probably would have had to leave the horses in Enderlin, anyway. I would have preferred to keep them together, so they wouldn't be on their own.

But I should have known that things wouldn't go according to plan. Plans were wishful thinking, at best.

"We'll come back for him," I said. "When we have a way to bring him home. For now, we keep going..." I was saying it more to me than to him.

"Okay," he said. "Makes sense."

We kept heading due south, or close to it, crossing several shelter lines of trees. At each one, I closed my eyes for a second, like a pre-emptive flinch, expecting something terrible to happen.

But the lines were clear of people.

Eventually we reached what David called out as the Maple River, which seemed more like a large creek that wouldn't be tough to cross.

"We can follow this down to the county line," David said. "From there it's just a couple miles to Enderlin."

"Where can we find the car?"

"Guy's place is on this side of the river, right before you cross into town."

"That's good... do you think he'll be a problem?"

"I don't know. We may need to be persuasive."

"I hope you don't mean shotgun persuasive, since we left that back with the tractor."

"You can be persuasive, Seffy. Just give him some of that Schmidt girl charm."

"That's more an Iris thing, actually."

"Come on, Seffy. Don't be stupid."

"What the heck does that mean?"

He paused. Like he was choosing his words with a little more care than you'd usually get from a guy like David. "Look… you're just as hot as Iris… I mean, it's a different… flavor, I guess… but still hot…"

I tried not to feel a rush from that. I tried not to let some good looking if slightly wimpy guy's opinion define my self worth…

I blushed.

And smiled again.

It felt like what I imagine it'd feel like if someone like Dr. Jillian Devreux told you your second-year ethology term paper was the best one she'd ever read. Like you were now known to be accomplished by an expert in the field.

David's an expert in the field of vapid outer appearance.

And apparently not much else.

We followed the river, loosely, since it wanders pretty slowly across the prairie.

We skirted around one last yardsite, crossing a field between it and an old dirt landing strip.

And we arrived at the county line, a paved two-lane road that would have had more traffic, had there been any way for that traffic to move.

"No sign of any quarantine line here," David said.

"Would have to be further south, wouldn't it? Since Enderlin is probably infected."

"If that's the case, they might have written off everything from here to the border with South Dakota."

"Isn't that two whole counties?"

"Yeah."

"Not sure they could hold a line that long…" I didn't say the rest out loud. That it's hard to imagine stopping the outbreak if it's already spread to a half dozen counties in North Dakota.

Being in the dark means *dark*.

We didn't know anything.

Somehow the only reassurance there was that civilization hasn't collapsed was a USAF bombing run we'd seen in the distance.

We followed the empty road toward Enderlin. There wasn't a roadblock, or a hastily-constructed fence, just a clear line of sight into the town.

We passed by a large ag yard, a long beige building with a pack of large white storage tanks hanging off the side. The place looked empty, like whoever'd been there had seen what was coming and high-tailed it to anywhere else.

I wondered if there was some place where people had run to, some refuge from the infection... but I couldn't picture how that would work, since all it would take is a few bright-eyed and fast-talking zombies like Iris to sneak through whatever defenses they'd set up.

I remember a passage from Dr. Devreux's autobiography, since I had her on the brain, from when that Russian mobster had tried to steal a prototype of the botshots from her lab in Haifa. He hadn't send in a van full of gunmen, he hadn't tried to kidnap anyone's kid or chihuahua to gain some leverage... he'd just sent a well-spoken Ukrainian biologist to the lab in a significantly nonclinical low-cut shirt, and she'd managed to get one door away from the sample storage before they'd realized what was happening.

Social engineering. Like tricking someone into giving you their banking credentials, or telling some frizzy-haired girl with an ever-growing chin zit that she's just as hot as her perfect blond sister.

The infection wasn't relying on brute force, on overwhelming isolation lines and death charges aimed on the National Guard. It was relying on things like Iris' playful smile... and probably, somewhere in the bowels of Fargo, on Errol's down-to-business crewcut and light brown khakis.

And even if the US government had set up a perimeter around half the state... someone like Iris could have gotten through.

The infection would get through.

"Stop the horse," David said, his mouth pressed up to my left ear.

"Why?" I kept Star moving.

"Something's moving... behind that little gray chemical tank."

"I don't see a gray one."

"We've passed by it."

I took a look over my left shoulder.

I could see the tank, but no movement.

"What do you want me to do?" I asked him.

"I don't know."

"Well... there's no point in stopping if we don't have a plan."

Two men stepped out from behind the tall forest of white storage tanks.

Both were carrying some heavy-duty rifles, the kind of weapons my father'd call "nukes to a knifefight". And both barrels were pointed at us.

"Stop the horse," one of the men said, a tall and thin thirty-something man with little to no hair on his face. I couldn't even see any eyebrows.

The other man was older, and stockier, and shorter... and looked a little out of his element. He was holding the gun well enough, but not looking all too comfortable with it.

Not looking like his friend at all.

But either way, there was no mistaking what either man would do if he felt the need. I wouldn't be lucky enough for them both to miss.

I slowly pulled back the reins.

"Off the horse," the first man said.

David went first, climbing down and putting his hands on his head, just like he had for me the day before.

"On your knees."

David knelt down.

"You, too," the man said to me. "Off the horse, miss." It was one of those loaded *misses*, like it was really just a synonym for "typical brainless woman" or, more likely, something way worse.

Like the way Lucas would call me *sweetheart*.

I hopped off of Star and got down on my knees, hands on my head, fingers laced.

The two men stepped closer, guns trained on our chests.

Two more people stepped out from behind the storage tanks, one man and one woman. He was tall and with only a little more hair than the bald one; they looked like brothers.

The woman was maybe mid thirties, maybe a little older than the two brothers. She was a little heavier, like heavier like I think I happen to be, on my bad days.

Neither of those two were holding a gun.

They hurried over to us, the man to David and the woman to me.

They bound our wrists behind our backs with cable ties; she cupped my left hand into my right, to make sure there was no give in the restraint.

"It'll be okay," she said to me. "Just try to stay calm."

I decided not to talk.

The woman stepped over to David, and she and the man each grabbed an elbow and lifted him to his feet. She gave him a gentle shove, pushing him toward the building.

The man came over to me.

He wrapped his arms around me, lifting me up.

I didn't need the shove; I started walking after David.

The man and woman took us around the side of the building, into a door. It led into a dark warehouse, lit only through the small open door, the walls lined with pallets of ag products, herbicides or fungicides or pesticides or whatever, a complete menu of soil-eroding and superbug-breeding crop science.

There were four folding chairs in the middle of the room.

And under one of those chairs, what looked like a patch of dried blood on the concrete floor.

I didn't say anything about it.

"Sit," the woman said. "Please."

I took the chair farthest from the blood.

David sat right beside me.

The woman walked over to a first aid kit, open in an empty space on a pallet rack. I assumed that she was going to see to the scratches that were basically all over David, as some kind of goodwill gesture.

She came back with a roll of purple vet wrap and a pair of disposable white gloves.

She came over to me.

"He's worse off," I said.

"Open your mouth," she said.

I clamped my jaw and shook my head.

She looked over to the man. "Josh…"

He came over to me.

He clamped his right hand over my nose, pinching my nostrils together.

I didn't wait for it to get worse.

I opened my mouth.

She shoved the gloves inside, then wrapped the bandage around my head a good four times.

I was starting to get a feeling for what Iris was going through. The taste and texture of the gloves were all kinds of terrible, but I knew it was more sterile than a moist and sweaty purple sock.

In that situation, was it better or worse if the sock wasn't yours?

I wondered if David would fight harder against whatever they were about to shove in his mouth.

But they didn't bring one out for him.

"What's your name?" the woman asked him.

I tried to tell her that what we were doing was important, that we needed to see if we could figure out the cure… it came out as a series of gurgles.

David was looking at me, as if he expected me to blink out an advanced counter-interrogation strategy.

"Your name," the woman said.

"David… David Horg."

"And her name?"

"Persephone Schmidt."

"Where you two from?"

"I live over in Alice. Seffy lives in Fargo."

The man stepped up to me. He stared into my eyes. He looked over at David. "Someone tied your wrists recently," he said. "Marks are still showing."

"Yeah," David said. "Extension cord, actually."

"Who tied you up, David?"

David nodded toward me.

The man laughed.

I tried to tell him to shut up.

It didn't come out right.

"She was worried I was a zombie," David said.

"You're obviously not," the woman said. "Your elbows are sliced up like shredded cheese."

"Are you sure she isn't?" the man asked.

"Who? Seffy?" David asked.

"Who else?"

"She's not a zombie."

"Did you test her?" the woman asked.

"Uh…"

"She asked you a question," the man said.

"I don't know how to test if someone's a zombie," David said. "I mean, Seffy pulled a bit of a trick on me, cutting into my hand…"

"That's not a test," the woman said.

"Then what's a test?"

"How are you still alive, David?" the man asked. "How could you not have gotten bitten?"

"You're still alive."

"Well, I'm not an idiot, so…"

"Why were the two of you alone out here?" the woman asked. "Where's the rest of your group?"

"We don't have a group," David said.

I wasn't sure why he'd chosen that exact moment to start making grot up.

"Why did you come here?" the man asked.

"Looking for a car. Something that hasn't been disabled."

"You're here to try and steal our equipment?"

"No… passing through… there's a guy in Enderlin, with a 1993 Cobra R."

"Classic car," the woman said. "No autonav."

David nodded.

"And what were you going to do with this car?" the man asked.

"Drive it."

"Drive it where?"

"I don't know."

The man looked over to me. "You're the smart one," he said. "Am I right?"

I nodded.

I'd expected him to start pulling off the vet wrap.

He just gave me a smile.

And then he and the woman walked out of the warehouse, into what was looked like a hallway; it was too dark to know for sure.

"Are you okay, Seffy?" David asked.

I rolled my eyes.

He leaned in toward me, his mouth to mine. Or to my vet wrap.

He started pulling on the wrap with his teeth.

It was awkward. And surprisingly soggy.

I tried to tell him to just turn around and try using his hands.

He kept going with his mouth.

Eventually he reached the skin.

And pulled the wrap down, where it nestled into my sticky-outy chin.

I started trying to work the gloves out of my mouth.

He stuck his face right up against mine and started gumming at the gloves with his lips.

The gloves came out.

And then he kissed me.

With tongue.

It didn't feel much better than the balled up medical gloves.

I pulled back.

"Sorry," he said. "Caught up in the moment."

"The chewing on my face moment?"

"Yeah…"

He went in for another.

I didn't really have any place to go.

So he kissed me again.

With that same slab of David tongue.

"Don't do that again," I said. "Please."

"I always figured you were into me," he said. "That you wanted to know what it was like."

"Wow. Are you serious?"

"What?"

"My sister's boyfriend thinks I want him to shove his tongue in my mouth while I'm tied up in a scary dark warehouse during the end of the friggin world?"

"I just thought you liked me, okay?"

"Well, just don't kiss me anymore, okay?"

"Yeah."

I looked over to the open door.

At least thirty feet away from us.

And at least two men with very big rifles on watch outside.

That was probably why they hadn't bothered strapping us into those folding chairs. That and the fact that you could probably just stand up and waddle out anyway.

"We need to get out of here," I said.

"I don't think that's going to happen, Seffy."

"It needs to happen. Iris doesn't have time for this crap."

"We don't know how much time she has."

"What is wrong with you? My sister is dying. Even if we manage to get the infection out... the chances of her getting through this..."

"What do you mean? We cure her, she gets better... isn't that the point of a cure?"

"The longer we wait, the weaker she gets. And the harder it will be for her to pull through."

He nodded. He still hadn't pulled back from being six inches away from my face. "So we need to get out of here," he said. "And how does that look, exactly?"

"I don't know."

All I did know was that running out through that open door was probably the wrong decision.

And I needed to start looking for a better one.

11

DIRTY FACE AND THROBBING HEAD

They came back after less than five minutes. The woman was smiling. The man was carrying a box of gas station donuts.

"You got the gag out," the woman said. "That's good."

"You could have taken it out for me," I said. "Saved me some trouble."

And an unwanted tongue.

The man opened the box, holding it out in front of me.

"My hands are tied," I said.

"Just use your mouth," he said. "I won't think less of you."

I shook my head.

He looked over to David. "When was the last time she ate?" he asked.

"She had a granola bar," David said. "Maybe an hour ago."

"You don't need to tell them everything," I said.

"You should eat," the woman said to me. "Really."

"I don't want anything, okay?"

"I'll feed her," the man said. He picked up a chocolate-topped donut and brought it up to my mouth. "Take a bite, Seffy."

"I'm not a donut person..." I was getting used to lying.

He pushed the donut up against my lips. "I'm gonna smush it all over your face... just open up..."

Now the whole thing was starting to mean something to me. I held my mouth closed. On principle.

And waited for the nostril pinch.

But he just shoved the donut against my mouth, smearing chocolate up into my nose.

I tried not to flinch. Or move at all.

He kept shoving. The donut started crumbling, pieces falling all over my clothes.

He threw the rest of it onto the concrete floor.

I had chocolate icing all over my face.

It smelled… really good.

"I'll take a donut," David said.

The man brought the box over, and David launched in with his mouth. Like a starving pitbull. Or a school of piranhas at Golden Corral. Or something hungrier.

The woman came over, putting her hand on my right shoulder.

She gave it a light squeeze.

"There's a place for you guys here," she said. "If you want it."

"If you can carry your own weight," the man said. "Contribute."

"We need to keep moving," I said.

"There's nowhere to go, Seffy," the woman said. "We're cut off from the outside world."

"There are ways out of here."

"No… there aren't."

"Just let us go, okay? Just cut these cable ties and we'll be on our way. And maybe let David keep the whole box of donuts."

"Where are you trying to go?" the man asked.

I shrugged.

"We're not stupid," he said. "Now tell me where you're trying to go."

"What does it matter? I just want to leave. I want to get far away from you and the skeevy way you welcome guests."

"She's not telling us something," the woman said. "Why aren't you telling us, Seffy?"

"We're trying to get back into Fargo," I said. "I think there may be a way to stop the infection."

"A cure?"

"A way to stop it. We kill the bots, and we see if we can print off a cure."

"Print off?" the man said. "Like at the hospital?"

"Yeah… at the Sanford Lab on Broadway. They should have what we need."

The man scoffed. "Forget it."

"What?"

"It's a stupid idea. And you're smarter than that… or at least you ought to be."

"It's better than your plan," I said.

"You don't even know our plan," the woman said.

"Hunker down... scavenge supplies... wait for rescue..."

"We're surviving," the man said. "Staying uninfected."

"The government can't stop this," I said. "The way this is spreading. If they even have an isolation line, I doubt it's going to hold for much longer. Did you see those bombers?"

"They have a line," the woman said. "They're holding it. At the Sheyenne River. They blew up nearly every bridge across."

"How do you know that?"

"I've been there," the man said. "The National Guard is holding the line. No one in and no one out. And I'm sure the CDC is working on a cure." He gave me that patronizing look that you get used to getting from practically every man you meet, particularly when you purport to know something about science. "Stop trying to be the hero, Seffy. Just stay here and be safe."

"My sister's infected. And she's dying. We need to get her to the Sanford lab before the infection kills her."

"That's not how it works," the woman said. "The infection doesn't kill people... if anything, it makes them stronger."

"That's temporary," I said. "Or at least it was for her. The infection is overwhelming her body now. *She's dying.*"

"I'm sorry," the man said. "But if you're right about that, your sister's already dead. You can't get back into Fargo, and even if you did, there's not going to be any electricity or running water..."

"They'll have emergency generators... stored water..."

"They'll run out of that before you get there. If you get there. How long do you think you'll last riding in on horseback? Not to mention that you guys were headed in the opposite direction..."

"I'm sorry," I said. "We need to go."

I stood up from the chair.

The woman grabbed my shoulder again. This time she was trying to push me back into the seat.

I shoved her down.

I started running.

David came along behind, kinda nipping at my heels.

I ran out the door, out into the parking lot. I cut to the left, trying to get as far away from the two men on lookout by the storage tanks.

"Stop!" a man called out. I wasn't sure which one.
I kept going.
David, too.
"We'll shoot!"
I called their bluff.
And then they fired.
I was still moving.
I turned and looked back.
David was on the ground.
I stopped running.

There wasn't enough in the first aid kit for David. The woman tried her best to clean up the gunshot wound in his thigh, with only a camp lantern for light. I knew it was only a matter of time before he lost consciousness, and then it wouldn't be much longer before David was dead.

For some reason, it doesn't matter if a guy hits on you even though he's dating your sister. Or that he did it in the most inappropriate and *moistest* way possible. You still don't want him to die.

The man had bound my feet with another cable tie, and sat me back down in my chair. No one had bothered to clean the chocolate icing off my face, but at least the gloves hadn't made a return.

They had David on the concrete floor, with only a sheet of cardboard between him and the cold beneath.

"Let me take him out of here," I said.

"He's going to die," the woman said. "I'm sorry."

"You're not sorry… it was your people who shot him."

"You shouldn't have run," the man said. "The guys on watch didn't know what was going on. They just saw two prisoners bolting… for all they knew you'd just finished bludgeoning us both to death."

"Let me take him," I said. "Let us go now. You've done more than enough."

"You need to stay, Seffy," the woman said. "You need to be safe."

"Why does it matter so much? Why do you want me to stay?"

"We don't want you to get infected," the man said. "We need

people to live through this."

"People?"

"Women," the woman said. "I'm the only one here, and I'm related to half these guys."

"How nice for you," I said. "You can have the pick of the inbred litter."

"We don't know how long we'll have to stay here," the man said. "We want you to stay, too."

"I get it. Tying me up, shoving latex gloves in my mouth, shooting my sister's boyfriend... that was all foreplay. You're just trying to get me in the mood for a roll in the hay."

"No one's going to force you to do anything," the woman said. "You understand that, right?"

"No, I don't. From what I can tell, you're forcing me to stay. And forcing me to watch my friend die."

"There's nothing we can do for him now." She started rifling through the first aid kit. "There's not enough in here to help him pass... all we can do is make him a little more comfortable."

"We have a group," I said. "Up to the north."

"I figured," the man said.

"Let me take him back there... so he can see my sister one more time. And then we'll all come down and join you."

"How big is this group?"

"Not big," I said. "Me and my dad, and two other girls around my age." I said two.

Two girls is more enticing than one. Better than just me and my chin zit.

"And your sister the zombie," the woman said.

"Yeah... and my stepmother the zombie, too."

"We can send a truck to pick them up," the man said. "But you should stay here."

A truck. Something bigger than a Cobra R.

"You'll need me to find them," I said. "And to get them to trust you. And I won't go without David."

"How far away are they?" the woman asked.

"I don't know... maybe a half hour drive..."

"David won't make it that long. The trip's too much. I'm sorry, Seffy..."

"What does it matter?" the man asked. "Why would he want to

see his zombie girlfriend anyway? Especially if she's dying…"

"You don't see it?" the woman asked. "She doesn't want him to see his girlfriend before he dies. She wants her to bite him."

"To keep him alive…" He shook his head at me. "You'd let him be infected, let him turn into one of them…"

"He won't bite anyone," I said. "We'll keep him restrained. And we'll get him to the lab in Fargo."

"That wasn't the deal you were trying to make," the woman said. "You said you'd bring your people back."

"We're not going to go through all that," the man said, "just to have you guys run off to Fargo and get yourselves bit."

"You can have the other girls," I said. "Jetta and Leona. They'll come and join you right away. They're both cute and in good shape. Leona's quite striking… Jetta's small and really bendy… You take them back with you, and I'll take David and the others into Fargo. And when we're done, we'll come back here."

"You won't be coming back. Even if you do manage to get out of downtown Fargo in one piece."

"I'm not going to abandon Jetta and Leona forever. They're family."

"Hold on," the woman said, "so those two are your sisters, too?"

"Close enough," I said. "Close enough that I don't want to lose them." I wondered how much of that I was actually starting to mean, about Jetta. "We don't have a lot of time…"

The woman looked over to the man.

I saw her give him a nod.

"We'll take you to your people," the man said. "Your two friends will come back with us."

"We'll need to take two trucks," the woman said. "We'll need some help."

"I'll get the boys."

He jogged out of the room, back to the dark hallway.

"I know you don't believe it," the woman told me, "but I really am sorry. We're not bad people. I want you to know that."

"I'll know soon enough," I said.

᧓

The boys were just as described, two guys who were not much past sixteen. Twin brothers, tall and lanky like the other ones, those older brothers.

It seemed like a bit of a family business.

Or a family who'd come in and taken the building over from whoever had been here before.

"These are my cousins," the woman told me as we both looked out an open garage door. Watching the boys help the older man load David up and into the back of a grain truck. It isn't easy getting someone in there when they can't climb in on their own; the back gate was just barely wide enough to get him through.

I was still in the folding chair, my hands and feet still bound. And still with chocolate icing all over my mouth and cheeks, and up into my nose.

"I'm Erin," the woman said. "You've met Josh already, of course. The boys are Yarden and Stanhope."

"Really?"

She smiled. "My uncle's an idiot. I've gotten past that. But the rest of these guys are great. All of them are."

"Even Josh? Because I'm not getting that vibe…"

"We're scared, Seffy. Like you. Zombies who act like people, people who act like freaking psychopaths… it's like the end of the world out here."

"It might be the end of the world."

"Come on," she said. "I'll carry you out."

"Can't you just cut my ankles free?"

She wrapped her arms around my waist and lifted.

She pulled me up over her shoulders, my head and chest dangling over the back.

"Fireman's carry," she said. "I know what I'm doing."

She carried me out to the second grain truck.

"What about my horse?" I asked.

"She'll be here, waiting for you. Now, you'll ride with me and Stanhope. David's going with Josh and Yarden. That way —"

"That way you keep us separate. Keep your control."

"It keeps us all safe. Us and you, Seffy."

"Whatever."

One of the boys helped her lift me into the passenger side.

"Scoot into the middle," she told me.

The boy climbed in beside me on the bench.

He didn't seem to mind the close quarters.

He looked at me and smiled.

I didn't feel particularly unsafe. He seemed nice enough.

I realized that he wasn't carrying a gun. I guess with a *sixteenish* kid a gun isn't always a great idea. I remember something about a fifteen-year-old girl and a compound bow…

"Is there a seatbelt?" I asked.

"No belt for the middle," the boy said. "Sorry about that."

Erin climbed into the driver side. "Tell me where to go," she said.

"Head north," I said.

"Like north left or north right?"

"North right, I guess."

"Don't guess, Seffy. Do you remember where your people are?"

"To the right."

She started the truck. "The grain and tanker trucks have nav exemptions," she said. "That's about it for running vehicles. Nice thing about all this is that there's plenty of fuel around."

"I'm glad there's a bright side," I said.

She playfully punched me on the shoulder. "We'll be alright, Seffy. You know that, right?"

"Sure."

I looked out the driver's side mirror, watching the other grain truck following behind.

"Is there anyone sitting with him?" I asked.

"Yarden's there."

"Why aren't you? Someone with medical training…"

"I don't have any training. And Yarden isn't that great of a driver."

"I'm a good driver," Stanhope said.

"You're fifteen," Erin said. "You think you're good at everything." She laughed.

Somehow they did seem like good people. Good people who had to make some hard choices, like my father had been forced to do. Like I still held out hope that I wouldn't have to make.

⤎

We weren't more than a few miles along when we came upon a tractor with a rectangular baler attached, blocking the road from one side to the other. I couldn't see clearly if anyone was hiding behind it.

Then they fired a shot.

I assumed it was a warning.

Erin stopped the truck a good hundred feet in front.

The second truck stopped just behind us.

"We can't outgun them," Erin said.

"Did you actually bring a gun?" I asked.

She unzipped her jacket and showed me the holster and the edge of a gun handle. "I'm not that great a shot," she said. "By which I mean I've never shot a gun before."

"Can he shoot?" I asked, nodding to the boy.

"I'm a good shooter," he said.

"Again, he's fifteen," Erin said. "He thinks he's invincible."

"I can shoot," I said. "If you cut me loose..."

Not that I've ever shot a handgun... or shot my father's rifle more than once...

"We can't fight," Erin said. "We'll have to go around."

"Okay," I said, not like I had a choice in the matter.

Erin backed the truck up, turning the wheel.

"They need to back the other truck up," she said. "I need more room here..." She cranked the wheel to the right. "We just passed a turnoff, right?" she asked. "Another road?"

"Yeah," Stanhope said, "heads east... we can take it to 140th Avenue." He looked over to me. "Does that get us where we need to go, Miss Persephone?"

"I think so," I said. "We need to get to the north side of Lake Bertha... you know where that is?"

"Oh my god," Erin said. She was staring at her side mirror. She'd stopped backing up.

I looked in the mirror.

Another tractor. Pulling out behind our trucks.

"An ambush," Erin said.

"What?"

"I'll bet they want our trucks."

I could see what the tractor was pulling. A trailer, not much different from the one we'd pulled out from my Dad's. But carrying three men with long guns.

"Pass me your gun," Stanhope said.

"Cut me loose," I said. "I can help."

"There's no point in fighting," Erin said. "That'll end up with more of us dead."

She turned off the truck.

"What are you doing?" I asked. "We need to keep moving… push through that roadblock."

"With one handgun?"

"With a five ton grain truck."

"I don't think we can get through," she said.

"What do you think will happen if we just surrender?" I asked.

"I've been through that before… you just shut up and give them what they want. You let them do what they want to do. That's how you stay alive."

"We need to push through, Erin… please…"

"I can't."

"They'll kill the boys," I said. "They'll shoot them on sight. You know that, don't you?"

"They might not… they might ask us to join them…"

"Please, Erin." I looked over at Stanhope. He was terrified. "You know I'm right," I said to him.

"I don't want to die," he said. "We're… we're better off trying to get through."

"Take us through, Erin," I said.

She nodded.

She turned the engine back on.

"Can we ram it?" she asked. "What will happen?"

"I don't think it weighs much less than this truck," I said. "Not to mention the baler. So I recommend you go around."

"Through the ditch?"

"Through the ditch and into the field."

She slammed on the gas pedal, cranking the wheel to the left.

The truck drove into the ditch and out the other side, hitting the ground up mud on the field that ran alongside the road.

"I feel it getting stuck," Erin said.

"Just keep going," I said. "Just don't slow down."

Two more gunshots from in front of us.

Then gunshots from behind.

"Josh has one of our rifles," Erin said. "Might be him."

"Just keep going," I said.

I looked out her mirror. Josh was following behind with the second grain truck.

I felt my head slam into the roof of the truck.

Then I hit the dash.

I looked over to Erin. She'd had her seatbelt on, but she'd still hit her head against the steering wheel.

Stanhope had taken a bad hit, too.

I looked out the windshield. The truck was tilted toward the mud.

They'd dug a steep ditch into the field. A trench.

A trap for anyone stupid enough to try and go around the road-block.

I tapped Erin on the shoulder.

She wasn't moving.

I slapped her harder.

Stanhope was staring at me.

I leaned my head toward Erin, sticking my bound wrists out in Stanhope's face. "Help?" I said.

He reached into his pant pocket and pulled out a screwdriver.

I'd been expecting a knife.

He had my wrists free before I could even tell what he was doing. He had my ankles done almost as quickly.

"We need to go," I said.

"What about her?"

I grabbed the handgun from Erin's holster.

I gave Stanhope a shove toward the door.

He opened it and hopped out.

I saw the other grain truck. Josh had slammed into reverse; he was backing up across the field, toward a belt of trees.

There was no way they'd get through that belt. No way past the second tractor and the gunmen.

I grabbed Stanhope's left hand and pulled him with me as I rounded the front of the grain truck, hoping that the men with the guns would be more focused on the imminent threat in that second grain truck.

I led him due east across the field. We were about halfway between the shelter belt and a yardsite. I knew that neither would be safe.

I dropped down to the dirt.

Stanhope did the same.

"What now?" he asked.

"We wait…"

"Give me the gun. I need to go back for my brother."

"You can't help him…"

"I need to try."

"No… you need to help me, Stanhope. Keep me safe. Keep the both of us safe."

"Why should I care more about you? I mean…"

"Because you and I are the ones with the best chance of getting out of here. Maybe the only ones with a chance."

"Are they going to kill him?" he asked.

"I think so… I'm sorry."

"That's my brother…"

"I know."

"I need to go back."

He crawled over to me. He held out his hand for the gun.

I shook my head. "This is for getting out of here," I said.

He grabbed the gun by the barrel.

I couldn't picture a realistic alternative; I let go of the handle.

He climbed up from the ground and started running back toward the trucks.

They'd kill him, too.

I stayed where I was, in the dirt.

Hoping they'd forget about me.

I watched as Josh and Yarden surrendered. And as one of the gunmen helped a dazed Erin out of her truck.

And I watched as Stanhope crouched down, trying his best to hide in the harvested field, and failing miserably at that.

They weren't paying any attention to him, though. Not yet. He wasn't the bigger threat, not at that distance. The gunmen were composed enough to know that, to secure their captives first.

I didn't know what had happened to David. I couldn't see the back of the second grain truck. I had no way of knowing if he was already dead.

The gunmen had all three prisoners get down to their knees at the edge of the paved road, hands on their heads, facing the ditch. I could see the looks on their faces.

They knew what usually happened next.

I didn't close my eyes.

Each of the three gunmen from the trailer walked up behind a captive, at close range.

Their guns were slung over their shoulders.

Each leaned down.

And grabbed their prisoner, a hand on each shoulder.

And then I watched as they lunged forward, biting into their captives' necks.

I heard Stanhope curse.

He looked back at me.

I waved at him, beckoning him to come back.

He shook his head.

I didn't want to leave him there. And I wanted the gun back.

I got up and started running toward him.

"We need to go," I said as I got closer. "Come on."

"I can't leave my family," he said.

"You have more family back home... we need to find our way back there."

"That's my brother..."

"He's infected, Stanhope. You can't help him."

"You're right," he said. "But I can stay with him."

"And be infected?"

"Yeah... and be infected."

"Stanhope, please... come with me... the infected don't stay like that... they can't get enough nutrients... they will die... you will eventually die..."

"I can't leave him behind. I can live with what happens to me."

"Come on..."

"I'm sorry. I can't."

I sighed. "Then at least give me the gun."

He handed it over to me, handle first.

"Thanks," I said.

He nodded.

And started walking toward the road.

I started running in the opposite direction.

12

PERSEPHONE SCHMIDT, BADASS
MOTHERLOVER

The field ended with a lake. And more water to my right. And a neck of land that I hoped would actually lead somewhere; for all I knew, it was just going to end in more lake.

I didn't know if they'd come after me. Was I worth the effort? Would they just reset their ambush for the next bunch?

Would there be a next bunch?

Did they know whether or not I was the last uninfected person in the county?

David was gone, and the best I could hope for was that they'd found him in time to take a bite into his jugular vein.

And Iris was still dying; I couldn't picture a way out for her if I didn't get her to the lab in Fargo. And if I was right about the whole thing, her mother would die soon, too.

And every other person who'd been bitten.

Errol. And Jetta's friend Leona.

Aunt Callie. My Mom.

I didn't slow down, even though I'd started to cry.

Which made the trip that much colder in the November wind.

I reached the line where one field ended and another begun. I took that as a sign that there'd be a way across the lakes to the other side.

Once I reached the road I'd head north again, keeping to that road until I found something I recognized... I wasn't far from the town of Alice... I knew that.

If I could skit around there, and get back to my father and Jetta. We could try again, look for another car... somewhere...

But I knew that was stupid.

We didn't know where we could find an exempted vehicle, classic or otherwise.

I knew where there were two grain trucks, one of which wasn't currently jammed into a trench.

I had a handgun. And I had the element of surprise, since I can't imagine those zombies would expect me to be stupid enough to loop around and come back.

I knew that it wasn't enough. That there wasn't much hope that plan wouldn't get me very far. That it was just as stupid as running away.

But I had to try.

⋘

My head was throbbing. My wrists were sore from the ziptie. I could still taste the combination of latex glove and even-more-awful gas station donut in my mouth.

I switched lakes once I was sure there were two of them, wrapping around to approach from the north. At the north tip there was a little creek that led from the one lake to another; I was actually surprised that my socks had managed to stay dry up to that point.

I followed the shore of the lake back down to the yardsite. A line of trees seemed to keep me hidden from guys with the guns.

Once I'd reached those trees I stopped to get my bearings.

They'd driven one grain truck up the driveway to the yardsite; I assumed it was the one that didn't have to get pulled out from the trench.

That meant that David might still be in the back.

If they hadn't checked the back for supplies.

I watched a third tractor, the smallest of the bunch with a couple of people riding on top, heading back down the driveway.

Probably to get the other truck, which wouldn't be that easy or quick of a process.

If the gunmen were still in position at the roadblock, waiting for another chance at an ambush, and these two were focused on pulling the other truck from the trench...

It's hard to know how crazy a plan is when you have no idea how many bad guy zombies you're up against.

I crept out from the trees, moving behind the sheds, heading toward the farmhouse. Trying to get as close the truck as I could without being caught out in the open.

Before I could get a view of the farmhouse, I heard footsteps on the back deck.

I crouched down and made my way to the nearest oak tree.

I saw a woman pacing along the deck, reddish hair and very skinny legs.

I couldn't see her face, but I could make an educated guess by how she was moving… she'd have a blank stare and bloodshot eyes.

Infected before Erin, but much more recently than Iris or Beth. Possibly the very kind of zombie who would blindly chase after a frizzy-haired brunette, who's holding a little gun she doesn't know much about firing.

And if I shot her, they'd hear it.

I looked down at the ground, all around me.

I found an old fragment of cinder block.

I slowly knelt down and picked it up.

I charged for the deck of the farmhouse.

She turned and saw me. She didn't have a chance to lunge. I slammed the piece of cinder block into her temple.

She fell onto the deck.

She looked up at me. She grabbed for my legs.

I hit her a second time.

Harder.

It smashed her skull.

I'd killed her.

I wasn't sure I'd needed to, if there'd been some other option… but I'd done it. That was that.

I kept moving on toward the grain truck.

The door was unlocked.

The key in the ignition.

It felt too good to be true.

But then again, I still had to drive it out of there.

I put the gun on the seat beside me, making sure the safety was on. My father taught me well enough.

And I tried to clear my mind enough to think.

Heading up the driveway to the road wasn't an option. They'd stop me.

I had to go the other way. The same way I'd ran to. Between the lakes.

I turned on the engine and started driving. I drove up to the sheds and turned, passing the grain bins and hitting the field.

As I got more comfortable with the bumps, I sped up. I hadn't seen any trenches in the field as I'd ran, but I kept an eye out in case I'd missed something.

I heard an engine; it wasn't a car, or a truck, or a tractor. It sounded lighter, tinny, almost. I looked out the side window.

I couldn't see anything coming after me.

And nothing in front.

I kept driving.

The sound grew louder. It was getting closer.

I saw it, in the mirror.

A dirtbike.

Riding up behind, as close to sticking in my blind spot as it could get.

I sped up, throwing away any shot at avoiding any problems in the field; I'd already driven farther northwest than I'd run, so there was no way I'd know if there was another trench in my path.

At least I had a seatbelt.

I maxed out at 45 mph... I couldn't get it any faster without losing control of the steering. I'd already gone long past having any control over the brakes.

The dirtbike was gaining.

I wasn't sure what would happen once it caught up.

They'd be armed... they had to be... otherwise they wouldn't have come after a grain truck with a little bike that could *easily get stuck in the hungry teeth of a grain truck.*

They'd reach me and they'd start shooting.

And then I'd be shot and half dead and they'd take a chunk out of my neck.

It wasn't the way I wanted the day to end.

I looked out the window again, trying to calculate if I could get to the road in time... if I pushed it a little faster...

Pothole up ahead, water right in front... I jammed the wheel to the left... too hard, too fast...

It all seemed to slow down as I watched the right side of the cab lift up, my body pulled down toward the driver-side door.

The grain truck nearly rolled over, before coming back to rest on its base. All four wheels back on the ground.

My mouth was bleeding. I could feel the sting of at least a half-dozen scratches and bruises in other places, including a pain near my crotch that was probably the worst of the bunch…

I found the gun lying at my feet.

Waiting for me.

I took it and stuffed it down my pants. I took it back out and re-checked the safety. Then back down it went, nesting unceremoniously in my slightly off-white granny panties.

I undid the seat belt and climbed out.

A man with a shotgun met me outside the truck.

The dirtbike was lying on the ground nearby.

"You're infected," I said.

"You look like crap," he said. "Can you get down on your knees, or should I just do it like this?"

"Why the knees? What's the point?"

"I think it's safer, don't you? Worst thing would be if somebody didn't stay still and something gets nicked…"

"I don't understand."

"A badly aimed bite and you might bleed out so quick the bots can't fix ya. Saw it happen once. Now… on your knees, please… for safety…"

I started to cry. It wasn't all for show…

I slowly lowered myself to the ground.

"I think I just peed myself," I said.

"Gross."

I started undoing my pants.

"No," he said, "don't do that. I don't want to know…"

I pulled out the gun and flicked off the safety switch.

I pointed it at him and fired.

"Jesus Christ!" he yelled, falling backward, dropping his shotgun into the dirt.

I kicked his gun away.

He scrambled a little along the ground, away from me. Like a crab.

I hadn't actually hit him on that first shot.

So I took a deep breath, carefully took aim.

And shot him in the chest.

I didn't have the luxury of being a nice person.
I shot him again, in the head.
I climbed back into the truck and kept driving.

I reached the edge of the little lake just after four PM, assuming that the plain digital clock in the grain truck was set to the right time. No autonav meant no console, which meant that the clock had little buttons to set the hour and minute. It made me wonder what the point of a clock was if you could just change the time on a whim.

My crotch was still hurting the most.

I wondered if that was what it had felt like for Felicia Traeger when she'd taken too many chances with that greasy guy from Minot. Crabs are a gift best ungiven.

I pulled off the road and followed the old rail bed. I flashed between high beams and low as I slowly neared the tractor.

My father had David's shotgun raised, but once he saw it was me he lowered it and smiled.

I climbed out of the truck.

"Are you okay?" he asked.

"I'm okay…"

"Where's David?"

"I'm not sure."

I realized that he might still be in the back.

Not that he'd still be alive.

Jetta came jogging over.

I ran to the back of the truck.

"What is it?" she asked.

I pulled open the gate.

And found David.

His eyes were closed.

There was blood all over the back of the truck.

There wasn't much chance he was still alive.

But there was a chance.

"How's Beth?" I asked. "Is she still eating?"

"She's eating almost everything we've got," Jetta said. "But Iris—"

"I need you to bring Beth over here."

"What?"

My father put down the shotgun and started running over to the back of the trailer. "Jetta…" he said.

She followed him.

I climbed up into the back of the truck.

I checked for David's pulse.

Nothing.

No heartbeat.

No breathing.

I grabbed his leg and shoved it out through the gate.

Dad and Jetta brought Beth over to the truck, her wrists and ankles still bound with duct tape. They leaned her against the bumper.

"Take the sock out of her mouth," I said.

Dad started pulling on the tape. He ripped the sock out of her mouth.

"I hate your guts," Beth said.

"Can you grab his thigh, Dad?" I asked.

He took David's left leg and brought it up against Beth's mouth.

"Femoral artery," I said to Beth. "You know you want to bite it."

"Knowing that you want me to means I won't," Beth said.

"He's going to die," Dad said.

Beth gritted her teeth. "I know that. I don't want that to happen."

"Then you need to bite him…"

"I'm not doing anything. Not until you untie me and my daughter. And let us go."

"We don't have time for this," I said.

I shoved the rest of David's body through the gate.

"God," my father said. "Seffy…"

"Hold onto her," I said. "Make sure she doesn't bite me."

I climbed down from the back of the truck.

"I need a knife," I said.

Jetta pulled one from her pocket.

I took it.

"Lay her down on the ground," I said.

My father gently lowered his wife down, onto her back.

"On her stomach."

He carefully flipped her over. "God, Seffy…"

He wasn't trying to stop me.

I took the knife and put it against Beth's bound hands.

I sliced open her palm.

She screamed. "What is wrong with you?" she said.

"Seffy... you're hurting her," my father said.

"She'll be okay, Dad," I said. "Just trust me, alright?"

He nodded, but I'd never seen his face so pale.

I prodded her wrist... there wasn't enough blood.

I needed more.

I grabbed her by the wrist.

I sliced a line along the fattest vein I could see.

Dad finally turned his head away.

I grabbed David's shoulder and pulled his body closer.

"You're going to feed him her blood?" Jetta asked.

"Not quite..."

I sliced a cut into David's gums, on the left side of his mouth. And a matching one on the other side.

I slid his mouth under Beth's wrist.

Taking both hands I began kneading her forearm, coaxing out as much blood as I could.

Trickling blood down into David's mouth.

The flow was slowing. The bots were starting to heal her.

So I cut her wrist again.

And waited until the blood stopped flowing the second time.

"You really think this will bring him back?" Dad asked. "He's been dead for how long..."

"I don't know when it happened," I said. "I don't know if there's enough in him to save."

"You need to tie him up," Jetta said. "Just in case."

"If anything happens, it won't happen for a little while."

It would take more than a minute or two to bring a dead man back to life.

Jetta and I loaded the grain truck with our supplies as Dad and Fender watched over David. Or while Dad watched over Beth, really. She was the one he was worried about.

If they hadn't ruined my life by being together, I'd probably have thought it was romantic.

Once the supplies were loaded, Jetta and I carried Iris over, lifting her body into the truck. She didn't look much better than David, but at least she still had a heartbeat.

I had to believe that a heartbeat and a rising and falling chest meant that Iris was still in there somewhere.

We went to grab Beth.

"I'll do it," Dad said. "Just me."

I nodded.

He picked up his wife and brought her to the trailer.

I knew he was struggling to carry her, but I wasn't about to butt in.

"She'll be okay," Jetta said. "We'll figure this out."

He didn't reply.

Jetta brought the duct tape over to David.

"Do we tape him up?" she asked me. "Do we... do we know... with him?"

"Can't detect any changes," Dad said. "Still has scratches... can't see what's happening under that bandage on his thigh."

"No fresh blood," I said. "Not a good sign."

I grabbed his right hand and checked for a pulse.

There was... something.

"It's weak," I said, "but it's there. More than there was five minutes ago."

I grabbed the tape from Jetta.

I taped his wrists. Then his ankles.

And Dad and I lifted him up into the back of the grain truck.

Dad drove the truck, the shotgun down at his feet.

Jetta shared the middle with Fender, while I took the far end of the bench, putting my handgun under the seat. I'd thought of sitting in the back with Iris and the others, but I knew that there'd be nothing I could do back there. And it was my crazy plan at work. I had to be up front. Front and center.

It felt like the whole world was waiting on me.

Waiting for me to eff it all up.

We went due east.

"There's a little town up ahead," Dad said. "Chaffee. Go around or through?"

"Definitely around," I said. "Basically, we should be skirting around everything. If there's a road without any farms, that's the one we want."

Dad turned right at the next junction.

"This road's too busy," he said.

"There isn't another car on it," Jetta said.

"Too many farms. We should be taking the crappiest-looking road we can find."

"So we should detour up through Winnipeg. Pothole capital of the universe. And mosquitoes the size of elephants…"

"And girls who won't shut up," I said with a grin.

"I'm growing on you… admit it."

I leaned my head against her shoulder.

My father saw that, and shook his head.

We took a less-travelled road eastward, passing a few farms, but no roadblocks. We reached a bend in the road at the Maple River, and Dad had to turn us around.

"Now things get dicey," he said. "At some point we're going to need to cross the Interstate. Do you think that'll be a problem?"

"I don't know," I said. Because I had no friggin idea.

We headed north, toward the Interstate, on a road that was probably only meant for farm machinery. The grain truck didn't have a problem with it, but I'm sure that changes pretty quickly whenever it rains.

We came to a dead end at a creek.

"Do we try to cross?" Dad asked.

I remembered the trench, and just how useless a grain truck could become. "No… we turn around."

"Shouldn't somebody be checking the map?" Jetta asked.

"I thought my father knew where he was going," I said.

"Do you think anyone knows all these damned country roads?" Dad asked.

"Then you should have said something… should have asked me to look at the map."

"Maybe use your head, Seffy… why wouldn't we use the map?"

"Where is the map?" Jetta asked.

"Not sure," Dad said. "Who had it last?"

"You mean, your tablet?" I said.

He reached into his jacket pocket.

"Out of juice," he said. "Dammit."

"Do we have anything else?" Jetta asked. "Glove compartment?"

"There is no glove compartment," I said.

"Oh. So where do they put their A&W coupons?"

"The visor…"

Dad pulled down the visor.

There was a roadmap on a clip.

He handed it to Jetta, who passed it on to me.

"One road over," I said. "To the east. There's a bridge over the creek. No, wait… head two over… that road takes us right over the interstate."

"Over?" Dad asked. "No onramps?"

"No ramps of any kind. Just an overpass."

"That's good."

"As long as the bridge is clear," I said.

"What do you mean?" Jetta asked.

"I'm probably just being paranoid. But I was told that the government blew up bridges on the Sheyenne to keep people in… made me think that a bridge is a perfect place for a roadblock."

"It's possible," Dad said. "But it's not like we have a choice. We're going to have to cross that creek somewhere."

"We had trouble at a roadblock."

"Is that how David got shot?" Jetta asked.

"No… that was another piece of bad luck…"

"So what happened at the roadblock?"

"I told her to run it," I said.

"Told who to run it?"

"A woman we met… that's how we got the grain trucks. But they'd dug a trench… we got stuck. I'm the only one who made it out. Well, me and David, I guess…"

"I'm sorry, Seffy," Jetta said.

My father didn't say anything.

"They were infected," I said.

"Who was infected?" Dad asked, apparently beginning to care.

"The people manning the roadblock. They didn't kill everyone else who was with us. They bit them."

Dad sighed. "And we're driving right into that."

"Into what?" Jetta asked.

"A city of smart zombies. Zombies who I gather can drive cars and shoot guns."

"Yeah," I said. "They can do anything we can."

"And not die as easily," Jetta said.

"What do you think we'll be up against?" Dad asked me.

"How should I know?" I said.

"Come on, Seffy. You've know better than anyone else. You're closer than anyone to figuring it all out."

"I don't know, Dad…"

"It's like a thought experiment," Jetta said. "So imagine a world where people are like people, only they like to take big chunks out of your neck."

"The roads will be blocked," I said. "The closer we get to town, the worse it'll be. People will be taking whatever still drives and trying to get out."

"Maybe we'll be able to tell from I-94," Dad said.

"You think everyone will try to run?" Jetta asked. "Even if they're already infected?"

"We all need to eat," I said. "And from what we've seen with Iris and Beth, they need to eat more than we do. I'll bet they've realized already on some level that there won't be enough food to go around."

"So how are we getting in?" Dad asked.

"I don't know…"

"Roads are blocked, so we find another way," Jetta said. "Bike trails, the river, the train tracks…"

"The tracks," I said. "Right into downtown." I looked at the roadmap. "There's no closeup of Fargo on here."

"Well," Dad said, "what can you see?"

"Cross the Interstate. We'll hit the rail line about a mile and a half north of I-94. Then we drive beside the tracks all the way in."

"What if someone else has thought of this?" Jetta asked. "The tracks might be just as blocked as the roads."

"Won't be as blocked," I said. "And we gotta try something."

Dad took us to the road I'd suggested, 158th Avenue SE.

The bridge was clear, and we made it up to the Interstate.

And that's where we found the fleeing residents of Fargo, North

Dakota.

They were walking along the interstate, thousands of people, the luckier ones with tractors or bicycles or dirtbikes, or even riding lawnmowers. Some were pushing wheelbarrows and a few were on horseback.

They'd taken all four lanes of the highway, all traffic heading west out of the city.

"Your great-great-grandfather fought in World War 2," Dad said. "He told me once that the biggest impediment to winning a war was the civilians getting in the way."

"You've told me that before," I said. "And that other story about dumping the planes in the ocean because they ran out of room to store them all." And I'd found it all so interesting I'd read up on it, and I'd even done my grade eight history project on the German invasion of Belgium, and how the British and French response to the German advance had been slowed considerably by the refugees blocking the roads.

Not that I'd ever let my father know that I'd been interested. That's not the kind of thing I'd tell him.

"The eastbound side isn't as busy," Jetta said. "I'll bet we could push through if we wanted."

"It's too risky," I said. "If we get stuck…"

"It's worse than that," Dad said.

"What do you mean?"

"We've seen the government response. A crowd of what could be zombies —"

"Probably all zombies," Jetta said.

"If they want to take them out," Dad said. "This is a great place to drop some bombs."

"We don't know what those bombs were for," I said. "I don't even want to consider the government doing that…"

"It's not about what we want, Seffy… it's about how far they'll go to try and stop this infection."

"It doesn't make a difference to the plan," I said. "We take the tracks."

"How do we know they won't just drop bombs on downtown Fargo?" Jetta asked.

"They might," Dad said. "My guess: this here… this is the low-hanging fruit. After they handle this… they might move on to something even worse."

I shuddered.

I knew that there was a good chance he was right.

13

POLICE ACTION

The rail line was quiet.

Two tracks running together, straight as an arrow lodged in a half-sister's lung.

With a service path along the north side, more dirt than gravel. But more than enough for our truck.

We headed east down the line, holding our breaths as we crossed the Maple River into the appropriately-named town of Mapleton.

There were cars abandoned in the middle of the streets, and several people in view. They watched us drive by with surprised looks on their faces.

"I guess no one else has been riding the rails," Jetta said.

"We're nowhere yet," Dad said. "The hard part hasn't started."

A few minutes later we were entering the edge of Fargo, the newest subdivisions on the West side of town. We were less than half a mile away from the interstate now, which made everyone a little uneasy.

We kept going.

Occasionally we'd run across refugees, most likely infected, but by the time they'd notice us we were already moving past.

As long as we kept moving...

We reached I-29, where the highway ran under the rail line. It was filled with people, but it didn't feel as packed as I-94 was past Mapleton.

"It isn't a bottleneck here," Dad said. "I imagine it's probably worse than I-94 up around Harwood... people thinking there might be help waiting in Grand Forks."

"Or stronger beer in Canada," Jetta said.

"Some people will be staying," I said. "Bugging in, as Lucas would call it."

"I don't want to run into those people," Dad said. "They'll be better armed than us. And probably a lot more hardcore."

After I-29 was the tractor plant.

I noticed right away that the tractors were no longer there.

"Probably a parade of stolen tractors heading out of town," Dad said. "I guess we saw a few from that overpass."

"But where did they get the fuel?" Jetta asked.

"A lot of siphoning. I remember having to do that back in the day…"

"Back in the day when you would steal other people's gas?" I said.

"Pretty much. It's guys like me who made locking fuel doors standard."

"What's a fuel door?" Jetta asked.

"Doesn't matter," I said. "Moral of the story is that my father's a terrible human being."

"Thanks, Seffy," he said.

I rolled my eyes at him.

"This is where we met," Jetta said, pointing toward the service station with the hand soap shortage. "Do you… do you think Leona's still there?"

"I don't know," I said. "If she… changed as much as Iris and Beth did… she probably didn't just stay in one place."

I thought about Errol.

Would he have wandered off, looking for someone to bite? Or would he have stayed at the shop, hoping that his father or uncle would find their way back?

Or would he have come looking for me?

That was stupid.

Errol wouldn't be in control anymore.

It's not like the infection had some skeevy connection to me that I couldn't seem to shake off.

Even if Errol was out there, or Leona, or my Mom… Iris had to come first.

The rail lines were getting more complicated, with the little track beside jumping from one side to the other, and with freight cars starting to fill up the area.

I started to wonder if it was time to try our luck on the streets.

We'd have to do it soon, since we were only a few blocks away from downtown. The lab was a ways north on Broadway; we'd have to turn left off the tracks just after the old train station, if I'd remembered it right.

But the tracks were blocked up ahead, by a couple of semi trailers between two railside warehouses.

We hadn't even made it across University Drive.

"A roadblock," I said.

"On the track?" Dad asked. "I don't get it."

"Some kind of perimeter or something… something meant to keep us out."

"Then let's keep out," Jetta said. "And go around."

Dad jerked the wheel to the left.

We drove through a field full of large pipes, toward 1st Avenue North.

"Keep an eye out," Dad said. "If someone's put up a roadblock, there's a chance they're watching us right now."

"If they're uninfected," Jetta said, "maybe they can give us some help."

"They won't know we're not infected," I said. "They'll assume we are."

"How do we know that?"

"Because that's what we'd think if we ran into anyone," Dad said.

I didn't argue with that; he was right.

People might shoot mindless zombies with blank stares and bloodshot eyes. They might know enough to get them in the head to kill them, not realizing that there is still someone trapped inside. But zombies who look and talk like everyone else…

Besides… if the uninfected people were winning the war, there'd be dead zombies with headshots littering the streets.

I hadn't seen a single body on the way into town. The only life we'd seen was trying its best to get out of town. In a surprisingly orderly fashion. No bodies there.

After two very messed up days, the lack of corpses could now be taken as a *bad* sign.

Dad didn't slow down as he cranked the steering wheel again, bringing us onto the street.

"Nothing ahead," he said.

"Why no roadblock?" I asked. "Why block the tracks if you've left the road wide open?"

"I don't know."

I didn't, either.

"We should get off here as soon as we can," I said. "Head farther north, away from the tracks."

"Why?" Jetta asked.

"Dad's right," I said. "Someone has to be watching us."

We were nearing another intersection. We could turn left there.

Head north, with one more set of tracks to cross before we could reach the lab.

Something hit the front tires.

The truck swung to the left, right across the road and up over the curb, slamming against a couple of trees. Jetta's head rammed hard into the dash, her body hitting me about as bad.

Her head fell backward, landing in my lap.

I wrapped my arm around her, bracing for what was coming next.

Dad slammed the gearshift into reverse, backing us away from the trees.

He jammed it into drive.

We were barely moving, bumping as we went, like crossing another muddy field.

I felt Fender nuzzling against my feet.

"Tires are out," Dad said. "At least the front two. I'll keep us moving for as long as I can."

"What the heck was that?" I asked.

"Spike strips... didn't see them in time."

Jetta looked up at me. She had a gash in her left temple.

She gave me a little smile.

"Thanks, Curlicue," she said. "Such a soft place to land."

"Thank the nacho cheese dispenser at the Kum & Go," I said. "I guess that stuff saves as many lives as it destroys. Just like my dad."

"Not funny, Seffy," he said.

I heard the sound of a police siren.

It pulled out onto First off the sidestreet ahead.

"We've got a problem," Dad said.

"The police?" Jetta said.

"That's where that spike strip came from," I said. "For some reason I don't think there's a good cop in the mix here."

"Any ideas?" Dad asked. "Can't outrun them, obviously."

"I think we're screwed," I said.

"So… pulling over, then…"

He drove toward the curb, bumping it with the front tire.

"They'll expect us to be armed," he said. "So keep your hands out."

"Like up?" Jetta asked.

"Maybe not up… it's not like we're giving up."

"Could have fooled me," I said.

The police car stopped behind us, half out to the left.

It felt just like a traffic stop, like that time Grandpa Schmidt had been pulled over on I-29 for going too slowly.

Two police officers got out of the car. Both men, and both wearing what looked more liked tactical response gear than the usual police outfits.

They'd upgraded when things had gone bad.

One of the officers stayed back by the front bumper, his gun already drawn on my father's location. The other slowly walked up to the driver's side of the grain truck.

He had his right hand down near his holster.

He stood back from my father's open window, practically standing in the middle of First Avenue North.

I noticed that he wasn't wearing a nametag. Fargo Police are supposed to wear nametags.

Fender was growling as much as I'd ever heard before. Like Lucas-level growls. You'd think given my father's past driving, the dog would be used to the occasional traffic stop.

"No driving allowed," the cop said. "Grain trucks or otherwise."

"I didn't know," Dad said. "Network's been down most of the day."

"Step out of the truck."

"All of us?" Jetta asked.

The cop shot a look over to her. "Just him," he said.

Dad slowly pulled on the door handle.

The cop stepped farther back as my father opened the door and climbed down. He was keeping a good five feet of buffer.

"I'm not going to bother asking for ID," the cop said. "You look like you're just trying to look out for your girls."

My father nodded.

"Sorry about the spike strips," the cop said. "Been reports of marauders in nav-stripped vehicles."

"Marauders?" my father said. "Not zombies?"

"You mean infected."

"Yes."

"We don't call them zombies. We take this a little more seriously around here."

"So no infected?"

"Been reports of both."

"And out of the two…"

"There's no need to comment on everything I say."

My father decided on another nod.

"I need to search your vehicle," the cop said.

"Search for what?"

"For evidence of looting or any other marauder type of activity."

"We have supplies," Dad said, "and a shotgun. But they're ours. Taken from our own houses."

"And this is your truck?"

"This is not my truck, no."

"That's evidence of looting right there, isn't it?"

"I don't know… maybe?"

I didn't know what to do. I knew enough about how life works to know that opening my big mouth wasn't going to help my father in any way… I knew that whatever was happening here, it wasn't a police officer looking to help out some local taxpayers.

And I knew that they wouldn't be too happy once they found the taped up captives lying in the back of the truck. It would pretty much blow the "we're not marauders" argument right out of the water.

"What do we need to do?" Jetta asked.

I slammed my knee against hers.

"We've got supplies," she said, still talking for some reason.

The cop glanced over to her before looking back at my father. "Get down on your knees," he told him. "Hands on your head."

My father complied, lowering himself down.

The cop walked over to the driver's side window.

"I see that shotgun," he said. "I don't want to see either of you ladies get close to it." He took a good, long look at Jetta, and then at me. "You girls don't look like sisters."

"I'm Canadian," Jetta said.

"That explains the mouthiness."

"Really?" I said, forgetting the situation.

"With cops, yeah," he said.

"What do you want us to do?" Jetta asked.

"What are you asking me?"

"Just tell us what you want, officer. Supplies, our shotgun… something else…" She nodded over to me.

I felt like I was being volunteered for something.

The cop turned away from the cab window.

He walked back to my father, closing the gap.

"If you're infected," he said to him, "my partner will shoot and kill you."

"I'm not infected," Dad said. "Shouldn't you guys be with your families right now?"

"My family's fine," the cop said. "I know how to keep them safe."

He pulled out a set of plasticuffs.

He brought my father's wrists together and locked them into the cuffs, pulling his hands behind his back.

"Stay on your knees," the cop said. "Don't move from this spot."

"What are you going to do to those girls?" Dad asked.

"Don't talk."

The cop walked back over to the window.

"You," he said, pointing at me. "Get out of the truck."

I slowly climbed out the passenger side door.

My handgun was still under the bench.

I put my hands on my head.

I started walking around the front of the truck.

"Wait," Jetta said, "you're choosing her?"

"I'm not choosing anyone," the cop said.

"Come on…"

"Stop talking."

"You don't like me?"

He sighed, exasperated enough with Jetta to have let his guard down a little.

It was like she had some kind of superpower. Jetta the Disarmer.

"Seriously, what's wrong with me?" Jetta asked. "Just tell me."

The cop didn't answer.

"Seriously," Jetta said again.

The cop gave another sigh. "I like brunettes, alright?"

"I'm a brunette."

"You're more dark-haired."

"Dark-haired *is* brunette."

"Jetta," I said. "Not now, okay?"

"What does your partner think?" Jetta asked. She stuck her head out the open driver's side window. "You have an opinion, officer?"

I didn't know how to stop her. "Jetta…"

"I don't have all day," the first cop said. He started walking toward me. "I'll take you to the backseat, alright?"

Like I was somehow a willing participant.

Maybe he'd convinced himself of that.

"What about me?" Jetta said again. "I'm not freaking chopped liver, you know."

"What the hell is wrong with her?" the cop said.

I guess he was asking me.

"She's a little competitive," I said. "Always been that way."

"And doesn't know when to shut up."

He wrapped an arm around my waist and started guiding me back toward the police car.

"Don't you dare touch her," my father said.

"I'm already touching her," the cop said. "Now shut up and maybe you'll all live through this."

We reached the second officer at the front of the patrol car. "You should cuff her," he said. "Just in case."

"I'll be fine," the first cop said.

"What if I'm a zombie?" I asked. "Wouldn't I… just take a bite?"

"If you were a zombie you wouldn't be talking to me right now, would you?"

He didn't know.

He opened the back door of the cruiser.

He gently lowered me in, probably more out of habit than kindness.

He put me on my knees, squeezing me down onto the narrow space between the hard white bench and the plastic and plexiglass divider.

And he climbed in behind me, leaving the door wide open.

"Get back in the truck," someone said.

It was the other police officer.

He didn't sound particularly panicked.

I assumed that meant he was talking to Jetta.

"I'm a brunette, right?" I heard her say.

"He's not going to hurt her," I said to the cop beside me, "right?"

"She'll be okay," he said, like he didn't mean it. Or care in any way.

And I kinda wished I was a zombie right then.

So I could bite it off.

He took off his duty belt, tossing it down by my knees.

Then undid the belt on his pants.

I'd never been involved in that kind of thing. I'd never even seen one outside of some very ill-advised messages on my phone.

I heard something, a gasp maybe… it took a few seconds to realize what it was.

The sound of someone choking.

"He's hurting her," I said. "You need to stop him."

"I don't care what he does," the cop said. "And you shouldn't, either. You've got one job here, alright?"

I heard the door to the grain truck open.

That made him look, too.

"Holy hell," he said.

He reached for his duty belt.

I grabbed it first.

I reached for the car door behind me.

No handle.

He grabbed for the duty belt.

He started pulling.

I wasn't going to win out.

I knew that once he had his pistol he'd probably just shoot me. Those plastic back seat benches in police cruisers aren't that hard to clean up.

I dropped the belt.

And took a big honking bite out of his forearm.

That made him let go of the belt, too.

I shoved him back.

He fell back onto the floor, his head falling right out the open door.

I grabbed the duty belt.

I scrambled right over him, onto the street.

And kept moving, lifting myself off my knees as I went.

I saw Jetta, standing over the other cop, who was on his rear, his legs sprawled out and kicking.

I saw his gun a good three feet away.

Jetta had wrapped her belt around his neck. She was pulling it tight, probably not enough to cut off all of his air, but enough to keep him down.

My father came out of the truck, his hands unbound.

And holding the shotgun.

He walked over to Jetta and the cop on the pavement.

He picked up the officer's handgun, shoving it unceremoniously into his pants.

"You're okay?" he asked me.

"Yeah," I said. I held out my stolen duty belt, its gun still holstered.

"You need to strap that on," he said.

I nodded.

I hooked the belt around, just above my hips. The last loop available kept it from hanging all that low. I guess they have plenty of officers with smaller waists than me.

"The other cop," I said.

"I don't see him," Dad replied.

I looked over.

He wasn't on the ground by the cruiser.

"You have his gun," Dad said.

"A gun... but he might have something else."

"Like a baton?"

And then someone opened the trunk of the police car.

Dad started running, toward the back of the cruiser.

I heard a grunt.

And the slamming of the trunk.

I pulled the pistol out from my duty belt.

It didn't feel anything like a shotgun, but I got that the principles were generally the same.

I pointed it at the cop under Jetta.

"Let him go, Jetta," I said.

"You sure?" she asked.

"You're going to have to let go sometime."

She whipped the belt off the cop's neck.

He dropped, falling onto his back, clasping his throat with both hands.

I started backing up, keeping my gun on the officer on the pavement.

Jetta followed me.

We walked toward the trunk of the cruiser.

I didn't know what had happened back there.

I had to keep my eye on the man on the pavement.

And hope for the best when it came to my Dad.

There was a shot.

"Dad!" I yelled.

Another shot.

"Jetta," I said, "can you see what's happening?"

"Not really," she replied. "And I don't want to go over there."

"We're both going over there. Just... slower than I'd like."

The cop on the ground sat up, still holding onto his throat.

"Stay down," I said to him. "I have better aim than you'd expect."

The cop just stared.

I wasn't sure how much damage Jetta had done to him.

He didn't get up.

I kept stepping back, toward the cruiser.

"He's in the trunk," my father said.

"What?" I wasn't sure I'd heard him right.

"I put him in the trunk."

"How the heck did you do that?" Jetta asked. "He totally should have been able to take you."

"Thanks," Dad said. "I guess he didn't see it coming. That and I know how to body check."

"So the gunshots," I said.

"He's got something in there... sounds like a shotgun. Just stay clear of the trunk. In case he shoots again. Or pulls the emergency release."

"We need car keys," Jetta said.

"We're stealing a police car?" I asked.

"I don't think we have time to find a Plan B."

"The other cop was driving," Dad said. "You guys check for the keys. But be careful."

"What about you?" I asked.

"I'll watch the trunk."

We walked back to the cop on the pavement.

He reached into his pocket.

I pointed the gun at his chest.

He slowly pulled out a set of car keys. He gasped. And then he started to talk. "Just… just d-don't… don't tell any... how… how easy this was for you."

I could barely hear him.

He threw the keys toward us.

Jetta bent down and picked them up.

"You should drive," she told me. "I'll be in charge of picking the music."

"We won't have room for everyone in there," I said.

"I'll sit on your lap," Jetta said. "There'll be enough room."

"We'll need my Dad to help load them… one of us needs to hold onto the gun."

"No guns for me… I'm not much of a heavy lifter, or laborer of any kind, but it's better than the alternative."

We stepped back toward the cruiser. I kept my gun aimed.

"We'll blare something girly," she said. "It'll drive him right out of that trunk. You know the stereo's usually louder back there."

My father came up to meet us at the door of the police car.

"You girls get in," he said. "I'll take care of that cop by the truck."

Jetta looked over at me.

She'd expected me to say something, some high-minded declaration that we shouldn't kill anyone.

But I wanted them dead.

Both of them.

"You're not going to kill him," Jetta said, "are you?"

"Just restrain him," Dad said. "Cuff him, tape him to a post. So you girls get inside, alright?"

Jetta opened the back door and started climbing in.

"What are you doing?" I asked her.

"Getting in," she said. "I've never been in the back of one of these before… I guess I'm not as worldly as you are, Curlicue."

She settled in on the middle of the bench.

"I don't think police cruisers have girly music," I said as I got into the driver's seat. "Or any music."

I turned the ignition, just to be sure. The engine started.

"We need something," Jetta said. "Some kind of torture for our buddy in the back. Something to make him want to rip right through the back seat…"

The seat.

All there was between him and Jetta.

Hard plastic.

It wouldn't stop a shotgun shell.

"Jetta… get out of the back seat," I said.

She moved to the door behind me. "I can't open the door." She shimmied across the bench to the other side.

I heard the gunshot.

The side window behind me shattered.

I waved for Jetta to get low.

She squeezed in between the bench and the divider.

I opened my door and climbed out.

He didn't try for me. I figured it was the angle, but I couldn't be sure. Maybe he knew I'd get closer to him, that he'd get a better chance.

If I opened the back door to let her out, he'd know just when and where to shoot.

I'd expected my father to come back.

But he hadn't.

I'd have to come up with something.

I walked around the front of the cruiser, trying to make as little noise as possible against the pavement. I approached the back of the car from the passenger side.

I saw the two holes in the trunk from his first couple of shots.

If he could shoot out, I could shoot in.

But how would I know if I'd shot him? It's not like people scream out "okay, ya got me" when you lodge a bullet in their stomach.

I didn't know, but my best guess was that I had somewhere between six and a dozen bullets in the pistol I was holding.

I could shoot three or four and wait.

Eventually I'd have to open that trunk.

And I'd managed to leave the keys in the ignition.

I aimed the gun at the lid of the trunk, making my best guess at where his chest would be.

I took a breath.

The trunk flew open. He'd hit the release.

I fired the gun.

He was out of the trunk, running down the street.

He was trying to get away from us.

And hadn't even taken the shotgun with him.

"Shoot him," Jetta screamed.

I kept the gun trained on him.

I watched as he disappeared around a small shed.

I opened the back door of the car and held out my hand.

Jetta didn't take it as she climbed out.

"You shouldn't have let him go," she said.

"You just asked my dad not to kill the other one."

"I never asked him not to."

"Oh… well, okay."

I saw that Dad was on his way back.

He'd cuffed and taped the cop to a streetlight, just as he'd said.

"You girls okay?" he asked.

"Where were you?" I said. "You should have come back."

"You did alright, Seffy."

"You're not supposed to say that, Dad."

"Why not?"

"Because I'm your daughter. Because you shouldn't want me putting myself in harm's way, shooting a gun at people who want to shoot me back…"

"It's okay, Seffy… you did just fine."

"Forget it," I said. "We need to transfer them to the back of the cruiser."

"He might come back," Jetta said. "We'll need to watch for him."

"He won't be coming back," Dad said. "But we'll keep an eye out, just in case."

He had something close to a smile on his face.

I didn't see how that was remotely possible.

⤚

We moved Iris first, Dad and I carrying her while Jetta kept watch.

She still had a pulse; I hadn't wanted to check, but there was no point in moving her into the cruiser if she was already dead.

Beth wasn't doing much better; it had been less than an hour since her last snack, but she looked like she hadn't eaten in a week.

The only one who looked healthy was David, aside from the blank stare coming from his bloodshot eyes.

The infection had kept him alive, and hadn't reached the point where it would pretend to be David.

For a moment I thought of the possibility that we'd lose both Iris and Beth, and that David would be the only one to pull through.

I couldn't think that way.

Jetta and I shared the passenger seat, with Fender sitting on my father's lap as if he honestly believed he was a chihuahua.

I turned on the overhead lights, but not the siren.

Dad turned north on 16th.

Three more turns and we were on Seventh, crossing the tracks without seeing any sign of life. That was the place where I'd first run into the infection.

We were close to the biomedical lab. We were almost there.

But I knew that we weren't really much closer to saving my sister

14

CROWD CONTROL

The crowd started just past the train tracks.

A mass of people... a crush of people, really, blocking the street. They were pushing into each other, trying to move farther down the road.

It was a crowd so far... not a mob, or some other group bent on messing things up... but I had a feeling that would be changing at any moment.

Once people realized that gentle nudges and tender pardons weren't getting them any closer to wherever they were going.

Some of them turned to see our flashing lights as we approached the rear. The people who looked at us seemed so normal, but I knew they weren't.

I was pretty sure. Sure I was looking into an entire city of infected people. They'd massed into one big group, like Lucas had said.

I just didn't know why.

"How many are out here?" Jetta asked.

"Hundreds," I said.

"Maybe more," Dad said.

"But why?" Jetta asked.

"Something's up the road," I said. "Something that's drawing them together."

"But what?"

I thought about it. Seventh Street. Almost to University Drive. "Locavore Market," I said. "One full city block of grocery goodness."

"They think they're people," Dad said, his joke of the week, apparently. "Hungry people."

"This is going to get ugly... we need to get out of here."

"Turn around?"

"Yeah… turn around."

I heard a siren.

It wasn't from us.

"OMG," Jetta said. "Like OMFG."

"I see it," Dad said.

"Can't turn around," I said. "So we go through?"

"Drive through a crowd of people? Are you serious?"

"Wouldn't be the first time this week," Jetta said.

"Just go slow," I said. "People will get out of the way if we look like we know what we're doing. Like we have a reason to be here."

I flicked on the siren, too.

The crowd slowly began to part, slowly being too fast a word for it. It makes sense, since there's only so much room for someone to go when someone elses are frickin everywhere.

People in the crowd were pointing, gesturing, some of them cursing, but for the most part they seemed to buy into the notion that we had a reason to cut through.

I glanced out the rear view window.

The other police cruiser was doing the same thing, about six or seven car lengths behind. If it wasn't for the sheer danger of trying to push through a crowd unprotected, I was sure those cops would already be out of their cars and on their way to us on foot.

Once they closed in on us…

Some people in the crowd started banging on the windows.

"That's it," Jetta said. "They've tuned in to the idea that we're actually not cops."

"So that means we're the bad guys," Dad said. "With people tied up in the back seat."

"And with the good guys on our tail."

The banging started turning into rocking.

Dad was having trouble moving us forward at all.

"So what do we do now?" I asked.

"They're going to catch up," Jetta said.

"They won't get out of their car," Dad said. "Especially if they're not infected."

"Do you really think all these people are infected?" Jetta asked.

"If just one was infected they'd be chomping on everyone else," I said, close to a yell, in order to be heard over the noise of people trying to screw over our lives. "So what's more likely, that not one person in a crowd of hundreds is infected, or that every single one's gone and gotten bitten by this point? We keep moving, start pushing through a little harder if we have to. Once we're through this... well, then we'll have a new problem to deal with."

"We won't make it through this," Dad said. "We're barely moving. This isn't a tank."

"So this is it?" Jetta asked. "We sit here and wait for them to break in and bite us?"

"Or we get out and they bite us," I said.

"There's got to be some way out," Dad said. "Seffy... this is kind of your department..."

I didn't have an answer. How could there even be an answer?

"There must be a crowd of *zombie* zombies out there somewhere," Jetta said. "I wonder where all those ones are, the ones who haven't gotten all smart and sophisticated."

"I guess that would be worse," I said. "Those guys back at the farm just kept coming at us."

"These ones might not," Dad said.

"If we promise to buy them a drink?" Jetta asked.

"No... if we make them think that trying to bite us will get them shot in the head. They're not invincible, and they know it."

"So we start shooting," I said.

Dad nodded. "We've got three guns, right?"

"I've never used a gun," Jetta said.

"Anyone can use a handgun, Jetta," Dad said. "That's why you get five-year-olds shooting their little sisters by accident."

"Wow, Dad," I said, "that's a little dark."

Dad handed me the handgun beside his seat.

I held it up for Jetta to see.

"Safety," I said, pointing at the switch. "Like a lightswitch, really. On, off..."

"Yeah..." Jetta said.

"And you know how a trigger works." I passed her the gun, handle first. "So the moment you've stopped shooting, that safety goes on. I've grown too fond of your broken faucet to see you shoot off your bottom jaw."

"Thanks."

"You'll need to use the shotgun, Seffy," Dad said. "Confined quarters."

"I can do it."

"Pass me the one on your belt."

I took my pistol and gave it to him.

I picked up the shotgun from beside Fender's butt.

Dad waved the handgun at the people outside his door.

They stepped back, giving him a tiny pocket of space.

He opened the window.

He pointed the gun low and fired, aiming for the legs.

"You guys, too," he said.

"I don't have the balls for this," Jetta said. "I'm more of a distraction than a weapon."

"Come on, Jetta," I said. "We need you."

She shook her head. "No... I can't do this." She held out the handgun for me.

My hands were full.

I opened my window and shoved the barrel of the shotgun out into the crowd.

And a man grabbed it.

He pulled.

I pulled, too.

Jetta grabbed the stock.

A hand reached into the crack in the window.

And started pulling on the pane, rocking it back and forth.

"They're trying to pull it off the track," Dad said. "Trying to rip it right out."

"Jetta," I said, "do something."

She jabbed her elbow at the hand. The man who owned it cursed her out.

Then I saw the baseball bat.

The window cracked, but didn't shatter.

But it was enough for the man with the bat to reach in and start pulling the window pane apart.

I lost my grip on the shotgun.

It disappeared through the window.

"Dad," I said.

"I see it," he said. "I'm going to open my door. You girls need to climb over and out this side."

"Then what?"

"Then we take this show on the road. We've still got two guns."

"And three people tied up in the back."

I heard Jetta scream.

They had her shoulders, two of the men, pulling her against the broken window glass. Trying to pull her out of the car.

I pulled off my jacket.

I threw it over the back of her head, trying to cover her neck.

And then I grabbed both of her arms and yanked.

I couldn't pull her away.

I found the handgun she'd had, lying on the seat beside her.

I picked it up.

I aimed for one of the men, for the bridge of his nose.

I fired.

One down.

I aimed for the other.

But he'd already let go.

Jetta wrapped her arms around me.

I started climbing over my father, pretty much dragging Jetta with me.

Fender did his best to trip us up, sticking his head between my legs.

Dad opened the door.

I climbed out, Jetta right behind me.

There was still a pocket there, maybe ten feet around us.

I held up the gun, hoping to keep that buffer.

Dad pulled open the back door.

"We can't take all of them," he said.

"We'll take Iris," Jetta said.

Two women started getting too close.

I shot one in the stomach.

And hoped that no one around us was counting bullets.

I knew that someone had just grabbed our shotgun with however many rounds. They could shoot us, then bite us. Mission accomplished. Infection passed to three new hosts.

But they weren't lunging, not like before.

Those men had grabbed at Jetta, but they'd been trying to pull her out. They didn't just go for the neck, or start biting her arm like that guy in the orange jumpsuit had done to that women in the little blue car.

They'd wanted her out of the police cruiser; getting her infected didn't even seem important to any of them.

Why had they wanted her?

"Seffy," Jetta said, poking my shoulder. "Come on."

"What?"

"You and me… we're taking Iris. We gotta move…"

Dad fired another shot into the crowd.

Fender stood his ground and barked.

I guess that might be intimidating to some people.

People who don't *know* Fender and his inner puppy.

The space around us was shrinking.

I followed Jetta to the back of the car.

She grabbed Iris by the shoulders and started dragging her out.

I put the handgun back into the holster on my duty belt.

I reached down and took my sister by the legs.

"I can't shoot if we're carrying her," I said.

"You need to take her," Dad said.

"I know that."

He reached in and pulled Beth out.

"You're not going to cover us?" I asked him.

"I can do both," he said. He threw his wife up over his right shoulder, steadying her with his left hand. He waved the gun at the crowd. "No one needs to die," he called out. "Just give us some space."

The buffer kept shrinking.

Some people had started screaming at us. Calling us names, yelling at us to let our captives go.

It seemed like they knew, not just that we weren't infected, since that seemed to be common knowledge among them somehow, but that Iris and Beth were just like them.

They could tell who had it and who didn't. From a distance.

I had no idea why.

"We need to move," Dad said.

"I can carry her," Jetta said to me. "Just like your father's doing."

"You sure?" I asked.

"Yellow belt… Judo… remember?"

I helped her get Iris up and over her shoulder.

She stumbled a little, but she seemed okay. She started pushing toward the crowd.

I pulled the gun out of its holster.

And waved it around.

There was maybe two feet of space between us and a horde of angry and frightened people. All infected.

We had to keep pushing through.

I heard a gunshot from behind us.

I turned to see my father, Beth still over his shoulder.

He and Fender were following behind us, but I could see that we were slowly getting separated, our little bubbles of space growing apart.

It wouldn't be long before I wouldn't be able to see him at all.

Something hit me.

I fell onto the pavement, scraping my knees.

I felt at least a half dozen hands grabbing at me, pulling at me.

It felt like they were going to tear me apart.

I screamed for Jetta.

I couldn't see her.

Someone took my gun.

I was starting to lose a shoe.

I heard the fabric ripping on my shirt.

The worst was when a clump of my hair got pulled clean out of my scalp.

But they hadn't bitten me.

I heard someone scream, not far from me.

It was probably Jetta.

They were tearing her to pieces, too.

"Someone just bite me already," she yelled.

She screamed again.

"Jetta," I said. "Jetta…"

"Just bite me!"

I didn't hear anything else from her.

Someone pulled me up off the ground.

I was up on someone's shoulders, fireman's carry winning the girl. I couldn't see who it was. All I could see were khaki pants and brown workboots.

I could hope it was him. I could hope.

The crowd parted as I was carried through, people moving aside much faster than they'd ever done for the police car or for my father with a gun.

I was thrown down in the back of a pickup truck, face first, hitting the bedliner hard enough that I felt a little dazed.

I could see through the corner of my eye, two men in the back of that truck with me, with masks on their heads. Masks… or helmets. Like the welding helmets from the shop. But I remembered the ones in the shop being a little more colorful.

They both had rifles.

They weren't looking at me.

I decided to stay put. Lying facedown in a pickup truck seemed better than some of the alternatives I'd been presented with so far.

I heard more gunfire, off in the distance. I didn't think it was from my father; it felt too far away.

I didn't feel like I'd see him again.

I closed my eyes. I wanted to drift away from everything, to just fall asleep and wake up long after, maybe with some grotty zombie-bots rewiring the Persephone… I didn't care. I just wanted to be done.

The crowd sounded different away from the police cruiser; people were screaming, yelling, shoving — I hadn't thought shoving would be something so obvious and loud — and they were busy, pushing toward what I still assumed was the supermarket, trying to grab what-ever supplies were still unlooted.

It seemed like a piss-poor strategy; several hundred — or thou-sand — people trying to pick through one grocery store, no matter how big… if I'd been scavenging, I'd be hitting smaller outlets, even people's houses. Every farm between here and Bismarck would prob-ably have ten months' worth of preserves in their basement.

I heard a thump on the truck bed.

I opened my eyes and turned to see.

Iris.

Another thump.

Jetta.

If it was Errol, I doubt he could have carried them both.

"I'm okay," Jetta said quietly. "No bites. You?"

I nodded. "No… no bites."

The truck started moving.

Not slowly, either.

The crowd gave it plenty of room.

After a couple of minutes we'd passed through the crowd.

Not that I could see anything; I'd kept to the bed of the truck, face to the side, looking over at Jetta, trying not to see just how lifeless Iris had gotten.

I worried that if I looked too closely, I'd see that she wasn't even breathing anymore.

How long do you get before brain death? How long until my sister was gone forever?

I couldn't deal with it.

I looked the other way.

One of the men was looking us over, helmet moving back and forth, that look that seems harmless enough on a Saturday night but completely uncomfortable in the back of a pickup.

Probably my first time hoping I was being ogled by Errol's skeevy Uncle Pat.

"W-where are we going?" I asked.

No response.

"Please," Jetta said.

"Just stay down and stay safe," the man with the wandering visor said.

It sounded like Uncle Pat. Or at least I wanted it to be him.

"I don't feel like things are going so good for us," Jetta said.

I heard the man chuckle.

"Why is that funny?" Jetta asked. "What the hell are you planning to do to us?"

"Relax," the man said. "It's okay."

"Are you... infected?" I asked.

"We're all infected, Seffy. You guys are the only ones left who aren't."

Seffy. He knew my name. It had to be them. Errol and Uncle Pat. And the other man... maybe Errol's father...

Unless that wasn't it. Unless he'd simply heard Jetta say it back in the crowd...

"Why haven't you bitten us?" I asked.

"Seffy," Jetta said, "I'd rather you didn't ask people to bite us."

She'd asked them to bite her like five minutes ago...

"Just relax, girls," the man said again. "It's going to be okay."

"Don't be offended," Jetta said, "but there's no way we're going to believe you on that."

The truck turned left. Like up a driveway.

And stopped.

"Is she going to be okay?" someone asked.

No one answered.

He spoke again. "Persephone…"

I looked up.

Another welding helmet. It was Errol's welding helmet. Right?

My eyes were getting blurry.

But it had to be him.

"Is Iris going to be okay?" he asked.

"She's dying," I said. "Or… or dead." I started to cry. As much as you can when you're exhausted.

"What do we need to do?"

"What?"

"What can we do to help her?"

"I… I don't know…"

He reached down and ran his hand through my hair. He cupped the back of my head.

I felt like that was when he should be biting me. I guess the welding helmet was a good thing for both of us.

"The hospital?" he asked. "Can they help her?"

"The hospital," I said. I wasn't really saying… anything, really. I felt tired, dazed… done…

"Seffy… come on… talk to me."

"Sanford Biomedical Lab," Jetta said. "Over on Broadway, apparently. Seffy thinks we can zap the bots and kill the infection. That's the only way we save her sister."

"Broadway…"

"Can you get us there?"

"Probably. I've been very persuasive lately."

"What… what does that mean?" I asked.

"I'll tell you later," he said. "We gotta get moving."

He hopped out of the back of the truck.

I wanted to say something about my Dad.

But I didn't. I didn't say anything.

I was just so tired.

And then Errol was gone.

We started moving a few seconds later.

Jetta helped me sit up, leaning me up against some boxes of something.

"You need to stay with us," she said. "We need to see this through."

"I know," I said. "I'm just…"

"You look the way I feel, Seffy. You see, I still look really good. But you… you look like dog poop."

That made me chuckle. A little.

"You girls should drink," the other man in the back said. He did sound like Errol's father.

A metal water bottle rolled over and knocked my elbow.

Jetta crawled around Iris and picked it up.

She gave it to me.

I took a drink.

Then she had some, too.

"Who was that guy?" she asked me.

"Errol," I said.

"He's in love with you."

"Well, duh," the alleged Uncle Pat said.

"I don't know," I said. "He's… he's infected, so… it's not like the infection loves me."

"The infection seems to want to save Iris," Jetta said. "I think that has something to do with you."

"I don't know, Jetta. I don't know."

I turned away from her and closed my eyes.

I'm pretty sure I fell asleep.

&

I felt something nudging me in the stomach.

And I had a headache.

That was not surprising.

And my crotch still hurt like a *sonofagoat*.

Something was still nudging me.

I opened my eyes.

It was a black leather boot.

"Time to get up and at 'em, bitches," a woman's voice said.

I followed the leg up to the belt buckle, two crossed handguns and "Pistol Packin' Mama". And up to the gray Winnipeg Jets hoodie.

"Yeah," Leona said, "Errol and I found each other, and now

we've found the two of you."

"You're not Leona," Jetta said. "Don't start acting like you are."

"Whatever, *stoopid*."

I noticed that Iris was gone.

"I think they just took her," Jetta said. "I... I just had my eyes closed for a second..."

Leona hopped down from the back of the pickup truck.

I followed.

Jetta seemed to hesitate.

"You might as well trust her," I said. "Because everyone else in this truck has held off so far on ripping our necks open."

I held out my hand.

She took it and jumped down.

We followed Leona into the adequately-labeled front door of the four-or-so-storey Sanford Biomedical Lab — four storeys if you didn't count the ridiculous solar tower they'd stuck onto the top during the latest Persian Gulf crisis — past the two men I was pretty sure I still officially worked for, wearing their welding helmets and holding their rifles, and apparently taking on the job of guarding the entrance.

I noticed a yellow "tornado shelter" sign right beside the door. I wondered if anyone was hiding down in the basement, waiting for the storm to pass.

The foyer was dark, not lit with anything, not even what I would have expected for emergency lighting. We wouldn't have much light at all once the sun set. We had maybe an hour and a half before the place was pitch black.

The lab looked like it had been shut down for days. Not like it had been overrun, or ransacked... it was like everyone who'd been there had decided to take the rest of the week off.

"Where's Errol?" I asked.

"He's moving Iris to an isolation room," Leona said. "He wants you to come in and help him with the scans."

I nodded.

"Errol's a good guy," Leona said. "You don't give him a fair shake."

"I don't want to tell you how weird this is," I said. "I don't want to talk about any of this with you."

"Just making conversation, Seffy."

The way she was talking to me... it felt too familiar, like we'd known each other for years. It was starting to feel like I'd known Jetta for nearly as long, but definitely not Leona...

She led us up a flight of stairs, a flashlight in her hand being our only light.

"Errol brought her up this way?" I asked.

"She's not that heavy," Leona said.

"But up a dark staircase."

"Those welding helmets see better than we do."

"How did you find him?" Jetta asked.

"Who?" Leona said. "Errol?"

"Yeah... Errol... you just ran into some random guy and started hanging out?"

"It's hard to explain, really. We know things about each other."

"Like soulmates?"

"Like short wave transmissions."

"What?"

"It's hard to explain, Jetta. I said that, didn't I?"

We walked down a second dark hallway.

Leona reached a door with a big red stop sign displayed on a banner.

"This must be isolation," she said.

She opened the door.

"Oh god," she said.

I followed in behind her.

She was shining the beam on a man, strapped to an examination bed; his face was gaunt, his skin pale. He looked like Iris, but worse. For one thing, he was dead.

"This is the wrong room," Leona said. "I'm sorry." She sounded genuinely upset.

"Patient zero," I said. I saw the blood on his exam gown, just below his neck.

It wasn't from being bitten. It was from biting someone else.

"I think it spread from him," I said. "Might have taken a whole bunch of people here. Whoever got out probably won't be coming back."

"They knew," Jetta said. "They've known from the start."

"We don't know who got this info... we don't know if it ever left this building."

"We need to get to Iris," Leona said.

I nodded.

We left the room.

She took us to the next room. No banner on the door.

Inside were Errol and Iris, in what came close to complete darkness aside from Leona's flashlight. Errol was still wearing his welding helmet.

Iris was on the exam bed.

He hadn't bothered to strap her down.

He had a tube running up into her nostril.

"NG-tube," Errol said. "Leona had one for a while, back in junior high."

I didn't get how he'd know that. It seemed like an awkward subject for casual getting-to-know-your-fellow-zombie conversation.

I rushed over to Iris' side. "That's not something you just shove into someone's nose," I told him. "Let me help."

"It's okay, Seffy. I know how."

I shook my head. "You've done this before, have you?"

"I have," Leona said. "Used to put it in myself."

"So you should be doing it," I said.

"It's okay," Errol said. "I know how she used to do it."

I watched him for a few seconds.

The way he guided it in…

He seemed to really understand how, even though the Errol I knew steered well clear of hospitals and sick people.

I didn't try to stop him.

I heard Iris gurgle.

"Air from her stomach," Errol said. "She's alright."

I nodded. I trusted him. Despite his infection.

Once the tube was all the way in, Errol walked over to the counter beside the sink. He picked a small pouch.

He brought it over to Iris and hooked it to the tube. "Isosource," he said. "Same thing Leona was given when she came in."

"Okay," Jetta said, "that's enough. You guys are freaking me out. How the heck does he know about all that, Leona?"

"You said I wasn't Leona," Leona said. "Remember?"

"Shut up… well, don't shut up. Tell me why he knows so much about you."

"The bots," I said.

"What?" Jetta asked.

"It makes sense, doesn't it?" Leona asked. "If bots in one body can talk to each other, bots can sometimes communicate between bodies, if the bodies are... uh, close enough together."

"What?" I said.

"When I say I know about Errol," Leona said, "I mean that I *know*. I know about him, and you..."

"There's no him and me."

"*Yee-ouch*," Jetta said.

"I'm used to it," Errol said, almost like an afterthought. "It's going in... the Isosource is getting into her stomach... we'll see what happens next..."

He was focused on keeping Iris alive.

Which was obviously where I should have been focusing. Not that Iris wouldn't have been distracted by the total and complete weirdness of bots swapping people's life stories.

"It won't be enough nutrition," I said. "I know it won't be."

"It might be," Jetta said. "You don't really know what will happen. Maybe her body will adapt. Or something."

"It's fine," Errol said. "It's just temporary. Because you're going to find a cure, right?"

"Why are you helping us?" Jetta asked. "Aren't you the bad guys in all this?"

"No... we're not the bad guys. I'm still Errol Kimmern, journeyman plumber and casual board gamer. I'm just... something more, too."

"That's not true," I said.

"It's creepy," Jetta said. "Okay? I said it. I don't want to be around it."

"You're surrounded by it, Jetta," Leona said. "And it's only us and those two gun-crazed plumbers out front who are keeping you from being exactly the same as us."

"Why haven't you bitten us?" I asked. "If you're so happy with what you've become."

"Because I love you, Seffy," Errol said. "And I know you don't want it."

"You know I don't want you to be like this, either. I want to find a cure for all of you."

"I'm not thinking about that right now. Let's just think about Iris.

Just her."

"My father didn't make it out of that crowd," I said.

"I'm sorry."

I grabbed the stethoscope from the tray.

I hooked it to my ears and placed the diaphragm against Iris' heart.

I listened. I heard it beating.

"She's still alive," Errol said. "That's why I put the tube in."

"It's clear I don't actually know what I'm doing," I said.

"But you look good doing it," Jetta said. "Paging Doctor Hot-Piece-of-Tail."

"She's going to think you're flirting with her," Leona said. "People don't get what you're about."

"No," I said, "I get what she's about. Even if we haven't swapped any bot signals or anything."

"I did accidentally jab my face in Seffy's lady parts that one time," Jetta said. "So we might be engaged now."

I smiled. I felt like I was allowed to, even if Iris wasn't out of the woods. Even if my father and Beth were still missing. And the others...

"We need power," Errol said. "For the scanner." He nodded to a small box on the counter with a small glass lens coming out the side.

"Emergency generator's probably out," I said. "If we need to find fuel..."

He shook his head. "Don't get ahead of yourself, Seffy. They might have just shut it all down before they left."

"Maybe if they were still themselves," Jetta said. "Like, not infected."

"I'll go down and check," Leona said. "Come with me, Jetta. I'll be on lookout of whatever, and you can mess with the panels and stuff."

"This is sounding more and more like a horror movie... we all just split off, one by one."

"It's two by two," Leona said.

"Not if you're the killer."

"It's okay, Jetta," Errol said. "Leona would never hurt you."

"Says the other zombie in the mix."

"Jetta," I said, "we need to get the power back on."

She nodded. "If she bites me, I want you guys to kill her. Like in the head and everything."

She walked out of the room with Leona and the only source of light.

"I can't see anything," I said. I had my left hand against Iris' temple; I wasn't going to leave her again.

"Sorry," Errol said. "I didn't really think that through."

"So is this the secret weapon? The welding helmet?"

"Part of it." He held his arms out. "Oh. I guess you can't really see it."

"What?"

"Around my chest."

I looked closer. He'd strapped something around it... almost like hot dog wieners. "Fake dynamite sticks?"

"No... real dynamite sticks."

"You're joking."

"It's called blast fishing, and it's highly illegal. And I, for one, am glad my Uncle Pat still does it."

"You look like a terrorist."

"That's the point. People don't go near the guy with the big helmet and suicide vest. How do you think we were able to pull you out?"

I heard more gurgling from my sister.

"She's okay," Errol said. "Don't worry."

"I wanted to ask you..."

"Yes. I'll go to prom with you, Seffy."

"Funny. Why weren't they biting us?"

"That's my dad and my uncle out there —"

"No... that crowd of people. Infected people..."

"They're not mindless," Errol said. "Once we get past that first awkward stage with the zombie waddle, things start seeming a lot more normal."

"They were pulling us apart."

"They were trying to take you... like capture you."

"What? Why?"

"I don't know."

"But the biting... isn't it automatic? Iris wanted to bite me..."

"Are you sure about that?"

"She went at Lucas."

"Who the heck is Lucas?"

"The douchebag who stole my father's rifle."

"That might be your answer right there. I don't think she would have ever bitten you, Seffy. Well, okay… she would have when she was first infected… but not now."

"But you don't know that for sure," I said.

"I'm just spitballing, Seffy. It's what I do."

I heard another gurgle from Iris.

"Thanks, Errol," I said. "You don't know how much this means to me."

Errol finally took his helmet off.

It was dark, but my eyes had adjusted enough to see his face.

He looked tired, a little weak.

A little too much like Iris.

He leaned over and kissed the side of my head, not far from my missing clump of hair.

I didn't say anything.

I didn't know what that kiss meant.

15

SPITBALLING WITH IRIS

The bombs started falling while we were standing in the dark.

I couldn't tell how far away they were; I'm sure Dad would have made a strong guess if he'd been there.

Every time one hit, the building shook.

"We should move to the basement," Errol said.

"Are you sure that's any safer?" I asked.

"It's reinforced... it's built to handle this kind of thing. Maybe not quite a bomb shelter... more a storm shelter..."

"Jetta hasn't come back... we don't know what's down there. And the equipment we need is up here."

"All it takes is one hit on this place, Seffy..."

"We'll be okay. They won't hit us."

"How do you know?"

"I'm just spitballing."

He nodded. "If they don't get that power back on, we'll need a Plan B."

"I don't have a Plan B."

"We can try to take the equipment with us, find a place to try again."

"That's a buttload of equipment," I said.

"I know."

I heard gunfire.

"They wouldn't fire unless people were trying to push into the building," Errol said.

"Your dad and uncle?"

"Yeah. We didn't think anyone would be interested in this place. It's not like people with a billion bots need aspirin."

And they weren't going to find any food outside of a few tupper-wares filled with rapidly-turning leftovers. So what was going on?

"They're looking for shelter," I said. "Whenever there's a tornado —"

"You head for the nearest storm shelter."

Errol pulled a small handheld radio out from his pant pocket. He pushed to talk. "Dad… Dad. Are you there? Are you okay?"

"We need to go," his father said over the handheld. "Too many coming this way."

"They want to get to the basement," Errol said.

"So we let them have it."

"No… Leona and Jetta are down there."

"Crap."

"Try to hold them off," Errol said. "For as long as you can."

"Five minutes, tops."

Errol shoved the radio back into his pocket.

"I need to go down there," he said.

"And leave us here?"

"You'll be okay. Just stay quiet and keep feeding her." He put on his welding helmet. "I love you, Persephone."

"Okay."

He left the room.

There was more gunfire.

And yelling.

Chaos.

I didn't think Jetta and Leona would get out of the basement.

Or that Errol and his father and uncle could get down there and fish them out, no matter how much dynamite they'd strapped to their bodies.

And I wouldn't know what was happening, since Errol had taken his handheld down with him.

And we wouldn't get power, not from the generator.

I wouldn't be able to scan my sister. I wouldn't be able to run the printer to find a treatment.

All I'd be able to do is feed her some more pouches of protein slime. Until we ran out. Or until some random zombie decided to come upstairs and bite me in the neck.

As an ending, the whole thing sucked.

I couldn't handle that.

Anything else seemed like a better way to end things.

Maybe a dramatic swan dive off the roof?

I almost laughed at the idea. Considering how the past twenty four hours had gone, I'd probably learn once I splatted on the pavement that the building just wasn't high enough to finish the job.

Maybe if I climbed up to the tip of the solar tower at the top…

The solar tower. That meant solar panels.

Electricity. Or something.

That wasn't really my department.

I moved my hand off my sister's temple, down to her shoulder. I gave it a squeeze. "Iris…"

A gurgle.

Then… a moan.

I started pulling the tube out of her nose, going as slow as I could stand.

She hadn't gotten enough… but if I could talk to her…

"Iris…"

No response that time.

I had the tube out.

She seemed stronger to me… not strong enough to do much of anything, probably not anywhere near ready to get up off the exam table.

But maybe strong enough to tell me what to do.

"Iris… I need your help."

She seemed to mumble something.

It seemed more deliberate than a moan or a gurgle.

"Iris… please."

She said something.

I couldn't hear it.

I dropped my head down near her mouth. And hoped she didn't have the urge or energy to rip out my throat.

"Iris…"

"Just… just stuff some money down my shirt," she whispered. "Then I'll be anything you want me to be."

I started to cry.

"I'm okay, Seffy. I'm still a zombie or whatever, but I'm okay."

"I need your help. There are solar panels on the roof…"

"AC or DC?"

"What?"

"How old are the panels?"

"Probably not very."

"Most panels in the past ten years or so have microinverters," she said. Her voice was quiet, halting, but she didn't seem unsure of any of it. "If that's the case, we can plug in directly."

"If we can get to the roof. And I can't carry you."

"I can't get to the roof," she said. "I feel like death after a... a booster shot of hepatitis."

"So what do I do, then?"

"It's pretty simple. You just need a whole heap of extension cords."

I went up to the roof first. There was no point in searching out and chaining together two floors' worth of electrical cords if I couldn't find a place up top to plug them in.

The door to the roof was locked.

I knew that I should have expected that.

I took a couple steps back.

I slammed my foot at the door, just above the lock.

It seemed to do *something*. Wiggle it somewhat...

So I kicked again.

Twice more.

The door came open.

I walked out onto the roof.

There were fires not far into the distance, maybe up at NDSU, to the northwest. And farther behind... I-29? If I had to guess, I'd say they were chasing the people, not the buildings.

Clearing out the disease.

I heard more planes in the distance. Sounded like they were coming, not going.

More bombs would be arriving, too.

More infection to clean up.

I looked down to the street.

Broadway was just like that parking lot, a crowd of people shoving each other. The only disasters we usually get in Fargo are blizzards and the occasional tornado.

No one's too worried about the blizzards, but the tornadoes are a different story. Every time there's a warning, you can bet that some people will shove their way into the first tornado shelter they can find.

Those kind of people were trying to force their way into the lab.

So many of them.

I had to get the power up. I had to make my sister better. So we could find our people and get the *hurr* out of there.

I found a green box next to the solar tower.

And another lock.

I wasn't equipped for that. I had nothing to pick it with, and I couldn't bash my way in.

You can pick locks with a bobby pin… I saw that in a movie once, where the plucky heroine was handcuffed in the back of a corrupt sheriff's police car — sounded so familiar — the best part of it was that there was nothing about the way she'd been wearing her hair to indicate that she'd even have a bobby pin on her.

I didn't have a bobby pin on me.

I wasn't getting into that box.

I started picturing that swan dive from the top of the solar tower.

And then I saw the outlet cover.

Two outlets right out the side of the box. Two regular outlets, for regular cords.

And I only needed one.

I had to test it out; I ran back down to the third floor and looked for something portable with a plug. I found a motion-activated thanksgiving turkey, one of those ones that are meant to gobble at you whenever you walk by.

I brought it up to the roof.

I plugged it in.

And walked in front of it.

"Gobble, gobble," the turkey said.

"Gobble, gobble, *motherlover*," I muttered. At the time I couldn't even remember where I remembered that from. Just that Iris had said it.

I ran back down the stairs to start pulling out extension cords. We didn't really use them at home; it's not like you'd bother when you've got the whole apartment set up for wireless.

But hospitals (and apparently research labs) don't do things that way, and for once, that was a really good thing. Every room had cords hanging from the ceiling, wrapped in reels like they were garden hoses.

Each one was a good hundred feet long.

But even still, I had a much longer chain than that to piece together.

Errol hadn't come back.

Neither had Jetta. Or Leona.

There was another round of bombs, to the southeast, I figured; maybe there'd been a crowd moving further into Minnesota, just trying to get away.

Each time, the building shook. Nothing that made me feel like the walls would come down around me.

But no bombs had fallen that close to where we were.

Not yet.

I had several hundred feet of extension cord running down to the isolation room. I plugged it into a shorter cord with a strip of outlets, where I'd plugged in the scanner on the counter. I ran one last cord from that power strip, out into the hall and over to the printer.

Over five hundred feet of power cords.

I wasn't sure that would even work, but then again, Iris had told me it would.

I went back to the isolation room.

I aimed the lens of the scanner toward Iris. I stepped out of the path of the beam. I pressed the button on top.

A reddish light swept across her, back and forth, three times.

That was it.

"Check the printer," Iris said, still barely loud enough for me to hear.

"I know," I said. I realized I actually sounded a little annoyed.

I went down the hallway to the printer. I was too busy to spend time wondering why Iris seemed ready to help me. Maybe the part that was Iris was just too curious not to have me run that scan.

I looked at the console on the printer.

Toxoplasma gondii. Unknown mutant.

The stupid cat poop parasite. Iris was loaded with it.
So effing redonkulous.
And with at least ten times the bots than should have been inside her. Like Dad had said, Iris was overclocked.
Too many parasites. Too many bots. Both replicating too quickly, eating away at my sister.
The console started displaying treatments, spitting out drugs and terms that I hadn't seen before. I knew enough to know that the printer was running through its simulations, trying out each known treatment against the unknown mutation.
I closed my eyes.
I said a prayer.
I waited a few seconds.
And then I checked.

Possible treatment.

And a big green button on the touchscreen.
The printer made a humming sound, quite a bit quieter than what you'd hear from blending a cocktail.
A small green light flashed at the output tray. The lid opened.
A printed-plastic vial.
A label that read "T. gondii mutant. Unverified treatment."
No FDA panel. The treatment had been printed right then and there.
Not that I had any way of testing it.
I brought the vial back to Iris.
"I don't know what this will do," I said.
"I don't want it, Seffy."
"What?"
"Think about it…"
"You're not really my sister."
"Yeah… I'm your stepsister."
"Uh… we'll get to that. But I need you to get better. This infection is killing you."
"It's part of me now. Don't you get it? I'm it and it's me. It's hard to explain… it's like… it's like now I'm perfect. Yeah… that's the

word, really. Perfection."

"Come on... that's not true."

"No... it's perfection. And true love. Iris and Toxo, sitting in a tree. K-I-S-S —"

"Shut up, Iris. Just... shut up."

She sat up. She started climbing off the exam table.

I grabbed her arm.

"I'll bite you," she said. Weakly.

And then she collapsed against me.

I barely kept her off the floor.

I helped her back onto the table.

I strapped her wrists. Then her ankles.

I took a syringe from the cabinet. I pulled back the plunger to the listed dose. I inserted the syringe into the vial.

"This... it's assault," Iris said. "You're assaulting me, Seffy."

I drew the liquid into the syringe.

I found a vein in Iris' arm.

I injected the needle.

"Well, ouch," Iris said. "You'd make a terrible nurse."

"Good thing I can't afford the tuition."

I ran another scan.

"It's no different," Iris said as the beam swept across her body. "It didn't work."

I ran over to the printer.

Treatment successful.

But the parasites were still there. The count was lower, but by maybe five percent.

Successful... just not effective enough.

If I just kept injecting...

I went back to the exam room. I ran the scan again.

The console told me what I knew was happening. The toxo count was higher than ever.

The treatment could kill parasites. But not if the bots kept repairing most of them.

I needed to get those bots out.

If I knew more about it all... you can control bots with a molecular MRI, and I knew they had those somewhere in the building; I remember reading about that antiviral for the "nameless" virus from Colorado. That one had come from rat droppings, and Sanford Bio-medical Lab had been one of the first places in the world to successfully treat a hantavirus.

They'd done that right there.

Somewhere in the building.

But an MRI isn't the same thing as an electromagnetic pulse; MRIs don't kill nanobots. But molecular MRIs can control those bots, if you know what you're doing.

Which I most definitely didn't.

I needed an rTMS machine. That I understood, at least in theory. *Or by pamphlet.*

But I had no idea where I could find one.

If they'd been conducting any studies on depression... if they'd been looking for non-medical and non-nano treatments... it was too slim of a chance.

rTMS was bush league, not cutting edge.

They'd have packed those machines away long ago.

If there was any chance of me finding what I needed, I'd have to find it in storage.

And with my luck, all the storage would be in the god-forsaken basement.

I left Iris strapped to the table; I didn't expect her to bust her way out.

I went down the same stairwell as before, clinging to the handrails in the near darkness.

I didn't have a gun, or even a shovel.

I wondered if maybe I should have brought a couple of syringes. I doubted that would have done anything for me.

I hadn't heard any gunfire, not since Errol had left to... I had assumed he was going to look for Jetta and Leona, not that he'd said as much.

Jetta was the one who was in danger, wasn't she?

Not the men with the welding helmets and hunting rifles...

As I neared the main floor, I heard them. Dozens of people, or hundreds, maybe, making their way down to the basement.

They didn't sound like monsters ready to tear me to pieces. I heard babies crying, young children babbling and whining... a few people were even laughing.

But I knew I couldn't go down there.

At least, not down that stairwell.

That's why Errol hadn't come back. He might have gotten down that stairwell, but couldn't get back up through a mass like that. Especially not with Jetta. No matter what he'd strapped to his chest.

I needed another way to get to the basement. And we'd all need another way to get back out.

I went back up to the second floor, hoping that no one had seen me.

I walked to the far end of the hallway, expecting another stairwell.

It wasn't there.

That left only one other way down, not including that swan dive.

I walked over to the elevator.

It didn't take me long to realize that I couldn't just pull the doors open. Something was keeping those doors shut.

I wondered if there was a way to get in from the roof, some hatch somewhere... but the notion of scaling down four floors and then one more to the basement...

I didn't see a way through.

I walked back over to the isolation room and Iris.

"We're both completely screwed," she said when she saw me. "So thanks for that, Seffy."

"Help me, Iris," I said. "If you don't want to stay screwed, that is."

"Let me go. Undo these straps and I'll get us out of here."

"You can't even stand up."

"Then find me a wheelchair or something."

"I don't know that they have any of those."

"Not that you've looked..."

"Look, Iris... we need to find everyone else and get out of here. That's at a minimum."

"We don't need them."

"No... we do."

"Just unstrap me, okay? Make me the happiest woman alive and get me off this frickin table."

I undid one of the wrist straps. "You're going to get weak again," I said. "You know that, right?"

"Yeah… I'm hungry. I need to eat. Probably more than I've ever eaten before in my life, outside of Golden Corral."

"It would be hard enough to survive on twelve hundred calories a day… you probably need twelve thousand… and it's not like the demand is decreasing. You can't sustain it, Iris."

"But what do you expect me to do? Just let you kill me?"

"I won't kill Iris."

"I *am* Iris. All of me."

"You're Iris mixed with advanced biotechnology and the worst thing about cat poo."

"Just accept it, Seffy. Don't try and change me."

"You're going to die."

"We'll find a way. Just promise me you'll respect my decision. Promise me, and I'll help you."

"Okay… I promise, Iris."

"No… swear it, Seffy."

"I *swear.*"

"Yeah, I can tell you're lying."

I didn't deny it. "So what do we do now?"

"You want to get down to the basement."

"Yeah."

"You can't take the stairs."

"Yeah."

"Then you need to climb down the elevator shaft."

"I can't get into the elevator."

"Because it's locked."

"I guess."

"Then you need to unlock it," she said.

"Oh, good. I'll just go grab the key."

"You don't need a key, Seffy. All you need it a wire hanger… maybe two…"

"So a closet…"

"Yeah," she said. "Too bad this isn't an abortion clinic… then there'd be coathangers everywhere."

"Are you kidding me?"

She shrugged.

I went out and found the coat closet.

And was so very lucky that the hangers weren't plastic.

On the way back I found a first aid kit. I opened it up.

A flashlight.

I took my couple of hangers back to Iris. "Will these work?" I asked.

"I think so."

"Okay… tell me what to do. And later on you can explain to me how you know so much about elevators."

"You've obviously never gone elevator surfing."

"What?"

"I guess I've fallen in with the wrong crowd at work," she said. "Listen… there's an access hole, maybe top left of the door… stick it in and try to reach around to get the latch, maybe to the left… uh, maybe… you'll have to feel around for it."

"And you think a clothes hanger will do the job?"

"Depends on the elevator… and the hanger… and how much forearm strength you have."

"In my case, very little."

"Then we'll need to get very lucky," she said. "I assume we're due for some good luck?"

"I wouldn't count on it."

She nodded.

I imagined that the past day or so was the worst run of bad luck my sister had been through since the ol' turkey shoot.

❧

I rolled Iris out with me to the elevator door, on a wheeled office chair.

She passed me the wire hanger, then shone the flashlight up at the door.

I stuck it into the small hole at the top left.

"See if you can find the latch," she said.

"I'm trying…"

"You gotta bend the hanger."

"You wanna do this?"

"Kinda, yeah…"

I pulled out the hanger and jammed it into her hands.

"You'll need to, like… help me up," she said.

I grabbed her waist and started pulling her to her feet.

"Now just… don't let go of me…"

She reached up and slid the hanger into the hole.

She jiggled it around.

"That's it," she said.

She sat back down on the chair and let out a big sigh.

"Well?" she said. "Pull it open."

I reached between the two panels and yanked them apart.

The shaft was dark enough to make the rest of the building seem well-lit.

"You would seriously climb down the shaft?" I asked her.

"Uh, no… we'd ride on the top of the car… getting on at the floor above… you'd have to be crazy to climb the cables."

"Crazy?"

"You'll do great, slightly-bigger sister."

"Whatever."

I took the flashlight.

I shined it down the shaft.

"I think the car's down there," I said.

"First floor?"

"I think basement."

"That's good… if it was sitting at the first floor you'd be hooped."

"Well, it's still in the way."

"You'll need to open it… it's probably bolted."

"This is becoming needlessly complex."

"Then take the stairs, Seffy."

I sighed. "I'll need a wrench, right?"

"Wow. And to think I'm the one who wants to be an engineer."

"Well, I don't have a wrench, Iris."

"Then get one. I'll wait."

I checked the desk where I'd found the first aid kit, near the printer.

Nothing. It's not like research scientists are expected to unbolt things between breakthroughs.

"Try the kitchenette," Iris said. She'd been getting progressively louder, which was probably more an indication that she was getting more frustrated than any improvement in well-being.

I walked over to the kitchen.

I checked the drawers.

I looked under the sink.

And found a pipe wrench.

Adjustable.

That could work.

Not that I'd seen the bolt on the elevator hatch. Or that I even knew there actually *was* a hatch.

I brought it back to Iris.

"Yeah," she said. "That'll do the job, sister. Old school."

"I don't know how I'm going to carry it down. I'm gonna want two hands for climbing."

"You've got a big mouth, Seffy. Might as well put it to use, right?"

I sneered at her.

And then I popped the pipe wrench into my mouth.

And the flashlight into my pocket, the bulbous end sticking out.

"Good luck, Seffy," Iris said as I peered over the edge. "Not that you'll need it."

I took out the wrench.

"What? Why?"

"You were born to climb elevator shafts."

"Why do you say that?"

"Just being optimistic."

I didn't bother continuing the conversation.

I bit down on the pipe wrench.

I reached out in the darkness for the ladder.

For a moment I couldn't find it. I felt close to falling.

But my left hand gripped it, and I was able to feel for the far side of it with my right.

I stepped down into the shaft, my right foot finding a rung.

I climbed down, the filthy pipe wrench clenched in my teeth, to the top of the elevator car.

I placed the wrench gently down on the roof; I didn't know how far the sound would travel.

I pulled the flashlight out from my pocket, flicking it on and pointing it down near the center of the roof.

The hatch was there, a green panel of metal bolted down to the roof of the elevator car. I put down the flashlight, aiming it at the bolt, and started to work with the pipe wrench.

There is nothing good about using a greasy pipe wrench to wrest off a pretty small metal bolt. It was colder than I'd expected in the shaft, too, and the wrench did its best to freeze up, too.

But after a couple of minutes I got the bolt off the door.

I flipped up the hatch, and shined the flashlight down through the gap.

A man in a welding mask was looking right back up at me.

"Seffy," he said. "Thank goodness." It wasn't Errol. It sounded like his Uncle Pat. "We've been trying to bust our way up. The stairwell's blocked."

"We couldn't get to the power," I heard Jetta say. "I'm sorry, Seffy."

I shined the light over to her. She was terrified.

Leona was huddled next to her, both of them in a corner of the elevator.

Errol and his father were at the open door of the elevator, guns pointed out.

"We don't need power," I said. "I've got power upstairs."

"How the heck did you manage that, sweetheart?" Pat asked.

"The solar panels on the roof."

"Then let's get out of here," Jetta said.

"I need an rTMS machine," I said. "I was hoping there'd be one in storage or something."

"I don't think that's going to work," Errol said, without turning around to see me. "We've got a bit of a standoff going on here."

"Hence the desperate attempt to climb an elevator shaft," Jetta said.

"How many?" I asked.

"There's probably fifty people down here," Errol said. "I'd say a good dozen are armed."

"So are they really a problem?"

"What?"

"Well, they're infected, you're infected… what's the point of shooting at each other?"

"There are supplies down here," Pat said. "Water, canned food…"

"Tell them we don't care about the supplies," I said. "Tell them we just need some medical equipment from storage."

"I don't think that'll work," Leona said. "We tried to reason with them about getting the power up. They can tell that Jetta's not infected. They don't trust us."

"And medical supplies aren't needed for anyone but you two," Errol said. "So why would they risk letting an armed group ransack the supplies for the sake of a couple of uninfected girls?"

That was the issue. We weren't the same as them. We weren't... what did Iris say... we weren't perfect... not yet.

And maybe that could be our problem...

"I'll talk to them," I said.

"This isn't debate team, Seffy," Errol said. "These people want to rip out your throat."

"It's not about that to them," I said. "It's not about that to you, is it?"

"What the heck are you talking about?"

"Jetta and I don't know how it feels... for everything to click, to feel so *perfect*."

"I'm confused, Seffy... you've made it pretty clear that you hate what this is."

"But they don't know that."

Pat and Leona helped me down through the hatch.

I walked by Errol and his father, out into the hallway.

There were a few men and women keeping watch over us, with a half dozen gun barrels pointed at the two men in the welding helmets.

No one bothered to re-aim any of those guns at me.

"My name's Persephone," I said, speaking mainly at a Filipino woman who'd already seemed to soften toward me. "I was part of a research trial here at Sanford Biomedical. So was my roommate Jetta, and... and my sister Iris."

"You girls shouldn't be here," one of the men said. "Not if you're trying to stay *unbit*."

"That's our problem," I said. "We can't get infected. Something to do with the experimental botshots from the trial."

"Maybe you've been bitten by the wrong people," the man said. "Come on over and I'll give it a try."

"No... that's why we're here. My sister, Iris... her boyfriend bit her, but she didn't turn. And now she's bleeding to death."

"But you said she had bots," the Filipino woman said. "So they should be fixing her."

"They're not repairing the tissue... I don't know why. So I had an idea, to disable my sister's bots, so we can get the right bots into her... so she'll get better."

"This doesn't sound believable," the man said.

I heard a few other people chime in on their disbelief.

"Why does it matter to you?" I asked. "So a couple of uninfected idiots have deluded themselves into thinking they can save one of their sisters with an rTMS machine."

"What's an rTMS machine?" the woman asked.

"It's a little rolling box that you hook up to people's heads," I said. "Repetitive transcranial magnetic stimulation. Disables bots."

"It's some stupid trick," the man said. "They want us to let our guard down so they can rush in here and take all the supplies. Or worse."

"What's worse?" the woman asked.

"Forcing us all back outside to get blown to bits, maybe?"

"Just me," I said. "Just let me come take a look around. I don't have a gun, or any sticks of dynamite..."

"Not worth the risk," the man said.

"My sister's dying, sir... she's bleeding out on an exam table upstairs. All we want is what you have already. I don't want my sister to die."

"Let her through," the Filipino woman said.

"I'm not letting anyone through," the man said.

The woman scoffed. "So you're scared of her, then? Maybe she's some crazed killer... maybe she knows Krav Maga and can murder each and every one of us with her pinky finger?"

Jetta stepped up behind me. "I'll come look, too," she said. "Two uninfected girls with perfectly exposed necks. Not exactly high risk."

"Yeah, okay," the man said. "You two. With your hands on your heads. You see something you want, you *ask* for it."

"I'll go, too," Leona said. "I'm unarmed."

The man shook his head. "Just the two uninfected girls."

"I don't like this," Errol told me. "There's no way for us to protect you."

"It's still pretty hypothetical that any of us are getting out of this building alive," I said.

"Thanks for the reassurance."

Jetta and I walked toward the Filipino woman, both of us with our hands on our heads.

"I saw some machines over this way," the woman said.

She led us down the hall to a storage area, leading with her own flashlight.

We followed her into a dark room. She let us pass in front, then closed the door behind us.

"Don't trust these people," she said. "I don't."

"They can't infect us," I said.

She shook her head. "They can do a lot worse."

The door opened behind her.

A man entered.

I didn't recognize him from out in the hall. He had a hunting knife strapped to his thigh; it looked like he'd wanted us to notice it.

He nodded to the woman.

She looked away.

And shut the door, standing right in front of it.

"What's going on here?" Jetta asked.

"Time for the test," the man said.

"We can't be infected," I said. "If you bite us, we'll just bleed out. You'll be killing us."

"No one here believes that."

He stepped toward us. Toward me, specifically.

Jetta pushed herself between me and the man.

"If we don't come out of here," she said, "those men with the dynamite will blow up this entire basement."

"I doubt it," the man said. "People can strap whatever they want to their chests... doesn't mean they have the means or the balls to carry it out."

"Maybe not," I said, "but then they'll just shoot you in the head. Is that what you want? A gunfight in a confined area?"

He grabbed Jetta's hair.

He pulled her down.

She fell to her knees.

"They will kill you," I said. "If you hurt her..."

"We can't be infected," Jetta said. "Don't you get that?"

He bent down and bit into her neck.

She gasped.

She fell forward, shoving her hands in front of her, but they collapsed as she hit the floor. The blood trickled along the concrete floor, travelling down the slope to some hidden low point.

"I wonder if she'll turn," the man said.

"You've killed her," I said. "And probably everyone else in this building." I started to cry.

The man knelt down and grabbed Jetta by the hair. He yanked her up, inspecting the wound on her throat. "Already starting to heal," he said. "This girl's been pretty well zombified." He dropped her hard onto the floor and glared over at me. "You lying bitch."

"We thought it was all of us," I said. "That we were all the same way from the bot trial."

"Just shut up already," the Filipino woman said, from her place by the closed door.

"So what is it you want with that machine?" the man asked. "You figure you can just zap our bots and that will kill us all off?"

"That's not what we're doing," I said. "I just want to save my sister. Please."

"She's still lying," the woman said.

The man stepped over to me.

"How many people you got upstairs?" he asked. "How many uninfected?"

I slammed my right hand against his forehead.

He fell back, his body slamming against a line of wire shelves, throwing several boxes of files down to the floor.

He smiled at me.

I hadn't expected a smile. It terrified me.

"There are worse things than being bitten," the man said, as he stepped back over to me. "I can make you beg for it, little girl."

"Skeevy doesn't equal scary," I told him.

He reached into his pocket and pulled out a pen.

I did my best Iris impression. "Autograph will cost you a hundo, pal."

"You don't have any bots, do you?" he asked.

"It's possible they put me in the control group. It's not like they're going to tell me that."

"So when I jab this pen into your hand... what will that do?"

"It'll make me knee you in the crotch."

"Stick out your hand."

"No..."

He grabbed my right elbow, pulling it toward him.

I couldn't think of anything defiant to say.

And I was pretty sure I was still crying.

He stabbed the pen into my palm.

At first I felt like it was happening to somebody else.

It seemed to stick a little in my hand.

He jiggled it, and gave it another shove.

I saw the tip come out the other side.

Then the pain set in.

I didn't want to scream. But it didn't feel like I was making any decisions, really. It was loud.

He pulled the pen back out.

My hand looked like it had sprouted a little red fountain. That hurt like a sonuvabitch.

I ripped a strip from the bottom of my t-shirt.

I wrapped it around my palm, tying it as tightly as I could with one hand and my teeth.

"So," the man asked again, "what's the machine for?"

I heard a couple of gunshots.

And the inevitable sounds of people running and shouting.

"They're coming," the woman said. "We need to go."

"Go?" the man said. "There's nowhere to go, Cherry."

He let go of my elbow.

He walked over to the wall, next to the door.

He pulled the hunting knife out of its holder.

I knew his plan. It wasn't hard to guess.

It's not like a welding helmet gives much protection from behind. One thrust up, from the back of the neck, right into the brain. That's not something you need a PhD in biology to understand.

So I yelled. "Don't come in here! He's behind the door, with a hunting knife…"

"Shut her up," the man said.

The woman just stared at him.

The door didn't open.

I heard one gunshot.

I saw the shell rip into the drop ceiling above.

The man with the knife collapsed.

"He's down," I shouted.

The door opened. Errol ran inside.

He took another shot, into the man's skull.

"Are you okay?" he asked me.

"Jetta's been bitten. I don't know… she's turning somehow." I was hoping to keep up the lie for another few seconds. "I don't get how that could happen."

"Don't kill me," the woman said, lifting her hands up. "I'm sorry."

Errol aimed the gun at her chest.

He looked over to me.

"Don't shoot," I said.

He nodded.

But didn't lower the rifle.

"I can help," the woman said. "I can find this machine…"

I looked down at her shoes. "Take out your shoelaces and get down and tie my friend's hands and feet."

I walked over to the shelves near the man's bloodied head.

Heart monitors, portable ultrasound machines, some other boxy objects I didn't recognize. And on the bottom, behind a box of sterile pads, an rTMS machine.

I heard the building shake as another bomb came down.

"Getting closer," Errol said. "Almost downtown."

Almost right on top of us.

16

THE EXPERIMENT REDUX

I asked Dan and Pat to stand watch at the stairwell. I got Leona to stand by the elevator doors, just in case.

Errol carried Jetta over his shoulders, her hands and feet bound with the Filipino woman's shoelaces.

We'd left that woman downstairs.

We'd let her live.

I rolled the rTMS machine down the second floor hallway, and Iris met us by the printer.

She gave the rolling chair to Jetta, wrapping her arm around my shoulder for support.

Errol grabbed some white medical tape and strapped Jetta to the back of the seat.

"You're going to test it on her, I guess," Iris said.

"I guess so," I said. "Since you don't want it."

"I don't want it, no."

We rolled Jetta over to the isolation room, where we'd kept Iris. Her eyes were bloodshot, and she was struggling hard, trying to free herself from the chair but not really knowing how.

I'd seen it happen to other people; I'd even seen a little bit of it with my own sister.

But seeing it happen all over again, to Jetta... that was breaking my heart. I guess there's something to that idea... once you've gone through hell with someone... you're connected to them. It's something we've gone through together... something we share.

Well, except for that last part.

That last part was just her.

She'd stepped in for me. Taken the bite.

"Is it safe?" Iris asked.

"Is what safe?"

"The zapping or whatever. What if something goes wrong?"

"I don't know what will happen," I said. "Once those bots are disabled, if they can be disabled... I'm not sure there actually is a way back from this."

"So she might just die..."

"Maybe... yeah."

Iris shook her head. "You can't do it, Seffy."

"She wouldn't want to be a zombie," I said. "She would have said yes to this."

"She'd rather die? I doubt it."

"She'd rather die," Errol said.

We both looked over to him.

He shrugged.

"I'll do it," Iris said. "Zap me first."

"You kidding?" I asked her.

"I'm still Iris. I'm here. I can still choose. She can't. So do me first."

"Are you sure?"

"Just checked. Again, still Iris. And I'm not going to lie... I'm a little curious to see what'll happen."

I nodded.

She climbed up onto the exam table.

She held out her arms, reaching out to the restraints.

"We don't need to do that," I said.

"Just in case," she said.

I strapped her down.

I rolled the machine next to her.

"You've never done this before," Iris said.

"Never even seen it happen," I said.

She laughed. "I love you, Seffy. Like a real sister and everything."

I nodded. "So, you ready?"

"Yeah."

I chose the settings. Repetitive, 30 Hz @ 50% output... that sounded nice and middle-of-the-road. I wasn't sure what I'd be able to observe; it wasn't like I'd see the bots shutting down.

But I had to start somewhere.

I placed the rubbery figure-eight coil against the top of her head.

I flipped the switch.

It didn't make any zapping noises, there weren't any lightning bolts.

"Can you feel anything?" I asked her.

She didn't answer.

Her eyes were open, but she seemed vacant.

I could see her breathing.

She gasped.

Her eyes closed.

"Iris," I said. "Can you hear me?"

I checked her pulse.

It was accelerating.

She seemed to be getting warmer, too.

"Something's happening," Errol said.

"Yeah... I just don't know what."

"How much more?"

"I don't know."

If I did too little, would we even get any results, any indication that the bots were being disabled? But what happened if I left it going too long?

I counted ten more seconds.

I switched off the pulses.

And turned on the scanner.

I ran over to the printer console.

Bot count was a little lower than before... not by much, but I'd expected that once she'd regained some strength her count would have gone higher.

I pushed for more detail... the bots in her brain had been affected, reduced by as much as half, while the ones in the rest of her body didn't seem touched at all.

That made sense; it wasn't like some weak electrical currents in the brain were going to shock out the bots swimming around her feet.

I'd have to reach more of her body.

I went back to see her.

She'd opened her eyes.

"How do you feel?" I asked.

"No different," she said. "I should feel different, right?"

"You're not dead... so that's something. I'm going to try sweeping your entire body with the coil."

"Okay… just don't shrivel anything up in there."

I flipped the switch.

I gave her scalp another thirty seconds before slowly bringing the coil down her neck. I swept her arms, then moved the coil down her chest, trying to keep it a good distance from her heart.

She'd drifted off again, and gave no sign that the pulses were hurting her.

I brought them all the way down to her feet, before sweeping up her body again, spending a final twenty seconds at the top of her head.

Once that was done, I ran another scan.

Bots were down by over 90%.

I decided it was time to try the treatment.

I took the syringe and loaded up another dose from the printed vial. I found the same vein and drew in the needle.

She didn't open her eyes.

I guess that wasn't a surprise.

I ran another scan.

Treatment successful.

And no parasites. None found.

"Oh my god," I said. "It worked."

"What was that?" Errol asked from the isolation room.

I ran back over to Iris and the exam table. "The parasites are gone," I said.

Errol put his hand on my shoulder. "So what happens now?"

"I don't know. We don't know what those parasites actually did to her brain… she might not be able to come back."

"What? So she might be some kind of vegetable or something?"

"Maybe."

He stepped back.

He was pissed.

"I… I don't get this, Seffy. How is that any better?"

"She was dying… we needed to get those parasites out of her."

"We needed to get her the nutrients she needed. We did that. But this…"

I hadn't expected that. Not from him. Errol was always on my side. "You think I've killed her," I said.

"I don't know… maybe…"

"Iris," I said, as I stroked her forehead. "Can you hear me?"

No response.

She was breathing, she was alive. But that didn't mean there was anything left.

I held open one of her eyes. I remembered the test from first aid.

I rocked her head to the left. Then to the right.

Her eye stayed with me.

I left her eyelid close.

I took my fingernail and dug it into her palm.

Her eyes didn't open.

She didn't move at all.

It had only been a couple of minutes, but I knew what was happening.

Sister in a coma.

I'd have to stick that tube back into her nose to keep her alive. I'd have to change how she's lying every few hours so she doesn't get bed sores. I'd have to find something to use as a bedpan.

We'd live together on the second floor of Sanford Biomedical Lab until someone found us and sunk their teeth into my jugular.

I shouldn't have tested it out on her. On my own sister.

Not that I should have done it to Jetta.

I should have taken someone from the basement… that Filipino woman who would have seen us dead…

I'd just killed my own sister.

"Iris," I said again, not that it would do anything. "Iris… please…"

"I don't know how long we can wait," Errol said. "We can't stay here forever."

"We can't leave. Something might change… she might wake up… people *can* wake up from this…"

"And how long is that going to take?"

I wanted to punch him. "As long as it takes, Errol. So just shut up and give me some time here, okay?"

Not that we had any time. It could take days, or even weeks. And there was no guarantee that she'd ever wake up, or that she'd ever be fully aware again.

Errol walked out of the room, grabbing Jetta and her rolling chair on his way by, pulling her along with him.

I heard Leona in the hallway. "What's going on?" she asked. "What's happening with Jetta?"

I didn't go out to meet her.

So she came into the isolation room.

"Seffy," she said. "What's going on?" She looked down at Iris. "You ran it on Iris?"

"Iris volunteered," I said. "She didn't think it was… right… to do it to Jetta first."

"Why's she sleeping? Is she sleeping?"

"The infection is gone… but I don't know what's left of my sister."

"I don't understand."

"She unresponsive."

"Oh…"

"I just need time," I said. "To see what happens."

"You don't have time."

"Excuse me?"

"Well, you don't. We need to figure it out now. You need to scan her again, don't you?"

"Why?"

"Won't that tell you anything?"

"I don't know…" I couldn't think…

"Well?"

It would just be easier to do exactly what I was being told to do.

"Okay," I said. "Hold on…"

I ran another scan. Leona followed me out to the console.

Errol kept a little distance, but I could tell he was trying to see the output.

The scanner didn't monitor brain activity, outside of a snapshot in time; I'd need to stick leads all over her scalp to get a recording of that.

The snapshot I did have couldn't tell me if anything was wrong with the functioning of her brain; all it could show is that nothing *seemed* to be missing. As far as the scan could tell, everything was still there, where it should be.

It was just Iris' brain, nothing more, nothing less.

But why wasn't she responding?

Why wasn't that brain connecting *to Iris*?

"Parasites are still gone," Leona said. "Bot count… isn't increasing. They should be replicating, right?"

"Yeah," I said.

"I don't think they know what to do."

I almost shushed her, thinking that might be the dumbest thing I'd heard in what hadn't been the smartest of days... but then I realized she might be onto something.

If those bots had been rewired by the parasite... however many bots had been replicated from those brainwashed models, they'd need to be rewired if they were going to bring Iris back. And they weren't going to rewire themselves.

"She needs new bots," I said. "Another shot. To undo whatever those parasites have done."

"Do they have that here?" Leona asked.

"Third floor," Errol said, pushing his way in. "I saw it on the directory downstairs. Nanomedicine."

"Let's go," I told him. I turned back to Leona. "Keep an eye on them."

"I'll be here," she said.

❧

We found the vials on the third floor, secured by locks and an alarm system that seemed to depend on there being power.

So Errol smashed open the casing, and we grabbed a handful of vials.

They had numbering, labeled as derivatives.

I had no idea what those meant.

We brought them down to Iris' table.

"These are experimental," I said. "I don't know which is the best one."

"How can you even tell them apart?" Leona asked.

"Last suffix... three digits' difference between all three kinds."

"Take the lowest number."

"Why?"

"Because that's hopefully been tested the most."

"I'm not sure it works like that," Errol said.

"No," I said. "I think it might."

I grabbed the vial with the lowest numbers.

"This is nuts, Seffy," Errol said. "You can't just inject this without knowing what it'll do."

"Do you think she's coming back from this?" I asked.

"We don't know."

"No... I know... she's not going to wake up in time... not if we don't do *something*."

"You said she could come out of it, remember?"

"So now you want to stay here and wait?" I asked.

"You know I want to support you, Seffy."

"Whatever."

I filled the syringe.

I injected the bots into my sister's arm.

"We need another scan," Leona said.

"I know what I'm doing," I told her. "Do you remember where you're supposed to be?"

She sighed. "Let me know before you do anything to Jetta."

I nodded.

"Promise me," she said.

"Yeah, okay... I promise."

She turned and headed back toward the elevator.

I heard a moan.

I turned to look at Iris.

Her eyes were still closed.

But she looked... different.

"Iris," I said.

Another moan, a little softer that time.

I leaned in close. "You need to let me know... that you understand me..."

"Unh-huh..."

"You understand me?"

"Unh-huh..."

"Iris..."

I saw her eyes open. Slowly, shutting once and then opening again, only a little more than halfway.

"Not... dead yet," she said.

I almost fell over.

I'd never thought we'd get that far.

I looked over to Errol.

"I'll bring Jetta back in," he said.

∽

After a couple minutes' recovery, Iris found a cushioned chair in the hallway to rest on. She hadn't even needed our help to get there.

Errol took over for Leona at the elevator, so she could be at Jetta's side for the treatment.

"It's weird that I want this," Leona said as we strapped Jetta down to the exam table.

"For you?" I asked.

"No, for Jetta. I don't want her to be like me."

"That is strange... Iris had told me that she'd felt more perfect... with the parasite."

"I don't know," she said. "I mean, I don't want to die, like who I am now... but I want Jetta to just be Jetta."

"She will be..."

"Hold on," Iris said from out in the hallway.

"Something wrong?" I asked. I started walking out to her.

"No... not like that... but don't treat Jetta just yet."

"Why not?" Leona asked.

"We need to run another test," Iris said.

"What kind of test?" I asked.

"We need to see if I can be re-infected."

"That's a simple test," Leona said. "I'll just take a bite out of you."

"You'd really do that?" I asked.

"I don't know... maybe..."

"Jetta would do it," Iris said. "No problem. Because she can't stop herself from doing it. So let her bite me."

"It might go bad," I said. "We don't know how those experimental bots will react to the parasite. What if they just let them in and they take you right over? What if those bots are more resistant to the rTMS machine? Or if they make the parasites more resistant to the treatment?"

"Someone's going to bite me eventually, right?"

"We don't know that for sure," Leona said.

"Well, I want to know."

"We might not even need her to bite you," I said.

"What do you mean?" Leona asked.

"Come here, Iris…"

Iris walked back into the room.

She didn't wait for further instructions. She leaned her head down over Jetta's mouth. Offering her neck.

Jetta didn't take it.

Instead, she turned her head away, pulling hard on her restraints. Jetta was trying to get away from Iris completely.

"They know," Leona said. "Those little bugs know that your sister is immune."

"It's more than that," I said. "I think she's more than immune. I want to try something…"

I took a new syringe and pulled off the packaging.

"Don't cure her yet," Iris said. "We should do some more experiments."

"She's not a goddamn lab rat," Leona said.

"It's not for her," I said. "It's for me." I nodded to Iris. "Well, for both of us."

"Hold on," Iris said. "I see what you're doing, Seffy. But you don't even know if we're the same blood type…"

"That doesn't matter. Not with what you've got."

"What have I got?"

"The vaccine."

"Maybe you should take a break, Seffy. Maybe a five minute nap."

"I'm serious. I think your new bots could keep those parasites out for good."

"Bots can't transfer between bodies," Leona said.

"These are lab bots," I said. "Experimental. It takes extra effort to genocode these things. I doubt they bother doing that when they're still under development."

"Okay," Iris said. "I think you've got something here, Seffy. Do it."

"You two are crazy," Leona said.

"Together we're a menace," I said.

Iris held out her arm and made a fist.

I drew some blood into the syringe.

And found a vein of my own.

"This could kill you," Leona said.

"I doubt it," I said.

I stuck the needle in.

∽

Test subject: Frizzy-haired girl with objectively hotter sister
Treatment: blood from same hot sister
Result: chin zit has disappeared

I felt fine. Not really different, just okay.

I was still tired.

I might have still had a bit of a headache.

It felt like maybe my crotch still hurt a little.

I unwrapped the strip of t-shirt I'd wrapped around my bloody palm.

It was healing.

Not nearly as quickly as what you'd find in your garden-variety zombie, but way faster that you'd get with potato soup and a good night's sleep.

There was only one test left to go.

I dangled my little neck in front of Jetta.

Zombie Jetta was just as scared of me.

"It's a vaccine," I said. "We're a vaccine."

Leona scoffed. "That's not science," she said. "That's wishful thinking."

She grabbed me by my shoulders.

She pulled me in.

I didn't fight it. I wasn't actually sure what was happening… until it happened. Until she bit me.

It felt more like a draft of cold air flowing through a hole in my scarf. I could feel the blood, too, like I'd dribbled some warm syrup under my chin.

I guess some things are too horrible for the pain to come. I felt myself falling, but I'm pretty sure that Leona caught me.

She brought me over to that cushy chair in the hallway.

I saw Iris running over, in what seemed like half speed, carrying a roll of bandage.

I felt the tightness of the wrap around my throat.

I couldn't talk.

I wasn't even sure I was breathing.

I closed my eyes.
I'm not sure it was sleep.

17

BUMP IN THE ROAD

I woke up with my head bobbing, and with a perfect view of khaki pants and brown workboots.

My nostrils were burning from the smoke and whatever else I was smelling.

We were outside, and it seemed darker than I would have expected. Like we were in the dark of the countryside, but with the smell and noise of homecoming weekend.

With bombs and stuff.

"Take a left up here," Errol said, obviously not to me.

I could tell from his voice that he wasn't wearing his helmet.

We jogged left, through someone's backyard.

I could see the lab building not far behind us.

"Errol," I said. "I'm here."

I didn't know what else to say.

"We're almost out of it, Seffy," he said. "I've got you."

I heard gunfire.

Errol dropped down to his knees.

He rolled me onto the pavement.

"I can walk," I said.

"Good."

He ducked behind a car.

I followed his lead.

Someone was already squatting behind the engine block.

A woman in Errol's welding helmet.

Holding a hunting rifle.

I was pretty sure it was Iris.

"Someone on the roof of that church," she said.

"Anyone hit?" Errol asked.

"Don't know. Jetta and Leona were up ahead. Can't see them."

"I'm right behind you guys," I heard Errol's father Dan say.

I turned in time to see him fire a shot up at the church. He still had his helmet on. The helmet placements made sense to me; the people with guns would be the people they'd want to shoot first.

"We won't be able to fish them out," Dan said. "We just need to keep moving."

I looked out over the car. We were in a parking lot now, a narrow one with banks of parked cars on both sides. There were trees up ahead, and a narrow slot between two buildings.

"We can get there," I said. "Between those houses."

Iris nodded.

"I'll take another shot," Dan said. "Just as you guys start running. Once you get clear… Iris, you'll need to take a shot from that end, see if it's enough to get me through."

"Keep your heads low," Errol said. "Remember… that's the one place you don't want to get hit."

"I don't want to get hit at all, thanks," Iris said.

And then she started running.

I went, too.

Then Errol.

Dan fired his rifle again.

No one shot back.

We reached the cars on the other side.

I noticed Dan right behind us.

"Saved us a round," he said.

"Any sign of Pat and the girls?" Errol asked.

"They must have kept going," Iris said. "Can't say I blame them."

"We'll catch up," Dan said.

"Where are we going?" I asked.

"Across the river," Errol said.

Iris started moving again, following the line of a wood fence, ducking behind the cars. I didn't know what she was planning to do once there weren't any more cars left for hiding.

"We can't cross the river," I said as I traced the fenceline. "We can't leave anyone behind."

"This isn't the time for a roundtable discussion," Iris said. "We need to keep moving."

"We are moving…"

"Can we try doing it quietly?"

We wrapped around the front of a two-storey house.

We were well out of sight of the church roof, but we had no cover from pretty much any other direction.

"We need to cross the street," Dan said. "Get between those houses on the other side."

Iris led us across, between the two houses and along a long garage.

I caught a glimpse of someone up ahead.

"I think I might see them," I said.

"You sure?" Iris asked.

"Not at all… could be anyone."

"We should skirt north around that next house," Dan said. "Keep out of sight of them."

"Then how will they find us?" I asked.

"I'd rather we found them."

Iris led us to the left, following the wall of a small beige house.

We reached the street. Tenth Avenue, maybe?

And someone started shooting at us.

I fell, not on purpose.

Iris fell, too.

Errol managed to pull back to the side of the house, where I assumed Dan had ended up, too.

Iris crawled back toward me. "Head down," she said.

"I know."

"We need to keep moving."

"I know."

I heard the sounds of boots on the pavement.

I saw a man in hunting camo run out. He kicked the rifle out of Iris' hands. He grabbed her, pulling on both of her arms.

He dragged her across the street, to an open garage door. There was some kind of barrier set up, cinder blocks and old furniture, and plenty of tarps.

He took Iris behind it.

The rifle was still on the pavement.

I reached out and grabbed it.

The man came back out.

He saw that I had the rifle.

He started running toward me.

I tried to get up.

I could feel the pain in my left leg, just above the ankle. And I knew my leg wasn't about to cooperate.

I wouldn't get anywhere in time. I wasn't getting away.

I threw the rifle out in front of me.

He grabbed my wrists and started dragging me across the street.

I saw Dan, watching from the corner of the house.

I knew he wouldn't be comfortable taking a shot.

The man brought me around the bunker and dropped my arms. The garage was ringed by candles, making it look a little like a mechanic's cult meeting.

Iris was lying on the concrete pad. The man had put her on her stomach, and bound her wrists behind her back with duct tape. He'd wrapped another couple layers over her eyes and right around her head.

She was bleeding from her right calf... I didn't know how long it would be until our wounds had healed. It would be pretty obvious at that point that there's something different about us.

"How many with you?" the man asked.

"Just us," I said.

"Crock of bull."

He bent down and flipped me onto my stomach. He pulled my hands behind me, crossing them and pinning them against my tailbone.

I heard the rip of the tape.

Someone else was binding my wrists.

"These girls aren't infected," that someone else said. A woman.

I couldn't turn my head around to see her.

The man was still pinning me down.

"No point in biting 'em right yet," he said. "They're probably quieter like this."

"There's nothing quiet about us," Iris said. "We'll kick and scream and bite until you finally just have to kill us."

I wasn't really following my sister's logic.

I felt someone pull me by the hair, lifting my head.

The woman wrapped duct tape over my eyes. Once. Twice. Three layers. Seemed like overkill.

"Where's Mason?" the man asked.

"He's on the crapper," the woman said. "You gonna help me

carry them in?"

"They've got more people out there... two men, I think. If we're lucky they'll come on over to try and get them back."

"This helmet's pretty cool... do you think it's bulletproof?"

"Well, duh, Stace... of course it's bulletproof. That's why she was wearing it."

"These guys seem hardcore."

"We're very hardcore," Iris said. "I'll bet our guys have surrounded the house already. You frickin peasants. You're all going to die."

"Peasants?" the man said.

"Says the girl who's trussed up like a game hen," the woman said.

"You realize that hunting camo makes no sense in the city, right?" Iris said. "Like, seriously. You guys get one lucky break and you think you're a paramilitary force."

"How many people with you?" the man asked.

"So very many," Iris said. "Somewhere between a battalion and a brigade."

"Can the other girl talk instead?" the woman asked. "Because I don't want to wreck my shoes stomping this bitch's skull."

"I agree with my sister," I said. "Unreservedly."

I heard a gunshot, to the side of the garage.

"They're coming at us through the house," the man said. "Stay here, Stace. These girls cause a problem, you cut their throats."

"With so much pleasure," she said.

The man ran out through the side door.

Iris didn't waste any time. She kicked her left leg back.

I heard the woman fall against the makeshift barrier.

I kicked in that general area. And kept kicking.

I uncrossed my wrists, loosening up my restraints. I started twisting my hands, weakening the tape.

Iris screamed.

"Not an idle threat," the woman said. "You feel that steel?"

"What's going on?" I asked.

"Your sister slipped on my cleaver. Her shoulder's bleeding pretty bad. But at least now she'll shut up, right?"

"Don't hurt her, please... just tell me what you want us to do."

"I want you to lie still and wait this out."

"Yeah... okay. Iris? Are you alright?"

I heard gasping.

"What the heck is wrong with her?" the woman asked. "Sounds like she's having a heart attack."

"Iris," I said. "Iris…" I almost had my wrists free…

"I'm not dealing with this crap," the woman said. She dragged Iris toward the side door, feet first.

I heard the door open.

I pulled my wrists apart.

The door shut.

I sat up and unwrapped the tape from my eyes, trying my best not to make any noise.

Someone whispered my name.

I turned to see Errol running toward the garage. He had his rifle back, up off the street.

"I'm okay," I said quietly.

And the pain in my leg… it felt more like a sprain than a gaping gunshot wound. Not as fast as a zombie… but it was healing quickly enough.

I nodded to the door.

Errol made his way over.

He pushed it open.

We both looked out.

The woman had one arm wrapped around Iris' ankles, while she held a blood-stained meat cleaver in the other. She wasn't making much progress, having only gotten halfway across the yard to the house.

She probably should have dropped the cleaver.

Errol ran out after her.

She turned and saw him.

She dropped Iris and started running toward the house.

Errol didn't bother to chase her.

I ran over to Iris. I helped her up and guided her back to the garage.

I started pulling the tape off her wrists.

"I know it's Errol untaping me," she said. "Such soft hands."

Errol was standing watch by the side door.

"Is your father in there?" I asked.

He nodded.

"We'll be okay here. If you want to see if he needs help."

"My uncle's with him."

"Your uncle? Where are the girls?"

"Across the street. Hopefully staying right where we told them to wait."

I started unwrapping the tape from Iris' head. "We can cross over to them," I said.

"I'm coming with you," Errol said.

I nodded.

The three of us made our way back across the street, behind the little beige house.

Jetta and Leona were squatting along the back wall.

"Are you guys okay?" Jetta asked.

"I got chopped up a little," Iris said. "But other than that..."

Jetta grabbed my hand. "I'm so glad you're okay."

I nodded.

She stood up and gave me a hug.

And kissed me on the cheek.

Maybe sometimes I'm not quite sure what she's about.

A door slammed. From across the street.

Errol ran back to the corner of the house.

"It's Pat," he said. "He's waving us over."

"Why would he do that?" I asked.

Errol shrugged. It was kind of cute. "I have no idea."

We walked over to the house, Errol watching the back while Pat kept an eye out in front.

I knew that I was probably a better shot than all three of the Kimmern men. But I also knew that any one of them was a more intimidating sight than me. And looking dangerous was more important than being dangerous. No matter what I wanted to believe, people would be less likely to challenge a guy with a gun.

Sexist bunk.

We went around to the front of the house.

Dan was standing just inside the doorway.

It didn't feel like there were three crazy people waiting inside.

He opened the door.

Fender came running out to see me. Then he saw Iris and all hell broke loose.

Iris was almost as excited to see him.

Not to mention how surprised we both were. Fender's a pretty cute dog, but even for him it was a stretch to re-home during the end of the world.

"It's not good, guys," Dan said.

"What does that mean?" I asked.

"We found something… it's pretty terrible. In the basement."

"Where are those psychos?" Iris asked. "That woman who sliced open my shoulder…"

"Just come downstairs," Pat said. He pulled off his helmet.

I guess the coast was clear.

Dan led us down.

Pat took up the rear; I could see him checking all the girls out again. You'd think if there was ever a time when you wouldn't be staring at a girl's rear end…

There was light at the bottom.

Another ring of tea lights.

And three people lying on cement floor, their hands and legs duct taped.

"They're still alive," I said.

"Yeah," Dan said.

"That's good."

Dan turned his head to his right.

I looked over.

Two laundry tubs. One had a faucet hooked up, while the other looked like it had just been dragged into place.

I could see the smears of blood on the outsides.

"I don't want to look," I said.

"You don't need to look," Dan said.

Iris walked over. She looked. "Oh… no…"

I took a step closer.

And saw something in one of the tubs.

It looked like a slab of pork. But bloodier than you'd see at the butcher's.

But there was a little bit of skin, a small strip that the meat cutter had missed. A small strip with tan skin and little black hairs.

It didn't look like pig.

"We've counted six sides of thigh in these sinks," Pat said. "That's at least three people butchered."

"This can't be real," Jetta said. "People don't do this kind of thing."

"Where's the rest?" Leona asked.

We all looked over at her.

"Well, three people makes more than six thighs," she said. "Where's the rest of their bodies?"

"That's what they were going to do to us," Iris said. "I thought they wanted to rape us."

"Why would they want to eat anybody?" I asked. "It's not like all the food in Fargo's been used up already."

"I can understand it," Errol said. "If you're going to kill people anyway..."

"Yeah, what the heck," Iris said. "Let's take a few bites off those three psychos while we're here."

"But they have too much of it," Leona said.

"What?" Errol said. "What are you talking about?"

"No electricity... so it's not like they can freeze it."

I thought I heard something.

"That closet," I said, pointing to a door under the stairs."

Errol pointed his rifle at the door.

He walked over.

"Who's in there?" he shouted.

No one answered.

But there was still noise. Like someone was moaning, not really talking.

Errol tried to open the door.

It was locked.

Dan walked over to the woman on the floor. "The key," he said.

"My pants pocket," she said.

He brought a key over to Errol.

Errol unlocked the door and opened it.

I couldn't see what was inside.

Errol leaned against the stairs.

He started vomiting.

I came over, not that I wanted to.

There were three people in the closet.

Sitting in chairs. They weren't tied up or handcuffed.

Two men and one woman, all naked below the waist.

I could see the wounds where their thighs had been carved, fading scars and fresh, pink skin.

If you carve a choice cut from a zombie, it eventually grows back. I guess that's what the thigh happens to be.

I didn't recognize my father at first. Or Beth.

Once I did, it felt like someone had kneed me in the stomach.

Dad's eyes were still bloodshot. He hadn't been turned that long before. They probably did it right before they sliced off his thighs.

Beth tried to say something.

I didn't understand.

She pointed at her tongue.

"It'll all grow back," the woman taped on the floor said. "We didn't kill anyone. Not that these people wouldn't deserve it."

"Why would you do this?" I asked. "How does this make sense?"

I started helping Beth out of the closet.

My father was more terrified of me than anything.

Errol stepped over to bring Dad out.

"The thighs taste... better," the woman said. "Not like the rest. So we were just going to eat the thighs again, and a few more times. And trade the extras for whatever else we need."

I brought Beth over to Iris, who led her to one of a set of old dining room chairs along the far wall. Errol helped my father to another one.

I offered my hand to the other man in the closet.

I didn't know him.

He wasn't much older than me. The only thing that stood out about him was his scraggly goatee.

"Eventually they'd die," Iris said. "It's my father and mother you had in there. You were going to harvest them like cattle until they finally just couldn't survive any longer."

"No... we would have fed them," the woman said, starting to panic. "Just... once things calmed down out there... we would have found something to give them. I swear."

"That's a load of crap."

"We should kill them," Leona said. "Otherwise they'll just do this all over again."

"We didn't want to hurt anyone," the woman said. "But we can't get enough to eat. We're always starving to death."

"That's the infection," I said. "It'll just keep growing inside of you until you won't be able to keep feeding it. It's killing you."

"We should board them up in that closet," Iris said. "Let them dry up and die like they wanted to do to my Mom and Dad."

"We should cure them," Jetta said.

"Why the heck should we help them?" Iris asked.

"Because that's the only way this will stop."

"She's right," I said. "Even if we remove these three from the equation… there are thousands more infected out there… they won't be the only ones to try something like this. Imagine what'll happen when the food actually does start running out."

"I don't want them to live," Iris said. "I really don't."

"We should take a vote," Jetta said. "Just like we did before, Seffy."

"A vote," I said. "I can live with that."

"As long as they don't," Leona said.

"So who wants to kill them?" Iris asked. She'd raised her hand before she'd finished saying it.

Leona raised her hand.

Errol looked at me.

"I'm abstaining," Pat said. "Because I honestly don't care what happens to them."

"I'll vote for that," Dan said.

"For abstaining?" Errol asked.

"Uh, yeah."

"You abstaining, Errol?" Iris asked.

"No," he said. "I'm with Seffy. We cure them."

"With Seffy?" Leona said. "Are you sure?"

"Something happened between you two," Jetta said. "I can smell it."

Leona frowned. "Well, I don't remember all of it. Zombie brain. A series of brownouts."

"I agree with Persephone," Errol said. "Because it makes sense."

She scoffed at him. "Whatever."

"How do we do it?" Iris asked.

"Same way Leona got it," Jetta said.

"How did Leona get it?" I asked. "I hadn't even realized she'd been cured."

"It was you, bitch," Leona said with a smirk. "Didn't take much."

"Oh… so when you tried to pull my esophagus out through my neck?"

"Uh, yeah."

"She must have swallowed some of your blood," Iris said. "Assuming she didn't have a cut in her mouth."

"She wouldn't," I said. "Not with the bots."

"So we force feed them some Seffy blood," Jetta said.

"Or your blood," Iris said. "Or mine."

"Or apparently mine," Leona said. "I'll slice my gums open and spit in their eyeballs."

"So I guess I can handle it myself," I said. "Anyone have a knife that hasn't been used to fillet my father?"

Errol handed me his pocket knife.

I sliced open my left palm.

Iris grabbed the woman first, holding her head up and squeezing her nostrils. Apparently that was a pretty well-known method of getting someone's mouth open.

I let a few drops fall onto the woman's tongue.

We did the same to the two men.

And waited.

Within thirty seconds, the woman started shaking.

She closed her eyes.

Then opened them.

She struggled a little against the tape, then looked up at me.

"What's going on?" she asked. "Why am I taped up?"

"You know why," I said.

"Who are these guys?" she said, looking over at the two men. "What do you want with me?"

"How do we know she isn't just making it all up?" Leona asked.

"We won't know for sure," I said.

"There's a way," Iris said.

She got down on her knees beside the woman.

She put her head right over the woman's mouth.

"She's not going to bite you," Leona said.

Iris shushed her.

Leona rolled her eyes.

"You can hear them if you listen," Iris said.

"Hear them?" I said.

"The bots. We all share the same ones. From the same place. So your bots can hear their bots if you're close enough."

"Like how it was with me and Leona?" Errol asked.

"Not quite the same. It's more a feeling I get. Like I can't make it out, but I know it's there."

"Not quite hearing, then," Leona said.

"Don't be a jerk, Leona," Jetta said.

"Can you cut me free now?" the woman asked. "Since I'm not infected anymore…"

"You guys figure it out," Iris said. "We've got better things to do." She walked over to Beth. "Do you think you can walk?"

Beth shook her head. She didn't try to speak.

"Ey-av-a-ah," the young man with the goatee said.

"Do we have a way for him to write it down?" I asked.

"He's a zombie," Errol said. "I'm a zombie. Hold on…" He walked over to the young man's chair. He leaned his forehead in, pressing against the other man's skin.

"I can't believe that works," Leona said.

"They have a car," Errol said. "That still runs."

"Another modded one," Jetta said. "Like Lucas."

"Can you take us to it?" I asked.

The man nodded.

"His name's Kellen," Errol said.

"Nice to meet you, Kellen," I said.

Kellen smiled and gave me a nod.

"A cute story for the two of you to tell your grandkids," Jetta said.

Leona and Iris laughed.

I think I blushed a little.

Kellen just smiled again.

Kellen brought us to a minivan.

Dan used the hardkey — that he took out of one of the taped-up men's pants — and managed to get the door open by hand. He put it in the ignition and started the engine.

There would have been too many of us if we'd been concerned about seatbelts.

We stuck to the quiet residential streets, heading north. Eventually we got back onto Broadway and made our way to the bridge into Minnesota.

I'd wondered if there would be an isolation line at the Red River, tanks and troops and blown up bridges.

But the road into Minnesota was empty.

If there still was a plan to isolate the infection, they were drawing the line somewhere else. There were other rivers out there.

The four of us girls sat together on the back bench, Iris and me, then Jetta and Leona. Iris was asleep on my shoulder before we'd even crossed into Minnesota. Jetta was on my other shoulder, but she wasn't even trying to sleep.

Leona was looking a little left out. And would occasionally shoot an angry stare up at the driver.

Errol didn't seem to notice the hate.

Or maybe he was just glad that someone cared enough to take the time.

18

THURSDAY AFTERNOON, AND A JAR OR TWO OF CHUNKY PEANUT BUTTER

No more bombs fell.

Not that we could see from where we'd stopped to rest, a farm just off the river, ten miles or so north of the bridge.

It wasn't a big house, just large enough that we could share three beds between us, and a couple of not-so-comfortable couches.

But by Thursday afternoon and forty-eight hours of fun, no one was interested in complaining about tight quarters or lumpy cushions.

I'd shared my blood with Beth and Dad and Kellen, just after we'd gotten out of the van. Their thighs had healed and their tongues had finally finished growing back enough that we could understand most of what they were saying.

Errol and his father found a three-quarter-charged sat phone in the house; Dan volunteered to spend the time trying to get in touch with the outside world, with anyone who'd listen.

Since we didn't know any contacts for any authorities outside of Cass County, Jetta gave Dan the number for one of Winnipeg's radio stations; I think it was the country one. I imagined it wasn't the worst place to start.

Once we told them that we had a cure, that there was hope... I wanted to believe that they'd listen, that there wouldn't be any more bombs. Once we could get out of the isolation area, show them our blood, our vaccine... this would all be over.

But it didn't feel like we were done yet. We were incomplete. We hadn't found David, and I hadn't even begun to look for my mother or my aunt. And there are others, too... Errol's Mom, Pat's girlfriend — who may or may not exist — and everyone Kellen had ever known.

I wanted to go back into town, as soon as we knew what to do about the cure. We wouldn't wait for the government to finally change its mind and decide that we were all worth saving.

But for that day... we needed to rest, to regroup.

So we made a decision. For the rest of that one day, or for a few hours of it, at least, we'd just take a frickin breath.

To feel human again.

☙

After a couple hours of dreamless sleep, Iris and I decided to take Fender for a walk. We weren't going far, just along the treeline, but Dad insisted we take one of the rifles anyway.

I'd asked him then if he'd had anything he'd wanted to say to Iris.

"Not today, Seffy," he said. "Just... not today."

So I let him have it. The one day.

Jetta asked to come along, but I just wanted some time with my sister. So I told her to give us ten minutes alone... then she could come and turn on the faucet.

We walked out the back door and headed toward a stand of poplars between us and the Red River of the North.

All we could see of Fargo was the smoke.

Iris had picked up a stick.

She threw it for Fender.

I watched him run out and get it.

And not bring it back.

I almost felt normal again.

"I feel like I need to reconnect with him," she said. "You know? Show him that I'm still Iris and he's still a mangy mutt."

"Yeah..."

"Like maybe some kind of doggy treat. Side of lamb..."

"You know what he loves?" I asked.

"What?"

"He's really big on that peanut butter thing."

"Yeah, okay..."

"So no?"

"Can you give me some serious suggestions here, Seffy?"

"Yeah. Peanut. Butter."

"God, Seffy. I'm not slathering peanut butter all over my naked body."

Naturally, Jetta came up behind us, just in time. Actually, around seven minutes early.

"Wow," she said. "I could come back later, but I so don't want to now."

"I wonder how long it'll be before you can head home," I said to her.

"Sick of me, eh?"

"We're jealous, actually," Iris said. "That you have a place to go home to."

Jetta smirked. "It's not all it's cracked up to be. My job's pretty awful, my family's about as dull as they come…"

"Just say it," I said.

"Say what?"

"Honorary sister."

"Are we doing that now?" Iris asked.

"We're doing that," I said.

Jetta smiled. "Do I need to do that peanut butter thing first?"

I heard the back door open.

Errol was running out onto the porch.

He called out to us, to come back.

We turned around.

He started jogging toward us.

"We're kind of in the middle of something," I said. "Pretty big deal, too."

"Huge deal," Iris said.

Errol didn't chuckle.

He wasn't smiling at all.

"What the heck is wrong with you?" I asked him.

"My Dad got a hold of someone in Winnipeg," he said.

"They won't have me back," Jetta said.

"The infection broke out."

"Broke out?" I said.

"Past the Sheyenne. Past the line at Gardner, too."

"What does that mean?" Jetta asked.

"It means that the infection is out of control."

"But we have a cure," I said. "And a vaccine."

"It might be too late," Errol said. "It's spreading so quickly."

"We need to get moving," Iris said.

"We need a plan," Jetta said.

I nodded.

We'd had all the breather we could get.

We had to keep going. We had to find a way to spread the cure. Because as far as I knew, we were the only ones who could.

ABOUT THE AUTHOR

Regan lives in Winnipeg, Canada with his wife, two children, and enough animals to bleed through ~~six~~ four layers of carpet.

You can find out more about Regan at his website:
www.reganwolfrom.com

www.ingramcontent.com/pod-product-compliance
Lightning Source LLC
Chambersburg PA
CBHW020055180626
46812CB00006B/2334